Lucy was alone. That made giving his gift of flowers easier. He caught them up and extended the bouquet toward her. "F-for you."

"For me?" Her eyes widened. "How lovely they are. Thank you, Ensign."

"James," he insisted. "You should c-call me James."

"Certainly, James. And you must call me Lucy." She cast her eyes down to the table.

Could he truly win her affection? He needed to have more time with her, to learn the truth of her feelings toward him.

When the clock began chiming the hour, Lucy stood. "Oh, dear. I must get back to the schoolroom."

"I w-wish you well in all your upcoming s-social d-duties, especially the b-ball," he responded with a slight bow. "B-but I am sure you w-will even outshine M-Miss B-Bradbury."

Something like amazement kindled in her eyes. "Do you really think so?" she breathed.

"Yes, I d-do." [illegible] Surely she knew [illegible]

"Well, if th[illegible]erson in Bath wh[illegible]t, and as she left t[illegible] smile his way as though she tossed a blossom at his feet.

Books by Lily George

Love Inspired Historical

Captain of Her Heart
The Temporary Betrothal
Healing the Soldier's Heart

LILY GEORGE

Growing up in a small town in Texas, Lily George spent her summers devouring the books in her mother's Christian bookstore. She still counts Grace Livingston Hill, Janette Oake and L. M. Montgomery among her favorite authors. Lily has a BA in history from Southwestern University and uses her training as a historian to research her historical inspirational romance novels. She has published one nonfiction book and produced one documentary, and is in production on a second film; all of these projects reflect her love for old movies and jazz and blues music. Lily lives in the Dallas area with her husband, daughter and menagerie of animals.

Healing the Soldier's Heart

LILY GEORGE

HARLEQUIN® LOVE INSPIRED® HISTORICAL

Recycling programs for this product may not exist in your area.

ISBN-13: 978-0-373-82978-1

HEALING THE SOLDIER'S HEART

This edition published by arrangement with Love Inspired Books.

www.LoveInspiredBooks.com

Printed in U.S.A.

For God hath not given us the spirit of fear;
but of power, and of love, and of a sound mind.
—*2 Timothy* 1:7 (KJV)

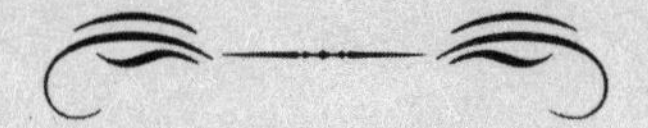

For my family and friends,
especially my husband and daughter,
who continue to endure my writing so patiently.

Chapter One

March 1818
Bath, England
Saint Swithin's Church of England

Lucy Williams rolled her eyes at her friend in playful disgust. Sophie Handley had no idea how to flirt. That much was certain. For all her airs and graces, for all her pretty face and lithe figure, her friend had no real idea how to capture a man's attention.

Why, they had come to Saint Swithin's for Sunday services just so Sophie could meet up with a man she liked, and here he was—on the point of departure. And Sophie just fretted at Lucy's side, murmuring how all was lost. Utterly ridiculous.

It was time to take matters into one's own hands. Lucy tugged on her reticule, unclasping it from her wrist. Then, as the parishioners began to file out of the church, she pushed through the crowd, keeping Sophie close by. The sea of humanity parted, and she could just glimpse Lieutenant Cantrill, her quarry. A young man stood beside the lieutenant, his angular face a mask of misery. Lucy stopped short. Why was he so sad? Her heart skipped a beat. Surely there was no reason in the world for such a handsome man to be so morose.

Sophie made an impatient tsking sound, jolting Lucy back to her senses. 'Twas time to accomplish her mission. With a smart twist of her wrist, she sent the reticule flying. It landed with a satisfying smack right beside the lieutenant on the wooden floor. He bent at once to retrieve it, his interesting companion bending down to assist. The lieutenant picked up her reticule, his eyebrow quirked, and turned to look for the party responsible for launching such a cunning little missile.

Time to spring into action.

"Oh, sir!" Lucy sang out. "You found my reticule. How very good of you." She hustled forward, tugging Sophie along behind her. "It was knocked clear of my hand by the bustle of this crowd." She skidded to a halt before the lieutenant and his companion, giving both the confident smile that had won her a position as governess to Lord Bradbury's daughters—no mean feat for a penniless orphan. Sophie stood beside her, pale and silent, her large blue eyes as round as saucers as she stared at Lieutenant Cantrill. Lucy jabbed Sophie in the ribs with her elbow, sending Sophie's curls bouncing.

Sophie winced and, rubbing her side, began the rounds of introductions. But it was clear from the way she stood ever so slightly closer to the lieutenant than propriety allowed that Sophie wanted a chance to be alone with the lieutenant. Very well, then. Lucy had her own task to follow.

It seemed that the young man with the lieutenant was none other than Ensign Rowland—the soldier Sophie had mentioned to her a few days prior. According to Lieutenant Cantrill, Waterloo had left the poor man mute. He had, in fact, barely spoken a few words since his arrival in Bath. The lieutenant believed that listening to someone else read aloud might ease his condition and had asked Sophie to find someone to read to the ensign. Sophie had asked her to assume that duty.

She turned to the tall man who stood beside the lieutenant. His wide green eyes regarded her solemnly, yet a spark flickered in their depths. His sandy blond hair waved over his forehead in a stubborn cowlick. She resisted the urge to reach up and pat it down with a tender gesture.

"So this is Ensign Rowland? How do you do, sir?" Lucy took his hands in hers. They were warm and capable—as strong as a man in service might possess. Now, how could she broach her assignment without making it sound as though she pitied him or felt sorry for him? Perhaps if she made it sound as though he would be doing her a tremendous favor in helping her. Yes, that would work best.

"Ensign, I was wondering if you could assist me with a problem. You see, I must instruct Lord Bradbury's daughters in the finer points of elocution and pronunciation, and the best way to do so is by reading aloud." She threaded her arm under his elbow and piloted him toward the door, letting Sophie and her lieutenant have their moment together. "But I am so rusty at reading aloud myself. Would you be my audience? I should so like to have your assistance."

The spark in his green eyes leaped. He understood what she had said, even if he didn't speak. He inclined his head ever so slightly, a lock of sandy hair falling over his brow. Again, she resisted the urge to pat it back into place, contenting herself with the feel of his arm underneath her hand.

He allowed her to guide him out of the side entrance of the vestry. He pushed open the rough wooden door, bathing their faces in pale, watery sunshine. Lucy blinked, tugging the brim of her bonnet down lower. Now she had him all to herself and no idea how to entertain him. Fine beads of sweat broke out under her brow. She would have to do all the talking and never pause for an answer. That was the only way to carry the conversation, without matters becoming awkward or embarrassing for the ensign.

Or perhaps the best way was to begin by acknowledging his obvious affliction. That way, one needn't feel quite so frantic about keeping up the conversational flow.

As they strolled into the courtyard, Lucy pulled away from the ensign's side. She turned to face him, her heart beginning to pound in her chest like a big bass drum. Why was she so nervous? She had faced scores of unsettling situations from losing her parents to leaving her only home, Cornhill and Lime Street Charity School, to strike out on her own. There was no need to panic just because she was facing a strikingly handsome young man.

"Ensign Rowland," she began, her words tumbling over each other in a rush, "I should let you know that I am well aware of your affliction. You cannot speak, can you?"

He shrugged, his eyes clouding over. She was losing that spark, that gleam of interest he had shown her just moments before. A frantic feeling seized hold of her, and she hurried on, her face growing heated under his uncertain gaze.

"It doesn't matter to me, of course. I can talk enough for two people. Indeed, I have it on good authority that I can talk the legs off a chair."

A strange sound, rather like a rusty chuckle, emanated from the ensign. His lips were quirked downward—with mirth. Good heavens, she made the man laugh. That was a good sign, surely. She pressed on.

"At any rate, do not feel you have to make a conversation with me. I really would like to have the opportunity to read to a captive audience. And if you don't mind my chattering, then I should love to talk with you frequently."

He nodded, his features softening.

"Very good then." She took his arm once more, and he steered her toward the stone steps that led down to the street. She could just pick out Sophie's voice behind them, but she wasn't ready to let the ensign go. Not yet. Now that things were resolved between them, she could let herself enjoy the pleasure of some company. Aside from Sophie, she had no one even close to her age in Bath to speak to, and sometimes loneliness threatened to overwhelm her. There were her two young charges to speak to, of course, but it was quite another matter to have a friend. It was nice to chatter on with the ensign; even if there was no possibility he would respond.

"You know, I work for Lord Bradbury. He has two daughters, and I am their governess. Sophie—" she nodded in Sophie's general direction "—works as their personal seamstress. Before Sophie came to Bath a few months ago, I had no one with whom I could speak freely. But now she is here, and I've met you. What a delight to have two young people I can chat with."

She slanted her gaze up at him. A delightful smile crept over his face, as though he too had discovered a treasure. A warm glow lit Lucy's heart. He was a gentle soul. That much was certain. And had probably suffered a great deal. It would be a joy to talk with him and to bring that smile back to his face.

From some distance away, a clock began tolling the hour. Botheration. She should be returning to Lord Bradbury's house soon. She needed to supervise her charges' luncheon; for if she were not present, the girls were likely to fire dinner rolls at each other like cricket balls.

"I must go." It was difficult to let him go. But perhaps she could see him again soon. "Will you be at the next veterans' group meeting? I don't know when they meet, but I can find out from Sophie."

He nodded, smiling once more.

"Sophie," she called up the steps. Sophie broke away from the lieutenant's side and began her descent. Lucy turned to the ensign. "Ensign Rowland, it's been a pleasure to meet you. And I look forward to tormenting you with the classics soon. I have a great fancy for Greek epic works, so beware."

His polite smile grew into a devastating grin, and her heart flip-flopped in her chest once more. She withdrew her hand from his sleeve slowly, savoring the moment. It would be nice to see him again.

Sophie danced up beside them, her eyes bright with merriment. They made their goodbyes, the ensign tipping his hat with a practiced, genteel gesture as he took his leave. Sophie linked her arm with Lucy's as they began strolling toward the Crescent, the balmy spring breeze rustling their skirts. And while Sophie babbled on about the lieutenant and her harebrained scheme to save him from his meddling mama, Lucy's mind drifted.

Though she made her usual barbed responses to Sophie's nonsense, Lucy was far from her friend's side. Instead, she wandered down the steps once more with the ensign, remembering his somber green eyes and his crooked, heartbreaking grin. The veterans' meeting, which she hardly knew about before this day, was now the most important event on her horizon.

As they approached his lordship's home, she looked up at the second-story window that housed the schoolroom. Of course, nothing could really come of her interaction with the ensign other than friendship. She was nothing but a poor governess, and she had to earn her own way in the world. Any girlish dreams of romance had to remain just that—dreams and nothing more. She had no time for love. And she had a duty to her charges.

And, after all, she had been asked to help the ensign not for her beauty or eligibility but because she was a governess. And a governess she would remain for the rest of her days. She dearly hoped that she and the ensign would become good friends. But friends were all they could ever be.

Ensign James Rowland smiled as he watched Miss Lucy Williams walk off arm in arm with the pretty blonde Miss Handley who had captured Cantrill's interest. Lucy didn't mind that he could not speak, which had made him quite comfortable in her company. In fact, he was more at ease with her than he had been with anyone outside his tight circle of fellow soldiers.

It helped, of course, that she was quite attractive herself, but in a more unique way than her blonde friend. She had glossy black hair piled high on her head, wide brown eyes and a fascinating sprinkle of freckles across her nose and cheeks. Most women, out of coquetry or sense of fashion, would use some type of artificial means to hide or remove those supposed imperfections. But not Lucy. They added spice to her person, like a sprinkle of cinnamon across a particularly tasty dish.

For the first time since his return from Waterloo, he was intrigued by someone else. Everything looked gray and sounded like it was wrapped in cotton wool since that horrible day he lay bleeding and silent in the rye at La Sainte Haye. But in Lucy's warm brown eyes, he captured a glimpse of life. And that brief spark glowed in his heart as Lieutenant Cantrill joined him on the street below Saint Swithin's.

"Come, Rowland, let us return home." Cantrill sighed. "I have much preying upon my mind this afternoon, and I need to think matters over."

Whatever Cantrill and Miss Handley had spoken of apparently drove the lieutenant to distraction. He spoke hardly a word on the fifteen-minute walk back to Beau Street to the modest flats that several soldiers had called home since their return from the peninsula. Of course, it didn't matter that the lieutenant didn't speak. In fact, Rowland couldn't expect anyone to make conversation with a man who only uttered a word now and again.

He nodded his goodbye to Cantrill, who lived on

the ground floor flat, and took the steps two at a time to reach the flat he shared with Lieutenant Sean Macready, a fellow officer of the 2nd Battalion 69th.

As he entered their humble flat, the delectable aroma of beef stew greeted him, causing his mouth to water. The housekeeper must be here. Thank heavens. They shared servants with Lieutenant Cantrill; this kept Mrs. Pierce bustling up and down stairs all day long, though she insisted she did not mind. And her stew, heated and reheated, formed their sustenance for many days, growing richer and mellower with each passing day.

"What ho, man?" Macready beckoned him into the kitchen, where he sat at the rickety oak table, a steaming bowl before him. "Mrs. Pierce just left to take the lieutenant his lunch. Try the bread first with a dab of butter. It's a poem."

With a grateful grunt, James grabbed a plain white china bowl from the cupboard and filled it to the brim with stew. Then he hacked off the end of the loaf of bread—so warm that it singed his fingers a bit—and sat across from Macready at the table.

"Good gracious, man. I haven't seen you eat so heartily since before the war." Macready leaned forward, eyeing James suspiciously. "What has gotten into you?"

James shrugged, keeping his eyes cast down. Nothing extraordinary had happened, had it? He was just hungry was all.

He split the bread open, patting butter on the inside and then closed it so the middle of the bread would become more moist as the butter melted. His favorite childhood treat, much more coveted than a cookie or a slice of cake.

Macready took another bite of stew. Then, assuming an elaborately casual air, he asked, "How was Sunday service?"

James bit into the crusty loaf, closing his eyes in delight for a moment as he savored it. Then he uttered his customary one-word response, "Fine."

"Hmm. Are you sure, Rowland? There's an air about you, as though something extraordinary happened to you. You even look different. There's more color in your person, as though you are warmer from the inside." Macready broke off another piece of bread, peering at James as he did so.

Blast Macready and his Irish gift of gab. He would never let up—not until James had told him about his entire morning. True, his meeting with Lucy Williams had given him hope—hope that he could move on from the past. She was the first person he'd met in Bath who wasn't a veteran of the war. And she was the only person to offer her friendship. The difference between how he felt before church this morning and now, sitting in the cozy kitchen, well, this was the difference that a new friendship could make in a fellow's life. She made life seem just a little less bleak and unforgiving.

'Twas strange indeed how he could speak to only certain people and stranger still how he could not speak to everyone else. His ability to speak naturally had fled as he lay crouched, playing dead, at La Sainte Haye. Macready was one of the only men to whom he could converse. And even though he could speak to the lieutenant, he did so slowly and haltingly. Macready had long since grown used to his stilted cadences, though, and waited with great patience to listen whenever James chose to speak.

But how to describe Lucy? She was merely offering to help him out of charity and friendship, surely. So it would be folly to describe her in grand terms that would have Macready expecting a romance in the offing. No woman wanted a poor, mute veteran for her own. Certainly not someone who was pretty and clever, like Miss Williams. So it was much better to stick with the facts, as a good soldier should.

"Met a g-girl," he grumbled. His voice was rusty and unpracticed, even to his own ears. He reached for the teapot and poured a steaming cup. "She will work with the veterans' group of Cantrill's. Helping out." He took a long draught of burning tea to calm his ragged throat and hide his emotions from Macready.

"Not Sophie Handley, surely? I don't know much about the female in question, but I believe she is destined to be Cantrill's," Macready replied, a warning note to his voice.

"No. Miss Williams. She wants t-t-to read to me. T-to help with…this." He shrugged one shoulder. 'Twas terribly awkward to talk about his strange affliction, even with Macready. After all, the lieutenant had deep gashes all along one arm and up one leg, wounds that were taking forever to heal. Whilst James himself had gotten only a few nicks.

It made a fellow wonder if, deep down inside, he was really a coward after all. Why else would he be so affected by injuries that had been so slight?

"Well, that could be most entertaining, you know. Is she pretty?" Incorrigible Macready, always ready to seek out a lovely new face. Even so, an unreasonable dart of jealousy shot through James. He played down his response so that Macready would leave him in peace.

"P-pretty enough," he allowed. "Let's hope she d-doesn't like G-gothic novels." But even as he spoke the words, James was prepared to take them back. He'd be willing to listen to the most overwrought of Gothic horrors if it meant spending more time basking in the warm glow of Miss Williams's company.

Chapter Two

'Twas Thursday, Lucy's day of rest from her duties in the schoolroom. Never before had she been so grateful for a day away from her charges. Amelia was making her debut in just a few days' time, and the entire house was in chaos as preparations mounted for her dinner party.

Amelia herself was absent from lessons all week, as Lord Bradbury had pressed Sophie into service, coaching Amelia on all the finer points of etiquette and deportment. Bereft of her sister and generally overlooked in the confusion, Louisa moped about her schoolwork, her large dark eyes filling with tears as she studied her Latin declensions.

And Sophie, working as both seamstress and mistress of proper decorum, was taxed to her limit. Lucy had not spent more than a few moments in Sophie's company since the past Sunday, and the absence of her only friend and confidante began to pall.

So, once she was dressed and ready to face the day, she marched down to Sophie's room to say good morning. Butterflies fluttered in her stomach at the thought of meeting with the ensign today. She'd never really read anything aloud before—and certainly not to a young man. It would help immensely to have Sophie nearby. She wouldn't be quite so nervous with a friend close at hand.

"Ugh. Enter," a decidedly sleepy voice muttered in response to Lucy's knock.

Lucy poked her head in as Sophie pulled the coverlet high over her head. "Sophie? You are awake, aren't you?"

"Yes. Awake but rebellious. I am entirely unwilling to face the day." Sophie wriggled farther under her covers as Lucy perched on the bed.

"Cheer up, chicken. We're going to the veterans' group this morning. You can see your lieutenant again." And, of course, she could see that interesting young ensign. The heat rose in her cheeks at that thought. Not that he would be hanging on her every word, of course. But it would be quite nice to see him and speak to him again.

"No, I cannot go." Sophie sat up and threw the coverlet back, revealing her woebegone face. Dark circles ringed her pretty blue eyes, and her pink-and-white complexion had taken on a sallow tone. She gave her tangled curls a shake. "I have too much to do. You'll have to go without me. And besides, I need time before I see the lieutenant again. I must practice and prepare myself, you see. We are pretending a faux courtship so his visiting mama will leave him in peace."

Lucy's heart hitched in her chest, and she barely registered the remainder of Sophie's words. "Go without you? Faux courtships? This is like a plot in a farce, Sophie! You are the only person I would know there. If you won't be coming along, whom will I sit by? How shall I get started?" She absolutely despised new situations. The way she had survived—and even thrived—at Cornhill and Lime Street Charity School was by knowing exactly where she had to be and what was expected of her at any given moment. And that only came through routine. If the routine changed—well, she had to start all over again, a most unpleasant practice.

Lucy grasped a long, dark ringlet of hair and began twirling it around her index finger, trying to think of a way to convince her friend to accompany her. "If you intend to go through with some sort of fake courtship, you might want to talk matters over with Cantrill."

"Oh, dear Lucy, on any other day you know I would be there. I love working with the veterans' group. And I love—" Sophie broke off, a flush creeping over her dimpled cheeks. Ah, yes. Her feelings for the lieutenant would be obvious to anyone, even a blind and deaf dormouse. She sighed and closed her eyes, rubbing her temples. "But there is simply too much for me to do. And I need more time to compose myself before I see the lieutenant again."

Lucy sighed. She was being too selfish. Here Sophie was, trying to help both Amelia and Cantrill, and all Lucy could think about was herself. She reached out and patted Sophie's shoulder. "Poor dear. You are working so hard to make Amelia's debut a success. Is there anything I can do to help? If you are willing to give up your day off for the cause, then I will gladly sacrifice mine, as well."

Sophie smiled and shook her head again. "No. Go—go and read to Ensign Rowland. You deserve a day off, and I know that you planned already to meet with the gentleman. And—" Sophie darted a quick, searching glance up at Lucy, a glance that seared through all artifice "—I have a feeling you are rather intrigued by the ensign, is that not so?"

"Don't be silly." Lucy rose, putting an end to the interview before Sophie's questions got too probing. "But I made a promise, and it would be most rude not to keep it. So, I suppose this means I shall see you after the meeting, then?"

"Yes." Sophie rose. "That blonde blur you'll see scurrying down the hallway will be me."

With a chuckle, Lucy descended to the kitchen and out the back door, breathing deeply of the balmy spring breeze to calm her nerves. She hadn't thought far enough ahead when she made her plans with Ensign Rowland. If only Sophie could come along. Courage was much easier to muster when one had a close friend nearby. When she met with the ensign a few days before, she was able to muster courage—to be breezy and nonchalant in her speech. But then, 'twas a brief meeting. She hadn't had to read to him that first day. Now she was alone, and her performance was imminent. Did famous opera soubrettes have an attack of nerves before going onstage? Probably not. If performance were a part of your daily round, 'twas quite likely that you'd simply get used to it.

Saint Swithin's perched majestically on a hill, its proud façade overlooking all of Bath. Why, it was intimidating even to look upon, much less consider what—or whom—awaited her there. By the time she reached the front steps, she was quite winded. She paused a moment at the top of the stone steps, exhaling as slowly as she could, her heart pounding in her chest. Bowing her head a moment, she counted to ten. It would never do to approach Rowland as though she had been running a footrace through the park.

As she drew herself up, shaking her skirts, she caught a glimpse of a handsome, angular face. Gracious, Rowland was here already! He turned toward her, a smile lighting his eyes as he extended his hand in greeting.

"Ensign Rowland," she gasped and then cleared her throat. She hadn't meant to meet him so soon. She needed more time to compose herself. But there was nothing to do but brazen through her nerves and her breathlessness.

He nodded, his smile growing as he surveyed her. She paused a moment, awaiting some sort of spoken response, and then shook her head. Of course, he was not going to speak. Botheration. That was the entire point of their meeting, was it not? To help him overcome his affliction?

To cover her confusion and deter his rapt attention from her now hotly glowing cheeks, Lucy took his hand and bobbed a curtsy. The brim of her bonnet would hide the pinkness of her face for a moment. But she hadn't anticipated on the tingle that shot up her arm at his touch. Goodness, she was making a cake of herself.

And if she went inside the church with him, her embarrassment would be writ clear on her face for everyone to see. Lieutenant Cantrill and Rowland's other cronies would surely laugh at her and jest to Rowland about it later after the meeting was over. No, if she was going to hide her roiled emotions, it would be much easier to do so from just one man than a dozen.

"Shall we sit out here and enjoy this fine weather?"

She indicated a nearby stone bench with what she hoped was a carefree gesture. "After such a wet and cold winter, I vow I am quite in adoration of this spring weather."

Out of the corner of her eye, she spied the ensign nodding. She allowed him to steer her over to the bench and then sat, gathering her skirts about her with as much grace as she could assume.

"Well, then." She waited as he took his seat, stretching his booted legs out before him. Then she opened her reticule—her curiously light and flat reticule. Oh, gracious. She had left her book at home.

She didn't know whether to laugh or to cry; she was such a bundle of nerves. An emotion bubbled up her throat, and for a dreadful instant, she thought she was going to burst into tears. Instead, she chuckled, unable to hold back any longer. At least laughter relieved the unbearable anxiety she felt.

Rowland glanced at her, puzzled, one eyebrow quirked. She turned her reticule inside out, showing him a few coins and bits of lint. "I came all this way, Ensign Rowland, and I never even had the book with me."

Lucy Williams had the most enchanting laugh. And when she giggled, as she was doing now, her brown eyes sparkled and her cheeks glowed a dusky pink. It was delightful simply to gaze upon her, drinking in her mirth at the absurdity of the situation. He handed her his handkerchief, which she used to dab her eyes—she laughed so hard that tears just touched their corners.

Her laughter slowed, and as her joy began to fade,

confusion took its place. He wanted to reassure her—to wipe any trace of discomfiture away. So he withdrew a battered book from his coat pocket and handed it to her.

She took the volume, handling it with a gentle touch to keep from pulling the worn pages apart. "Poetry? Ah, some of the finest. Sir Walter Scott, Dryden…" She continued perusing the pages. "I shall have to be very careful with this, ensign. I can tell just by looking at it that this is a book you have consulted many times."

He nodded, eyeing her carefully. His throat worked, but no sound came out. He remained silent and watchful.

She traced over a dark splotch on the cover. "In fact, I would wager this book has been to battle." She kept her eyes lowered, her dark lashes fanning out over her cheeks.

He nodded again. He read those poems often in the field. More than once, Sir Walter Scott had given him the courage to see another battle.

"I bet I can find your favorite." She grasped the book, settling the spine on her lap. Then, with infinite caution, she let the volume fall open. And just like that, the pages settled, revealing *Marmion.*

She began reading in clear, dulcet tones, as though reciting for a schoolroom of young ladies or as an elocutionist in a performance. Her voice, lit from within with warmth and fire, began the introduction to the first canto,

"November's sky is chill and drear,
November's leaf is red and sear:
Late, gazing down the steepy linn,
that hems our little garden in…"

The spring breeze ruffled her lavender skirts as she continued to read, stirring her black curls so that they touched her cheek as she read. He gazed at her, saying the words in his mind as she read them aloud. He knew the poem like he knew the hills and fields back home in Essex—it was as familiar to him as breathing. And yet he had never felt the passion and the pathos of Flodden Field until Lucy Williams read the poem aloud.

She paused a few times, darting quick little glances up as she read through the six cantos. Whenever her eyes left the page, he studied his boots as though they were the most fascinating things in the world. She was nervous enough as it was without having a mute soldier ogling her like a green lad.

"To thee, dear school-boy, whom my lay
has cheated of thy hour of play,
Light task, and merry holiday!
To all, to each, a fair good-night,
and pleasing dreams, and slumbers light!"

After repeating Scott's final words, Lucy sighed and closed the book, taking a few deep breaths. "Goodness, Ensign Rowland, I have not read for so long aloud in many a year. Growing up, when I was in school, I often had recitations. But as a governess, I have the luxury of passing on the task of reciting to my charges." She turned to him, a smile hovering about the corners of her mouth. "Did I perform well enough?"

Again, his throat worked. He strained against his infirmity, longing to offer a flowery compliment. Or at least a thank-you. But no matter how hard he tried, his voice was gone. So he merely nodded, struggling to let his gratitude show in his expression.

She inclined her head as though he'd really spoken. "Thank you, Ensign. I do appreciate the compliment. And the captive audience." Her smile widened to a grin. "Shall I read another?"

He grasped the book and flipped to another page, with another favorite, and handed it back to Lucy. "Ah, *The Lady of the Lake*. Excellent choice. I had my eldest charge, Amelia, recite this last year."

She read again, putting the same fervor and enthusiasm into her performance as she did before, though she must be getting tired. Those were long poems and did not precisely come trippingly off even the smoothest-speaking tongue. And yet, she sat here, under the shade of an elm tree, reading him poems that he fancied. On her day off. When she could have been doing a hundred other interesting things. His heart surged with gratitude, and a bit more of the cotton wool fell away from his view of the world.

Behind them, the doors of the church banged open, and the general hubbub announced that the veterans' group was dispersing. Lucy paused midverse and closed the book, smiling with what might have been a pang of regret. But if it was real disappointment or feigned for his benefit, he could not be certain. She rose, dusting off her skirts, and returned the poems to Ensign Rowland.

"I suppose I should be going," she announced. "The house is in uproar. Amelia's debut is later this week, and everything is in chaos until that fateful night."

"Ah! I see you found one another." Lieutenant Cantrill broke away from the crowd and started over, holding his good hand out to Lucy. "When I didn't see you inside, I was worried that perhaps neither of you could make it."

Lucy bobbed a curtsy. "Lieutenant, I do apologize for worrying you. The weather was so lovely, and I have been cooped up of late. So Ensign Rowland and I decided to stay outdoors."

"No, no. That's fine. All well and good, then?" The lieutenant glanced over at Rowland for confirmation, and he gave a short grunt. It was all he could muster under the circumstances.

"Excellent." Cantrill turned back to Lucy. "Will I be seeing you at Miss Bradbury's debut, then? I—uh—that is, I had planned to attend as my mother will be in town—"

"Yes, Lieutenant." Lucy nodded briskly. "Sophie told me of your plans, sir. I hope that everything works out well for you."

James's head snapped up. Cantrill had plans with Sophie Handley? This could be rather diverting. It would take his mind off his own infirmities at least.

Lucy prattled on in the same no-nonsense tone. "But of course I won't be present at the party. I must take care of Miss Louisa, and she is none too pleased that she will be missing her sister's debut." She turned to James. "Louisa is two years younger than her sister and quite distressed that she cannot attend all the grand functions that her sister will be enjoying. It has been my job, of late, to ensure that Louisa's feelings are not too sadly trampled."

James smiled and nodded. Miss Williams really seemed to enjoy her two charges. She spoke of them almost as an indulgent older sister would. It brought to mind his sister Mary and how much they enjoyed each other's company.

Miss Williams continued. "Of course, Sophie plans to turn Amelia into a diamond of the first water. And being so pretty and graceful herself, I know she will accomplish her goal." She turned to Cantrill with a playful grin. "Wouldn't you agree, sir?"

James couldn't suppress a grin. He turned to Cantrill, one eyebrow raised.

Cantrill reddened. "Yes, yes. Of course." He turned to Rowland. "Well, then? I suppose we must be off."

However much he wanted to see the lieutenant squirm about Sophie, James had no intention of going back to his flat with Cantrill—not with such a fine spring day ahead of him, and such pretty company. He offered Lucy his arm. "C-C-C-r-r-r…" he stammered. He cleared his throat. "C-C-Crescent?" It was all he could say, but hopefully Miss Williams would catch his meaning. She was rather astute after all.

She did. Tucking her arm through his elbow, she cast him a dazzling smile. "Yes, thank you, Ensign. I shall be delighted if you would see me to his lordship's door in the Crescent."

Chapter Three

James Rowland had spoken. A single word, of course, and stammered to be sure, but he had spoken. 'Twas an excellent sign. Whether this development was due to her reading or some other mysterious aspect, she could not fathom. But it was progress. That much was certain.

She cast a sidelong glance at Rowland as they strolled back to the Crescent. If he was surprised or elated by his utterance, he kept his counsel. His face had settled into its usual angular lines, and he remained silent. Did he know that her entire purpose in reading to him was to help him overcome his infirmity? Did he know that Lieutenant Cantrill and Sophie had put her up to it? Oh, she was entirely willing to help, but their brief session together made her feel awkward. As though she had helped a child to win a race by holding back as she ran. It was a confusing emotion, because she hadn't held anything back from him—other than the truth. It was time to tell him.

She paused, tugging on his sleeve. "Ensign, I would speak to you if I may."

He stopped, and several passersby bumped into

them. The ensign steered her away from the crowded sidewalk to a small side street where fewer people jostled along. As they reached the corner of a garden, she turned to face him, the warm sunlight touching her face as she spoke.

"Do you want to regain the power to speak, sir?" Her words sounded too harsh, too frank even to her own ears, so she rushed on. "The lieutenant thinks that if I read to you perhaps that can help you overcome your infirmity. But I don't want to help you unless you wish for me to do so."

A flush crept over his face, and his bright green gaze remained rooted on the ground. Oh, this was awful. She had hurt his feelings and made him feel ridiculous. And meanwhile, she didn't feel so wonderful herself.

"I want to read to you, because I enjoy your company," she continued hastily. "I have very few people with whom I can converse. I have no family and little acquaintance beyond the schoolroom. So reading to you was actually quite a bright spot in my world for me to look forward to this week. But…I shall stop if you don't like it."

He shook his head, his Adam's apple bobbing in his throat. "C-c-continue."

"Do you want me to continue meeting with you, then?" She wasn't certain what that single word meant. Or did he want her to continue blathering away like an idiot? By the way he was nodding his head, he indicated that he wanted her to keep meeting with him. "Very well, then, sir." She took a deep breath, unsure if she should go on. But then, if he wanted to recover, he would have to work as well. It was the same sort of agreement she offered the Bradbury sisters in the schoolroom. She would offer what help she could, but her pupils would also have to work hard.

"I will continue to read to you, but we will work together to help you regain your voice." She looked up at him, willing him to look her straight in the eye. "You spoke to me today. Can you speak to anyone else, sir?"

"M-M-Macready and C-C-Cantrill." His voice was rough, like sandpaper across her skin. She suppressed a shiver at his tone and continued in her same businesslike manner.

"If they are your brothers in arms and you are able to speak with them, then that indicates something profound, Ensign. I am not sure how we shall go about making matters better for you. I am sure we shall have to try several different methods. But I wanted to be honest with you. I wanted to make sure this is what you want. And if it is, then I shall help you in any way I can."

The poor man—his eyes were cast down and his hair mussed, a flush still stealing over his face. Well, one could hardly blame him. It would be difficult indeed to admit to needing help for any particular weakness or to have anyone—especially a woman who was practically a stranger—question him on it. She took his arm again and allowed him to steer her back onto the main street from which they had deviated.

They plodded on in silence, a silence that Lucy relished. She was tired, too. And addled a bit. And rattled, if she were to admit the truth. She had just agreed to help the ensign regain the power of speech—the very thing he lost on a Belgian battlefield. It was no small promise and no small task. And what if she failed? She said a silent prayer for help and for hope. She would need a great deal of both in the coming weeks.

His lordship's fashionable townhome—situated right in the heart of the Crescent—loomed up ahead of them. If his lordship saw her with the ensign, there might be trouble. Servants—even high-placed governesses—were supposed to conform to certain kinds of behavior. And even though her relationship with the ensign was entirely above-board, she wasn't about to do anything foolish that might cause talk.

"We can stop here. The house is just about a block away, and I don't want to get into any kind of trouble," Lucy explained in haste, heat flooding her cheeks. "His lordship wants his female servants to remain unmarried, and so I don't want to do anything to stir up gossip. Not that it would. Or that it should—" She broke off, feeling like an utter fool.

He patted her shoulder. "V-very well," he responded. He took her hand in his and raised it to his lips for a brief, chaste kiss. "Th-th-ank you, M-Miss Williams." He bowed, releasing her hand.

Butterflies chased themselves around her stomach, and she struggled to remain composed. Outwardly composed, that was. "Of course, Ensign." She bobbed a curtsy. "And thank you for the pleasure of your company. I can assure you, I spend many of my days off traipsing around the booksellers, hoping to scout a new volume. It was a rare treat to have pleasant company with which to share my day off instead of being all alone." Botheration. Now she sounded like a dried-up old spinster. If only she had as much gift for pretty speeches with Rowland as she did with Cantrill—but then, she didn't care about Cantrill.

On the other hand, she suspected that she might be caring more about Rowland than she should.

Rowland stretched out on the settee in his humble flat, his mind spinning. On the way back from walking Lucy home and then for the better part of the afternoon, he had replayed their conversation—well, her conversation with him—in his mind. That she was willing to help him, that she cared enough about a fellow human being to offer assistance—that alone was enough to fill him with gratitude. But he couldn't stop thinking of Lucy as she read and as she spoke to him.

She had a certain manner of flicking her glance sideways—a sharp look out the corner of her eye that sent his heart racing. There was no coquetry in this gesture. It was not practiced. It was simply part of who she was, but it was enough to send his heart pounding every time she did so. He was much happier concentrating on how this glance made his heart leap than in dwelling on her words from their walk to the Crescent. But, unbidden, they crept back into his mind. Her clear, dulcet tones asking, "Do you want to regain the power to speak, sir?"

No one had asked him that. Everyone assumed he did, but no one asked him in such a direct and forthright manner before. The doctors in Belgium had scratched their heads at his predicament, and after his superficial wounds healed, had sent him on his way. "He'll speak when he's ready," they pronounced.

Back home in Essex, Mother threw her hands up in despair. "You're just being stubborn," she wailed. "Your sister Mary can't find a match—not with her stammer. And you—you were our only hope. Be a man, like your other brothers in arms. Look at Captain Brookes, missing a leg. And now he's married and running the family farm! Look at Lieutenant Cantrill, supporting himself in Bath. And you, barely wounded, can't get a position anywhere because you won't speak? James—our family is in desperate circumstances!" And so it had been until Macready, Rowland's closest friend in the 69th, had invited him to share his flat in Bath as he recovered from his battle scars.

Among his brethren soldiers, his inability to speak was a given, as much as his green eyes or blond hair. It was a part of him, much as the others now carried more visible scars of the war. And yet none of them had asked him if he wanted to recover, just as they were recovering thanks to the curative waters of Bath. Cantrill had gone so far as to recruit Lucy for the job without asking Rowland if that's what he wanted.

He brought his booted foot down hard on the floor, the force of the blow smashing a china plate as it fell from the mantel. He gazed at the fragments. They were as jagged as the pieces of his life. His lack of ability to flirt with Lucy, or even chat about mundane topics like the weather, drove him to distraction.

He grasped his head in his hands, willing his temper to stay controlled. No one understood what he wanted. No one had bothered to ask before.

No one, that was, but Lucy. She respected his privacy, acknowledged his right *not* to get well. And that spoke volumes about her character.

The front door banged open. "Rowland? Are you here?" Macready's voice, hale and hearty despite his many wounds, echoed throughout the little flat.

Rowland grunted. Macready must be back from taking the waters.

"So, how was the meeting?" Macready limped in, discarding his jacket on a nearby leather chair. "You look like you are having a bit of a study. If your forehead had any more lines, you could compose music upon it."

"Funny," Rowland replied, keeping his tone sarcastic. He didn't want to share everything about Lucy yet. Certainly not her beauty or her sparkling character. Macready, with his Black Irish looks and his gift with words, might find her beguiling. He could charm her in ways that Rowland lacked—until he regained his power of speech.

"I met Cantrill in the Pump Room. He mentioned that a certain Miss Williams read to you today and that you squired her back to her employer's home in the Crescent," Macready yammered on. He sank into a worn velvet chair, eyeing Rowland closely. Too closely. "He even said you spoke to the lady."

"Nothing much." He kept his face turned toward the wall. If Macready saw how deeply he was flushing, he'd never hear the end of it.

"But think of it, man! You haven't spoken a word to anyone besides myself and Cantrill since La Sainte Haye. This is an amazing accomplishment. You are on the road to recovery. I think this Miss Williams is excellent medicine, you know."

"She's not." She was much more than a pretty face or a pleasing diversion. Macready made it sound as though she had worked her feminine wiles on him and gotten her way. What transpired was much more profound and deeply shaking than that. But trying to say that aloud—why, it would sound beyond ridiculous. So he merely settled for shrugging his shoulders.

"You know, I think you've been much too hard on yourself, Rowland. Think of it. Most of us were far too young to be in the military. I was twenty. How old were you? Eighteen? We were green as grass and broke formation. That's how the Frenchies were able to get the best of us." Macready paused, rubbing his battered arm. "Hiding in the rye as we did, well, that was simple survival. We had almost no chance against the cavalry."

Well, they had hidden. That much was true. But while Macready lay delirious from dreadful wounds, Rowland had been awake and fully alert when he played dead. Like a coward. He had feigned death to the point that the peasants who came to collect them after battle thought he had died. And he didn't cry out for help but remained mute even as his body was loaded onto a cart bound for Brussels.

The shame of his deception burned strong, deeper perhaps than any physical wound he could have sustained at Waterloo. And there was nothing he could do to right the wrong. His inability to speak seemed as though no more than justice. There was, after all, nothing he could say to defend or excuse the cowardice he had shown. And if he regained the power of speech, would he ever find a way to express his disgust with himself? His profound disappointment at how little he had done to save his fellow men?

The silence between them stretched out, punctuated by the ticking clock on the mantel. At length, Macready cleared his throat. "That's why I asked you to come to Bath, you know. You needed to recuperate as much as

I did. And Cantrill, he's looking out for your welfare, too. I think that this Miss Williams shall probably play a significant role in your healing."

Macready knew everything. He knew about Mrs. Rowland's tears and recriminations. He knew about the doctor in Essex who had told James Rowland that fear had tied his tongue. He knew about the shame and the anger and the horror of the battlefield. And yet, Macready sought only to offer help. Never once had he blamed James for his injuries. But he should.

James struggled painfully with his voice for a few moments. It seemed he couldn't force the words over his tongue. "I—I—I…" He trailed off, and inhaling deeply, he began again. "I—I am s-sorry."

"Whatever for, old man? We were all of us terrified. We did what we could under the circumstances." Macready rubbed his hands together briskly. "How about some tea? I could do with a bit, myself. Not to sound flippant, but that Bath water tastes like rotten eggs. And, uh—" Macready nodded his head at the heap of broken china on the floor "—I'll bring a whiskbroom so you can tidy up."

Macready heaved himself up from the chair and made his way to the small kitchen. The rattle and clank of the kettle and dishes signaled that he was readying the tea and had no more wish to converse about the past than James.

James rubbed a weary hand over his brow. Of course he didn't want to think about it. No one wanted to examine the unpleasant or foolish side of himself. But all the same, James had a driving curiosity to know the truth. What kind of fellow was he after all? There was a saying that the battlefield brought out what was genuine in a man. If so, then he had failed the test miserably. Sure, he was young. But then, they all were. What made a man suffer nobly, like Macready? And what made a man hide and cower with fear as he had? Where was the defect in his character? Would that he could root it out and tear it away, like attacking weeds in an overgrown garden.

He wasn't sure he deserved the friendship of his fellow veterans, like Macready. That's what made attending those veterans' group meetings so difficult. Those men had sustained real injuries while defending home and country. Many men had given their lives, leaving wives and children behind. He couldn't even look the widows in the eye, so riddled with shame was he. Their husbands had paid the ultimate sacrifice while he lay silent in the rye at La Sainte Haye.

If he wasn't sure he deserved the friendship of those brave men, then he felt doubly undeserving of Miss Williams's attention. She seemed to care about others quite a bit, judging from her conversation with Cantrill. Every mention of her charges or Sophie brought a merry twinkle to her eyes. She would never sit back and allow others to suffer in her place. Someone like her would recoil in horror at his cowardice. Not that he had a chance with her anyway, poor and mute as he was. It was just that, in general, a friendship with someone like her could be nice. It took the rough edges off of life.

How could he come to deserve friendship again? Perhaps he could begin by confronting his shame and his cowardice first. These twin emotions had robbed him for two years now, leaving him bereft of speech.

Only by ridding himself of them could he regain what he lost.

It was going to be a difficult journey. But, like the soldier he should have been, he could take it battle by battle. He would regain his power to speak. He would find a way to support his mother and sister. And in doing so, he would become a man. Not, perhaps, the man he should have been had he not been such a quitter on the field of battle. But, perhaps, the man he was meant to be.

He sighed.

Would he ever become the kind of man who might, one day, deserve a pretty girl like Lucy Williams sitting by his side?

He certainly had his work cut out for him.

Chapter Four

Lucy perused the bookshelves before her, tapping her fingers across the spines of the leather-bound volumes. Lord Bradbury possessed an excellent library that he used but infrequently. Surely he wouldn't mind if she looked among them for something that could help her to cure the ensign.

She moved along the row of books pertaining to natural history, drifting toward the middle of the room until she spied the medical texts. Botheration, the titles of some were in Latin. Oh, it was all jolly well to teach Latin and to importune his lordship's daughters with the proper declensions of each noun but to read it oneself? Highly taxing to the nerves, and hard on the eyes. She shifted her gaze higher, looking for any treatise that might be of help.

Ah, there was something. *A Treatise Upon the Treatment of Invalids, the Infirm and Those Wounded in the Course of Battle.* A handsome volume, too, bound in heavy green leather. She fetched a step stool from the corner and stood upon it, straining to reach the text. She was still too short. What a nuisance it was to be so small in stature. Leaning forward on her slippers, Lucy grasped the dusty bookshelf in one hand, and flailed about for the book with the other. She caught hold of the spine just as the shelf wobbled, shifting her weight forward. In one ungainly movement, she leaped to the floor, book in hand.

Lucy straightened and darted a glance about the room. Good thing no servants had passed by—or worse, his lordship himself. Such an ungraceful display would no doubt be quite amusing to anyone who witnessed it. She wouldn't have fallen if the shelf hadn't wobbled at that precise moment. Really, his lordship should take better care of the library. The shelves alone could stand some straightening, a good deal of cleaning and perhaps some shoring up with hammer and nails. In fact, it was rather odd that the rest of the home was in immaculate condition, but the library—which was often a gentleman's pride and joy—should go so heartily neglected by the household staff.

She dusted the volume with her handkerchief, tucked it under her arm and then quit the library for the comfort of her room. The girls were both busy with their dancing lessons and would be occupied for another half hour or so. Perhaps she could at least begin delving into the ensign's problem before they returned.

Opening the door to her room, she was flooded anew with the peace and the beauty of it. Never before had she been given a room to call her own. The little low white bed in the corner, the settee by the fireplace and even a vanity table with a looking glass were all solely hers to enjoy. She paused for a moment, drinking it all in. How very different and how very wonderful her life was now that she was earning her own way. She must never forget or take for granted all that she was given in return for teaching Louisa and Amelia. For a penniless orphan, she'd done quite well for herself. Really, one could expect no more of life than this—a good position in a nice home. And some day, perhaps, she'd save enough to open her own little school. It wasn't much of a dream, but it was all she could permit herself, given the circumstances of her childhood.

She wedged herself into the corner of the settee with her favorite pillow at the small of her back and tucked her feet beneath her. She was now comfortable and ready for a good read. But the book was a difficult slog. So many dreadful wounds could be sustained in battle. She'd really had no idea of what the soldiers had endured.

It was no small wonder, then, that the ensign was speechless since the war. Had he been witness to but a few of these injuries it would be enough to scar him for life. And he must have been so very young during the war. A boy, really, just judging by how youthful he still looked, despite his war service. She flipped through the pages, but the wounds the author discussed were all physical in nature. There was nothing about the distress that could take over one's mind in the aftermath of a battle.

She closed the book and gently laid it to one side. She cupped her chin in her palms and concentrated on the ensign himself. After all, he could speak. It wasn't as though he were completely bereft of speech. So there could be nothing wrong with him, physically speaking. He could communicate with other soldiers and had spoken to her. So what could be helpful to him?

What could help him regain the faculties of speech completely?

Louisa and Amelia burst into her room, chattering at high volume. Snapped back from her reverie, Lucy rose, sending the volume under her settee with a swift kick. Explaining just why she had such a treatise in her room to two curious young ladies was a greater task than she was equal to at the moment. Better to hide it than to explain it.

"Oh, Lucy, such fun," Amelia panted, fanning herself with her hand. "The dancing master said I am a natural, so graceful. I cannot wait for my first Assembly Rooms ball, when I shall dance until dawn."

"Not if Papa says anything about it. He's already said you must be home after the supper is served." Louisa's face clouded. "And besides, he liked my dancing, too," she grumbled, flinging herself on the settee.

"That may well be, but you shall have to wait two more years before you can flaunt your skills," Amelia retorted, spinning around on one foot. "I shall only wait a few short days."

Lucy gave an inward sigh. Trouble was brewing yet again. Time to split the girls up for a while. Though Amelia's upcoming debut was rather exciting, her manner of crowing about her good fortune to her younger sister was wearing to everyone's nerves—particularly Lucy's, as she often had to act as peacemaker between the pair. "Amelia, my dear, you should go to Sophie's room at once and be fitted for some new dresses. Louisa, you may stay here with me. We shan't go back to the schoolroom today. You two are far too overwrought to concentrate on any more lessons."

Amelia giggled and executed an extraordinarily

deep curtsy to Lucy and Louisa, then flounced out of the room. Louisa sat glumly, plucking at the needlepoint pillow she had drawn into her lap.

Lucy took her small hands and gave them a gentle squeeze. Louisa and she were very close—closer than her and Amelia though she strove to hide it. She loved them both—but felt more kinship with Louisa. She was smaller than her sister, more hesitant and quieter. She had little of Amelia's verve but was sweet and dear to Lucy—as dear to her as family. "I know how difficult it must be for you now, Louisa. But you must know that your turn will soon come. And then you'll be dancing in a ballroom, wearing a fine frock just as your sister shall in a few weeks' time."

Louisa sniffed, turning her face downward. "I know it seems silly of me. But I can't help it. And when Amelia starts crowing about her new gowns and her parties, well, I just want to throw things against a nearby wall."

Lucy could not suppress a smile. "Louisa, dear, you must have patience and faith."

Louisa sighed and pulled her hands away from Lucy's grasp. Her brow remained deeply furrowed.

Oh, bother. None of this was helping. Lucy searched Louisa's anguished expression. Though it *did* seem silly, a pang tugged at her heart as she remembered just how quickly Louisa's debut would come. Though the time would feel like an eternity to the young lady, they must cherish the few years they had left together. She must find a way to distract her charge, to entertain her, as Amelia enjoyed her first glittering season in Bath.

"Well, then. Why don't we suspend our regular schoolroom lessons?" Lucy asked, eyeing Louisa carefully. "It will be difficult to move forward anyway, with

Amelia going for fittings and the like. Perhaps you and I could have more outings together. Bath is alive with history. We should enjoy it."

Louisa glanced up, hope dawning on her woebegone face. "Could we, Lucy?"

Lucy shrugged. "I don't see why not, as long as your father approves."

"Oh, Lucy!" Louisa wrapped her arms around Lucy's neck, giving her a fierce hug. "You are so kind. And what fun that will be—just we two. Can I ask Papa today when he returns from his club?"

"I think it would be better if I asked his lordship. But it wouldn't hurt if you showed him you approve of the plan." Lucy grinned. Good. Things were turning out better than she had hoped. She hated to see Louisa sulking. "Would you like to take tea in your room?"

"No," Louisa replied with a definite shake of her head. "I like your room better."

"Silly gel." Lucy ruffled Louisa's curls with an affectionate gesture. "I'll go downstairs and make some tea and bring it up. The others are busy with Amelia's party. You don't mind, do you? Do you want to help me?"

"I'd rather stay here." Louisa stretched out. "My head is beginning to ache."

"Ah, then you need food and drink," Lucy admonished. "I'll be back as soon as I can."

She returned to her room just quarter of an hour later, bearing a tray with steaming hot tea and chocolate biscuits. Louisa was still sprawled across the settee, but she was reading that certain familiar green volume her governess had tried so desperately to conceal.

Lucy set the tea tray down carefully, busying herself with the cups and saucers. The questions were going to start soon; why, she could feel them bubbling to Louisa's surface. She must compose herself and think of a way to explain the book without inciting further curiosity. She poured a cup of tea for her charge, adding two spoonfuls of sugar as Louisa loved.

Louisa sat up, casting the book aside, and accepted the teacup. "Lucy, why did you borrow this book from Papa's library?"

Ah, there you go. The questions had begun. "I was using that book for some research, Louisa. That is all."

Louisa took a careful sip of scalding tea. "But you are no nurse, Lucy. What do you need to research war wounds for?"

There was no way to hide the whole truth. "I am helping a veteran of Waterloo. There is a group of veterans who meet at Saint Swithin's, and I have been charged with the task of helping one of them regain the power of speech."

Louisa set her cup aside. "Really, Lucy? Can I help, too?"

Lucy choked on her tea, spluttering and wheezing into her handkerchief. "H-h-help?" she coughed. "H-how on earth can you help?"

Louisa sighed. "I don't know." She dropped her eyes to her cup, and the corners of her mouth creased. "I could read about cures or something. I feel so useless, Lucy. With Amelia getting to have her debut—it's like she's already a lady and grown up, and I am just stuck here. . . ." A single tear traced down her cheek.

"Oh, Louisa." Lucy gathered her close. In her innermost heart, Louisa had always been her favorite.

"Listen, Louisa. You may help me. In fact, I should love to have your assistance. Perhaps we could scour your papa's library for more volumes on treating war injuries. He has quite a large collection, you know, and few people seem to ever go in there."

"Oh, Papa cares little for the library. It was my mother's favorite room in the house, but since she died, he hardly ever goes in there." Louisa hiccupped and pulled away from Lucy. "He won't mind if we use it, though."

Lucy stroked Louisa's cheek. Her ladyship had passed away just a few years before of a wasting disease. Even the curative Bath waters had offered little relief. No small wonder, then, that his lordship had allowed that particular room to fall slowly into disrepair. She ran her hand over Louisa's forehead and paused. "You feel warm, my dear. Are you quite well?"

"I feel miserable," Louisa admitted. "My head aches, and my throat burns." She reclined against the settee, closing her eyes. Dark shadows ringed those closed eyes. And her cheeks were a trifle flushed, too.

"Time for bed, then," Lucy replied briskly. The headache, the sore throat and the moodiness—signs that Louisa was likely coming down with a head cold. She tugged at Louisa's hands, pulling her from the settee. "Go to your room and put on your nightgown. I'll warm some broth and be in to take care of you in just a few moments."

Louisa stood, rubbing her forehead with one shaky hand. Then, in one sudden movement, she grasped Lucy by the waist, holding her tightly. "Lucy, you are too good to me. As good to me as my own mama would be if she were but here."

Tears stung the back of Lucy's eyes as she watched her charge leave. Did Lucy really think of her as a mama? Lucy touched her fingertip to the corner of her eye. She would never have children of her own, of course. Marriage was not for her. So Louisa's love meant the world to Lucy. She was so fortunate to have such good, caring girls to teach. So many of her friends went into service upon leaving the orphanage—and such tales they would tell! Letters sent back to chums still in school detailed the horrors of working for spoiled children, lazy or even libertine parents. From these letters, she gleaned that finding a frog in one's bed was a matter of course in some governess's lives. She was so very fortunate. She must never forget that or take it for granted.

She picked up the book that Louisa had set aside. Of course, there was no way that Louisa could really assist with healing the ensign. Why, if Lucy felt overwhelmed by the task—and she did—then a fourteen-year-old miss could hardly do better. On the other hand, 'twould be nice to have Louisa with her often in the coming weeks. A new project, some interesting outings—these matters would keep the girl occupied, her thoughts further from her sister's dazzling debut.

And, of course, Louisa's presence would help distract Lucy from the ensign, as well. It was no good to think about the man as anything but a pleasant friend—the kind of person one would help when he was in trouble. She had no business entertaining any but friendly thoughts for him. She was a governess, after all. She must stick to her purpose and earn her own way in life.

She laid the book on her dressing table and then rushed down to the kitchen to see to Louisa's broth.

* * *

James lay in the twilight hush of his room, his hands folded behind his head. The ropes under his feather tick gave a squeak of protest as he shifted his weight, trying to ease his restless body and mind. He wanted to overcome his problems and become a better man, but he had not the faintest idea where to begin. He had no real purpose in Bath. He could join his mother and his sister Mary in the poky cottage they called home in Essex, but they were depending on him to make their lives better or easier. There was nothing he could do to achieve that in Essex, no matter what his mother believed.

His mother still clung to the idea that the Rowlands were somehow still of the nobility, minor though his family was in the great scheme of things. An air of ruined grace still clung to her—the way that dried roses still retained some scent. And she didn't want him to work with his hands, didn't want him to seek employment in any profession that would somehow "disgrace" the Rowland name. In fact, Mother held out hope that he would, in time, marry an heiress who could restore the family's dwindled fortunes.

He laughed—a bitter, scraping sound that echoed off the bare walls. Poor Mother. As if any heiress would want him. No woman with a grain of sense would. Would she? He caught his breath a little, as an image of sparkling brown eyes and a clever mouth drifted across his mind before he pushed it away. Lucy Williams would never take him to heart. She was a sweet girl, a thoughtful one, the kind of girl who would help anyone in need. And she happened to take an interest in him because Cantrill asked her to and nothing more.

'Twas folly to think anything but friendship would come of knowing her. Although friendship with Lucy could be quite sweet. She was such a nice girl.

Forcing his mind back to the matter at hand, he decided that he needed to have some occupation. Something to distract his mind from its ceaseless wandering over the fields of La Sainte Haye, back to his family in Essex and over to Lucy Williams. He must have some purpose in life—this endless drifting was insupportable, unbearable even.

He flung the pillow to the floor. Macready had an occupation—devoting himself to nursing back his wounds until he was hale and hearty. He worked at it every day, taking the waters, getting fresh air and food, learning to return to civilian life. Cantrill worked by helping others, eschewing material comforts so that others worse off than he might thrive and prosper.

It was time, long past time for James to get on with his life. To become a man and not the scared, shrinking boy who'd returned from the war. When he met with Cantrill on the morrow, he would ask the captain to help him find some kind of occupation. Even if Mother fainted at the thought of her son working with his hands, he must do something.

He could not idly stand by and remain a lily-livered coward forever.

That life had to die—as it should have in the rye field at La Sainte Haye.

Chapter Five

Thank goodness she had sent for the physician. His mere presence was enough to calm Lucy's nerves. Her heart slowed to a normal beat as he took Louisa's pulse, his brow furrowed with concentration. Dr. Phillips was the best doctor in Bath, and his word on any illness could be considered the best diagnosis one could hope for. When Louisa awoke this morning with flushed cheeks and a damp brow, it was time enough to send for the good doctor. And in this, Lord Bradbury assured her, he was in complete accord.

His lordship's connections could be most reassuring. And the care he always showed for his two daughters was heartening. She took a deep breath and said a silent prayer for Louisa's health.

Dr. Phillips placed Louisa's wrist gently back onto the counterpane and turned to Lucy. "I really think it's only a cold, Miss Williams. Keep giving her the chicken broth, and add some weak tea. Perhaps a few crusts of toast when she begins to improve. She should be quite well within a matter of days."

"Matter of days?" Louisa lamented hoarsely, turning her head on her pillow. "But I shall miss Amelia's debut."

"Well, we shan't be going in any event, sick or well," Lucy reminded her crisply. Dr. Phillips's advice was so welcome that she snapped back from her worry without even missing a beat. "After all, you aren't old enough to attend such an event. But thank goodness you aren't seriously ill. You must learn to count your blessings, Louisa." She used her best governess tone of voice, for it covered how very shaken she'd been. She was so certain Louisa was on the brink of a dreadful illness.

Louisa grumbled and turned away from them both, burying her head in her pillow. Ah, she was already beginning to improve, then. Wanting to have her own way. When Louisa grew passive, that's when you knew she was sick.

"Well, Dr. Phillips, I do appreciate your coming on such short notice." Lucy helped him collect his things from the little birch wood bench at the foot of Louisa's bed. "With so many guests expected so soon, I wanted to make sure we weren't dealing with a gravely sick little girl."

"Not at all. I am always glad to come and see to our Louisa." Dr. Phillips straightened and shot Louisa a merry look from under his brows. "Mind you, listen to what Miss Williams says. I'll be back to check on you in a matter of days." He wagged a warning finger at her and turned to go.

Louisa sat up, casting her pillow onto the floor. "Dr. Phillips, I wanted to ask you a question. If a man is in battle and later has trouble speaking, could you cure him?"

Dr. Phillips turned from the doorway and looked over at Louisa, his brows beetled in confusion.

Lucy gasped. "Louisa—surely the doctor has no time—" Oh, the doctor would think them most assuredly too forward. And if James ever knew they'd spoken of him…oh, dear. He was such a proud man. He would not like it in the least.

"Nonsense. It would be an interesting case for him, wouldn't it, Dr. Phillips?" Louisa replied in her most wheedling tone.

Dr. Phillips cocked his head to one side, as though considering the matter. "A soldier? Not one of your beaus, I should think, Miss Louisa?" His expression was both kindly and skeptical. "How do you know of such a young man?"

"Oh, he's not my beau. He's Lucy's beau." Louisa beamed up at the doctor, ignoring Lucy's pained gasp.

"He's not—" Lucy began. Oh, this was dreadful. A governess with a beau was as good as sacked in Lord Bradbury's home. She shot a look that was half pleading, half threatening in Louisa's direction. Her charge merely widened her already large brown eyes and gave a small, noncommittal shrug at her governess's distress.

Dr. Phillips turned to Lucy, overriding her small protest and ignoring their obvious—if silent—disagreement. "Well, Miss Williams, what do you know of his injury? Was his throat injured, or did he sustain any kind of head wound?"

Lucy sighed. She'd deal with Louisa's brazen behavior later. As for now—well, in for a penny, in for a pound. Dr. Phillips's opinion could actually be quite helpful, given how highly regarded he was in Bath.

And as his fee was so expensive, neither she nor James could consult him on their own. "No. As far as I know, there's no reason why he shouldn't be able to speak. He can, in fact, speak to some people. His brothers in arms, for example. He's spoken to me a bit—small phrases, you understand, and with a noted stammer."

"Hmm." The doctor drummed his fingers on his worn leather bag. "I imagine, then, that his injury has less to do with the physical and more to do with the mental distress he underwent in battle." He straightened and fetched his bag from a nearby mahogany chair. "I'd have to see him, though, to make any kind of informed diagnosis."

"Well, could you?" Louisa flicked her long braid over one shoulder. "When you come back to see me later this week. Lucy could bring him here."

"Absolutely not," Lucy broke in, her mouth agape. "Forgive us, Dr. Phillips. We've intruded too long on your good nature." She gestured toward the bedroom door, fixing Louisa with her best governess-in-charge look.

"Well, why not?" Louisa wailed, her tone belying how very feverish and miserable she must be feeling. "After all, I am sure Dr. Phillips can help more than all those dreadful books in Papa's library."

Dr. Phillips held up one hand, silencing them both. "Miss Louisa, I understand your desire to help. But you must realize that the young man may be offended or hurt if Miss Williams dragged him here—to his lordship's home—for me to poke and prod at him. But—" he turned to Lucy, a kind expression lighting his eyes "—you can let the young man know that I would be happy to see him. He's part of the veterans' group, is he not?"

Lucy nodded. The feeling that she had somehow betrayed Rowland welled in her throat, making speech impossible.

"Well, then, I would be delighted to see him at no charge. I do quite a bit of work for the veterans' group, as Lieutenant Cantrill will attest. You may tell him I said so, or you might find it easier to have the lieutenant reassure him. I don't want the lad to think I am seeing him out of charity. Rather, it's my way of thanking those lads for all they've done for our country." He nodded at them both and wagged a warning finger at Louisa. "Now, listen to what Miss Williams says. I expect to see you hale and hearty when I return later."

Lucy walked with him to the bedroom door and ushered him out. Then she turned to Louisa, who sat, sniffling, her eyes red, her pallor dull.

"Don't be mad, Lucy," Louisa pleaded. "I want to help, and Dr. Phillips will be of assistance—I hope." She plucked uncertainly at the coverlet, her flushed cheeks and sweaty brow betraying her illness.

Lucy sighed, sinking onto the foot of the bed. She could never stay mad at Louisa long, especially when she obviously felt so poorly. "I'm not angry with you, Louisa. And you're right—Dr. Phillips can help a good deal more than any old Latin text we'll find in your father's library. But—the ensign is very proud. He might not like that we've spoken about him to Dr. Phillips without his consent. I shall have to handle this matter very carefully if I am not to offend him."

Louisa gave a mighty sneeze, wiping her reddened

nose on her embroidered handkerchief. "Oh, I'm sure you can find a way, Lucy. You're so clever."

Clever? Hardly. She gave a rueful inward chuckle. The only way she had managed her life thus far was to move into unfamiliar situations with wariness and crouch there until she became entirely comfortable. But this—this was different than trying to do well at the orphanage, or seeking a position as a governess. This meant meddling in another man's life.

There was no guarantee that Ensign James Rowland would like or appreciate her interference, however good her intentions might be. He might be ashamed of her for discussing his impediment without his permission. Or he might be offended that Dr. Phillips was offering his services free of charge. The doctor's offer might smack of charity to the ensign. And as a proud man, he might not be willing to accept it.

Or he could be angry on both counts.

She twirled a lock of her dark hair, staring out the window. Only one thing was certain. She must proceed with infinite caution.

"What ho, Rowland, it's good to see you," Cantrill said in a hearty tone of voice as he opened the door to his flat. "Come in, come in. My place is in a bit of uproar, pardon the mess. Mrs. Pierce is tidying up for my mother's impending visit."

Rowland stepped over the threshold, his hat in hand. Indeed, Cantrill's flat—normally as neat and spare as a soldier would have it—was a welter of dusters, brooms, and carpet-beaters. Rowland shrugged and allowed Cantrill to lead him, zigzagging through the mess to the relative peace of the little parlor.

"What can I bring you? Tea? We'll have to make it ourselves—Mrs. Pierce is far too busy at the moment to bother with refreshments, I'm afraid." Cantrill motioned Rowland to a small chair near the hearth.

"Nothing…for me." James cleared his throat and took a deep breath. He could speak to the lieutenant, it was true—but that didn't mean his speech was free-flowing and unfettered. He must get to the heart of the matter. There was always the lurking fear that speech would elude him entirely if he took too long to come to the point.

Cantrill sat across from James, his normally pleasant face reflecting, perhaps, some of the confusion and exhaustion that his mother's impending visit was causing in his flat. Funny, mothers could cause such mixed emotions. After all, James loved his mother and wanted to support her. But what if she were on her way to Bath right now to see him? He shuddered at the mere thought. No. He had definite sympathy for Cantrill today.

"I've come…about a job." James cleared his throat again. "I must have—some occupation."

Cantrill sat back in his chair and rubbed his hand across his brow. "Are you quite sure you're ready for work, old fellow?"

The old anger and self-hatred began welling under the surface, causing James to swallow convulsively. "I'm not injured," he muttered after an eternity.

"No, no of course not. But many of the other veterans, you know, are having a difficult time making this transition to civilian life. Some of them have elected to refrain from work for several months until they feel equal to the task of going to work every day." Cantrill furrowed his brow, gazing over at him with a piercing gaze. "No need to rush things, you know."

"I—I—I'm not." James breathed deeply, calming the anger as it began bubbling over. Cantrill wasn't meaning to condescend, after all. "Long p-p-past due. N-n-need to be useful for s-something."

A flicker crossed Cantrill's expression, as though he finally understood how very positive James was about seeking a position. "Very well," he responded in a genial tone of voice. "What can you do?"

He paused. Not very much, he must admit. He'd been educated in the little country village with Mother bewailing their lost chances at Eton. But he liked the village and liked learning and had no desire to run off to boarding school with a lot of tony chaps who'd look at him as a charity case. And then he'd lied about his age and gone to war. He had very little to show for his life. But still, one had to say something.

"I—I—I don't know, really," he finally responded, his voice sounding sheepish even to his own ears. "S-something that doesn't require s-speech, I imagine."

Cantrill gave a rueful chuckle. "I should think some occupation with your hands would work well. Would you have any objection to working with a carpenter? There's a fine one here in Bath, Henry Felton, who does quite a bit of cabinetry and the like. He was apprenticed during John Wood the Younger's days and knows more about woodworking than anyone in the country, I wager."

Working with his hands? Mother would perish at the thought, but the idea was strangely appealing. He'd only ever whittled a few things as a hobby, but the idea of building fine, strong furniture and cabinets—well, that gave a fellow something to do. And it would never matter whether he could utter a single syllable.

"I-I-Is F-Felton hiring?" A glimmer of hope welled in his chest.

"Yes. As a matter of fact, he came by the veterans' group meeting about a fortnight ago, seeking to apprentice someone in his new shop. Felton had an assistant, but the fellow married and moved to Brighton. So he's in need of someone to help—and quickly, too." Cantrill glanced at the little mantel clock. "I'd step 'round there today, if I were you. Tell him you are one of the veterans. I'm sure he'd be more than happy to have you."

"I—I—I'll go n-now." James rose, knocking his chair backward a few feet in his haste. "Apologies, L-L-Lieutenant."

"Not at all. It matches the higgledy-piggledy nature of my entire flat." Cantrill held out his hand with a grin. "Felton's shop is located on Bennett, near the Assembly Rooms. Best of luck to you, Rowland. Though I am sure you won't need it."

James thanked the lieutenant and saw himself out of the flat. 'Twas midmorning, and the weather was fine enough for a walk. In a mere quarter of an hour, he would change his life.

As he strolled up Broad Street, his nervousness grew. Perhaps he wouldn't be able to speak at all once he arrived. What then? Would he just stammer like an idiot?

He could turn back now. Head back to his comfortable life in the humble flat on Beau Street. He'd been such a failure that no one expected anything of him, besides Mother—and even her hopes were vague and rapidly dying. Cantrill had all but turned him away from seeking employment at first. That's how very little everyone thought of him.

He paused, grasping the cool iron of a nearby fence rail until his knuckles whitened. He'd been a coward before. He'd never be one again. Even if he couldn't utter a word to Felton, he'd find some way to communicate. Hand gestures. Writing on foolscap. Scratching words in the dirt. Anything to finally overcome this impediment and get on with his life.

He released the fence post, his palm smarting from the pressure. Good. Pain, strangely, kept him calm. It gave him something to focus upon. As he drew closer to George Street, the sight of the walled-off garden on one side street brought Miss Williams sharply back to mind. It was here that she had asked him if he wanted to be well. It was here that she had offered to help him.

What would Miss Williams think of this plan? Would she approve? She, who earned her bread through her own work, surely would. He wanted her approval. Why? 'Twas hard to say. She was just, well, the kind of girl who any man would want to be friends with. She seemed to have such a tremendous sense of spirit. If he got the position, then he'd have good news for her the next time they met—news that would bring a light to those lovely, velvety brown eyes of hers.

He hastened his steps, fear melting away as he imagined her quick, slanted gaze, the freckles dusting the tip of her nose. It would be nice to have something good to tell her. To show her that he was becoming more of a man.

And there was Bennett Street. The Assembly Rooms loomed ahead, gracious and aloof. And there, with a handsome wooden sign bolted sturdily to a pole, was Felton's shop.

He poked his head in the door, breathing deeply of the fresh, exhilarating scent of newly shaved wood. He stepped inside, his boots scratching against the sawdust that littered the floor. The shop was strangely hushed, as though not a living soul were present. James scanned the room with a nervous eye. What if they were all gone? He needed to speak with Felton now. He needed to go through with the matter now that he'd finally screwed his courage to the sticking-place.

He scuffed his boots across the floor. The sound echoed through the building. He strained his ears to hear any scrap of sound. And then he caught the faintest tsk-tsk-tsk of metal scraping against wood and strode toward the sound.

A tall, graying man was bent over a workbench, using a chisel of sorts to carve an intricate scroll onto a piece of fine, unblemished mahogany. Without thinking, James let out a cheerful whistle of appreciation. Startled, the man dropped his chisel and turned an affronted gaze toward Rowland.

"Well then, who might you be?" He challenged, a glint of either mirth or annoyance in his faded blue eyes.

'Twas now or never. "Rowland. I—I—I'm a veteran. Cantrill sent me here to see about a position."

Chapter Six

'Twas Thursday, so the veterans would surely be gathering at Saint Swithin's for their weekly meeting. Lucy hastened her steps. She must find the ensign alone, before the large crowd of men began clustering into the vestibule of the chapel. If she were to have any hope of convincing him to see Dr. Phillips, she would have to make her argument to him when they were alone. His pride would make it impossible for her to convince him around his brothers in arms, even though they—if they had any sense at all—would agree with her.

The bells tolled the hour as she trotted up the interminable steps. She flicked a glance around the courtyard, seeking out the willow tree they'd sat under when she read to him before. He was not waiting. Oh, well. The weather wasn't especially fine today. 'Twas humid with only the occasional fitful breeze. Perhaps Rowland was inside, waiting with Cantrill.

She paused at the top of the steps, panting. Goodness, she was always arriving to meet Rowland with a flushed face and bated breath. He must think her a very curious sort of person, always rushing about.

Funny, she wasn't like this with anyone else. She was always cautious and deliberate in her dealings with her charges and the household staff. What was it about Ensign Rowland that made her scurry about, like a mouse after a delicious morsel of cheese?

She wrenched open the door and was confronted with a roiling mass of humanity—men, some wounded and some whole, talked in small groups, while women, old and young alike, stood slightly apart. Children darted in and out of the pews, playing hide-and-seek. But nowhere in this throng did she spy the man she sought. She stood on tiptoe, straining her gaze past a cluster of men who were talking in measured tones amongst themselves. But nowhere was a lanky young man—easily a foot taller than these others. Not that she noticed his great height. Well, not especially.

"Looking for someone?" A pleasant voice rumbled behind her. Lucy started and turned around, heat rushing to her cheeks at being caught gawping. How embarrassing.

"Lieutenant Cantrill." She bobbed a quick curtsy. "I was...looking for the ensign. Our reading lesson, you know." She wasn't ready to admit to Cantrill that she was trying to help cure Rowland. Or that there might be anything more to their meetings than what he'd asked—which was just companionship for the ensign. Nothing more.

"I'm afraid he won't be here, not for the foreseeable future." The lieutenant gave her a rueful grin. "He got a position here in Bath with Henry Felton, the carpenter. So this new job in woodworking is occupying most of Rowland's time."

For a moment, her tongue was tied. Rowland had an

occupation? That was excellent news of course. But—did that mean he didn't want her to read to him anymore? Her heart dropped like a stone in her chest. "Is he ever coming back to the veterans' group?"

"Well, I gather he must make a good impression his first few weeks of working. And that must mean sticking to the schedule Felton gives him. In time, perhaps, he can join our meetings again if Felton can spare him on Thursday mornings." Cantrill checked his pocket watch. "I should start the meeting soon, Miss Williams. It's getting rather late in the morning."

"Yes, of course." Lucy gave a quick nod. She shouldn't detain him. There really was nothing more to say. Rowland had a new position, so he was doing quite well. And Cantrill didn't seem to think she needed to continue working with Rowland—or if he did, he didn't say so. But, even so, she couldn't hold her tongue. "Do you think the ensign will continue to need me to read to him? To help with his speech problems?"

Cantrill hesitated a moment, a kindly light kindling in his brown eyes. "I think that friendship is still important to Rowland, job or no job," he responded in a heartfelt tone. "But since his time is rather occupied at the moment, perhaps you should talk to him about the matter yourself. As I said, he's at Felton's shop, near the Assembly Rooms." He bowed. "I must start the meeting, Miss Williams, but thank you again for helping young Rowland."

Lucy nodded, and Cantrill worked his way through the throng of veterans and families who filed after him, filling up row upon row of pews. Thus left alone in the aisle, Lucy must present quite an odd picture to the assembled group. Neither wife nor sister, she had no reason to be included in this mass of people seeking comfort and aid. Her face heated to the roots of her hairline. She hated being conspicuous.

She quit the vestibule, her slippered feet making nary a sound as she creaked open the door and stepped outside. A feeling of loss, almost of homesickness, washed over her. Rowland would not seek her out, at least for the foreseeable future. What could she do? And, well, it hurt a bit that he hadn't sent 'round a message. Anything to let her know that he wouldn't be at the meetings anymore. Or even just a note to share his triumphant news. For it was quite extraordinary that he had landed a job. Why, within just a week or so, he had come so far. She was proud of him. Too bad she could not convey this feeling of pride to him in some way.

She scuffed at a pebble with her toe and started down the steps. Now she had an entire day off and nothing to do. Sophie was off doing something and would be coming to the veterans' group later in the morning. Her charges had happily planned a day out with their papa, now that Amelia's debut had gone successfully and Louisa was quite well. No one had any need of her today. And that made one feel quite lonely and insignificant. As though she didn't really matter in this world.

At the bottom of the steps, she paused. She could run by Felton's shop and just congratulate the ensign. After all, it would be the friendly thing to do. And, while she was in that part of town, she could stop by the bookseller and find a few new books for the schoolroom. That would be a pleasant diversion, and though the weather was rather peevish, it would be a shame to head back straight to Lord Bradbury's on her day off.

As she strolled toward the Assembly Rooms, she racked her brain for a way to approach the ensign. She'd have to tamp down her injured feelings, that was for sure. If she showed him how very hurt she was that he didn't tell her of his good fortune, he might think her quite silly. Or suspect that she had some reason for caring about him beyond the constraints of friendship. Which of course wasn't true. In fact, she wasn't even sure why she felt so hurt. It was none of her affair, after all.

She hastened her steps, as though by quickening her pace, she could run away from her thoughts. 'Twas worth a try. How wonderful it would be to run and run and run until her heart beat wildly against her breast and be far, far away from her troubling thoughts.

She was a governess, after all. She had no family. She had to make her own way in the world. She had no time whatsoever for any silliness about caring about a young man. In even thinking about it, she was making herself ridiculous.

By the time she reached Felton's shop, she was out of breath. Again. It was her lot in life to always arrive breathless before any meeting with the ensign. She would never present a picture of composure to him. Never.

She tried the door latch, her hand shaking a bit. Inside, the shop smelled pleasantly of sawdust and lemon oil. Her slippers scrunched across the floor, but as she peered around, she could discern no one. Perhaps Rowland wasn't here after all.

Well, in for a penny, in for a pound. Holding her head up high, as though she were quite used to mucking around carpentry shops, she wound along behind a large table. An older man, with graying hair and spectacles, glanced up sharply, as though astonished by her presence.

"May I help you, Miss?" His voice was pleasant enough.

"Yes. Are you Mr. Felton?" She gave him a nervous smile. Somehow, it was easier to say his name than the one of the man she truly sought.

"I am." He rose, dusting his hands on his rough work apron. "Are you in need of some carpentry work, Miss?"

"No, sir." She coughed. The sawdust was choking her. Surely 'twas that and not the embarrassment of having to utter the real purpose for her call. "I've come to speak to Ensign Rowland. I understand he's working with you."

A sudden grin broke across his face, like the sun peeking through storm clouds. "He is. Just follow me." He beckoned her over his shoulder.

A torrent of words poured out of her as she followed him toward the back of the workshop. "I work with the veterans' group, you see. And Lieutenant Cantrill told me I might find him here. So I came to see him about—" She broke off, colliding with Felton as he paused in a doorway.

"You've got a visitor," Felton announced. "You may take a bit of a respite, if you like, Rowland. You've been working hard all morning." Turning, Felton gave Lucy a rather cheeky wink. "Miss." Then he wound his way back through the shop, leaving Lucy standing on the threshold like some ridiculous and lovelorn statue.

Rowland's heart pounded in his chest. She was here. Lucy was here. What was she doing here? How did she know he was working for Felton? She stood, still and silent, with dust motes and bits of sawdust falling around her like snow. He stood, schooling his expression to remain pleasant and neutral. He had no right to show his wonderment at her presence.

She stepped into his workroom, her honest, forthright gazing boring into him. "I understand congratulations are in order, Ensign," she began in that quiet, musical voice of hers. "I went to the veterans' group for our meeting, and Cantrill said you wouldn't be going to the meetings for quite some time."

The meetings. He hadn't forgotten so much as he had been wrapped up in his new prospects. He'd wanted to tell Miss Williams about his new position many times, but why would she care? Even if he had sent 'round a note, it would seem awfully forward of him. After all, he was nothing to her except a charity case. No need to make himself ridiculous.

"M-m-my apologies," he began. His throat worked, but nothing else would come out. Any explanation was choked off, and he stood there, staring at her like a fool. Yet again his stammer was robbing him of any dignity.

"No apologies necessary." She turned away from him and began fidgeting with a block of wood he had hewn earlier in the morning, rocking it back and forth on his worktable. "Lieutenant Cantrill said that I could continue our lessons if you wish, but of course, I don't see how you would have the time. Being busy with your new position here and all."

He watched her graceful fingers. Of course, she was busy, too. One of her pupils was making her debut soon—or had already. So likely Miss Williams was stretched thin. Perhaps this was her way of politely letting him know. He understood. James nodded, but her face remained stubbornly turned away from his and she did not see his expression.

"I am happy you got this job, you know." Her voice was quieter now; he had to strain to hear it. "It shows how determined you are to improve." She gave the block of wood a final pat and turned his way. "I also wanted to tell you that I spoke to Dr. Phillips about you. He works with the veterans' group, you know. He said if you wanted his opinion on your condition he would be happy to speak with you."

Rowland's blood turned a shade cooler, and a buzzing sound caught his ears. Miss Williams had spoken about his condition to someone else? This wasn't right. He thought—he thought—well, no matter what he thought, it wasn't quite fair. "W-w-what?"

She looked up sharply, as though the word shocked her. Or perhaps she was reacting to his tone. "I spoke to Dr. Phillips last week," she repeated. "Louisa was ill with a bad cold, and while he was there, I asked him what he thought could be done with your speaking problem."

He looked down at his hands as they gripped the side of the worktable. His knuckles were growing white. Anger and despair poured through him like molten lead. He really was nothing more to Lucy Williams than a charity project. And she, whom he had trusted—she, who had asked if he really wanted to be well—had discussed his problem with someone else. The fact that she spoke to a physician as if his condition was an ailment to be cured was ludicrous anyway. There was nothing wrong with him except his own cowardice. He knew it, and the fact that she spoke about him as though he were a particularly interesting specimen with some tony doctor served to double his humiliation.

"N-n-nothing c-c-can be d-d-done," he managed, his face growing hotter as he tripped over the words. His stammer was growing worse, hang it all. "T-tis my own cowardice. N-nothing more. D-do not speak of it again, Miss Williams. T-t-to anyone."

Her velvety brown eyes grew wider and her face paled until the freckles stood out in bold relief across the bridge of her nose. "I beg your pardon, Ensign Rowland?"

"I c-c-can't speak because I was a coward on the b-b-battlefield," he spat, clenching the workbench until a splinter stabbed his palm. Oddly, it caused no pain. "N-no physician c-can help me. There's nothing wrong with me."

"I see," she murmured. But something in her expression gave him pause. What was she thinking? Was she pitying him, even now? He didn't want her pity. He wanted her to like him. Not, of course, that she would fall madly in love with him, but it would be nice to be anything to her besides a mere curiosity.

"D-don't." He gave a long, shuddering sigh. He didn't want her concern.

"Don't what?" She gazed at him with those same fathomless eyes that had haunted him for days after he first met her.

Don't pity me. Don't coddle me. Don't think of me as less than a man. But the words would not come.

It was time to put an end to this interview. He was dangerously close to losing what little grip he had on his infamous temper. 'Twould do neither of them any good if he began throwing tools against the wall in a fit of rage.

"D-don't ever speak of my condition with anyone else again." Rowland released his grip on the table and regarded her as evenly as he could. "T-tis my affair and no one else's."

"I see." Lucy drew herself up to her full height, but even with perfect posture, she still was so small. His heart lurched. He'd been a bully and a buffoon, and here she was—the only person who cared enough about him to seek to ease his affliction. When would his temper cease to get the better of him?

"I apologize, Ensign Rowland. I knew, in some ways, that speaking to Dr. Phillips was an invasion of your privacy. I hesitated to do so but thought perhaps he could really be of assistance. Please understand it was done in an attempt to help you rather than as a way to hurt you." She turned to go and then whirled around, her skirts flaring about her slippers. "And I understand from Lieutenant Cantrill that you will be far too busy in your work here to attend any more meetings. Shall I consider our reading sessions finished for the time being?"

He nodded. His heart was lodged in his throat, making speech impossible once more.

"Very well." Were those tears in her eyes? Surely not. He must be imagining things—putting thoughts and emotions on Lucy that weren't really there. "I wish you the best of luck, Ensign. I hope your new position gives you a great deal of happiness."

He nodded once more. She patted the table with one graceful, gloved hand and gave him a long, searching glance. "Did you know that you regain your speech almost entirely when you are angry, Ensign? I just thought you should know." Then she left, taking with her the last bit of beauty, of life, of hope in that small, dusty workroom.

Rowland sank onto his step stool, the weight of her departure sinking like lead into his very being. He had been so close to having her friendship, and then he threw it away.

When would he stop being a coward?

Chapter Seven

Lucy was still shaking when she let herself into the back door of Lord Bradbury's townhome. Whether she was shaking with fury or fear mattered not a whit. In fact, she refused to examine her emotions too closely. She needed the privacy of her room. No, she needed first a bracingly hot cup of tea. Which she would then carry to the comfort and solitude of her bedroom. She would relax then for never had she been so rattled in her life.

Lucy retrieved the kettle from the cabinet and began boiling water for her tea. Thank goodness the kitchen was blessedly empty. She didn't want to make small talk with any of the other servants at the moment. She smoothed her still-trembling hands on her apron. She needed to gain some measure of calm before speaking to anyone else.

She'd never really argued with anyone before—certainly not with a young man. She'd spent her life trying to get along with others, playing the part of helper in the background of other, more important people's lives. She never had mattered enough to anyone to even get into a disagreement. Much less a fight.

She retrieved the canister of tea leaves and placed them into the strainer, breathing deeply. The smell of tea leaves was so pleasant, so soothing. She closed her eyes and breathed once more, just as the whistle of the kettle rent the air. She splashed the hot water into the cup and carried it upstairs, not bothering with a tray and all the accoutrements of a proper tea break. She just needed to be alone, and the quicker the better.

She settled into her window seat, pressing her hot cheek to the cool glass. But her solitude was short-lived. As soon as Lucy settled behind the curtain with her cup of tea, a knock sounded on the door.

"Enter?" Perhaps it was the girls, returned from their day out with their papa. But no, Sophie poked her head in the doorway. Lucy sighed with relief. Perhaps she could confide in Sophie.

"Oh, good. I was hoping you were back." Sophie bounded into the room, plunking herself down on the settee. "I've some news. I think I shall be headed for Brightgate soon."

"Really?" Lucy's heart lurched a bit. With no more lessons, and Sophie gone, 'twould be a dreary existence indeed. It was good for her to go and all—but when Sophie left, Lucy had only her charges to talk to.

"Yes, if Charlie can arrange matters. You see, his mother is determined that I should come to Brightgate for a proper introduction to the family. I don't know how we shall manage it, but Charlie feels that perhaps Aunt Katherine could help." Sophie toyed with a loose thread on the upholstery fabric, her face turning a lovely shade of pink.

"But…your engagement isn't real, is it? I thought this was merely a ruse to keep Cantrill's mother from hounding him about marriage." Honestly, this farce of Sophie's grew stranger by the moment. Why wouldn't she just admit her love for Lieutenant Cantrill and be done?

"It was, but now our plan has taken on a life of its own." Sophie kept her face downcast, her brilliant blue eyes turned toward the Aubusson rug. "How did you fare?" she asked after a moment's pause. "Did you see your ensign today?"

"Yes, I did. But not at the veterans' group." She cleared her throat. How much of this should she tell Sophie? Sometimes, Sophie only appeared interested in her own problems. Would she even listen if Lucy spilled the whole truth? Still, Sophie was her only confidante, and she would be leaving soon for Brightgate. It wouldn't hurt to tell her everything. In truth, it would be a relief to unburden herself.

Lucy confided the whole of her morning to Sophie, whose eyebrows shot up in surprise as Lucy finished her tale. "Goodness," she breathed, patting Lucy's hand.

"So, you see, I had to run home and just give myself a moment to mull things over. I don't know what to do, Sophie. I—I have no purpose in life now. The girls are growing up and won't need me soon. Helping the ensign was going to be so interesting, and now that's gone, too. And soon you will be leaving me for Brightgate…" Hot tears welled in her eyes, and she broke off with a sniffle.

"Oh, sweet Lucy. If it makes you feel any better, have a good howl." Sophie enfolded her in a warm, violet-scented embrace, breaking down the last of Lucy's reserve. She cried until the bitter disappointment flowed from her being, washed away by her salty tears. Then, hiccupping a bit, she pulled away from Sophie and fumbled for her handkerchief.

"I'm sorry. I don't know why I am so upset." She blew her nose and gave a deep, shuddering sigh.

"Well, I imagine it's for many reasons, though I am not certain you are ready to admit them to yourself just yet," Sophie replied in a gentle tone.

Lucy glanced up, her defenses bubbling to the surface. "I don't love the ensign if that's what you are implying. He is—he was—a good friend to me. Someone of my own age, whom I could speak to. It's nice, after years of being alone, to have friends."

"Why are you so stubborn, Lucy? Why not admit that you can—and should—fall in love?"

Lucy leaned back against the comforting arm of the settee. How to explain her feelings to someone like Sophie? After all, though Sophie had never suffered poverty, she'd never been truly alone. Truly independent. She'd always had her sister and no end of swains. There was always someone there to love her, to want to take care of her. She hadn't had to learn—as Lucy had, while still quite young—that there was no one for her to depend on but herself.

"Not all of us are beautiful," she snapped, regretting her tone as soon as she'd bitten the words out. Sophie drew back a little in surprise. "Oh, I'm sorry, Sophie. It's just that I realized at a very early age that I was truly alone in this world. I cannot hope for someone to come along and take all my troubles away. I have to earn my own bread through my own wits."

"Does that mean, then, that you can never fall in love?" Sophie eyed her expectantly.

"It means that, though I may lose my heart just as anyone would, I may not allow myself the luxury of love. I'm far from an eligible match, so there is nothing to gain and much to lose should I put my heart at risk. I shouldn't lose my temper or waste any more thoughts on my situation with the ensign. We were friends, and through my own stupidity, I lost his friendship." Hateful words, they were. But it was better to be honest with oneself. There were no hearts and flowers in her future. "The only question is, what shall I do to occupy myself now that the ensign no longer wants my help?"

"Well, there is always a lot of work to be done with the veterans' group, even if the ensign is no longer attending meetings," Sophie replied in a determinedly cheerful tone of voice. "I've got a bee in my bonnet about a sewing club for the widows. Bringing everyone together to sew clothes. I think it would do the women a world of good. Some of them have such threadbare dresses. Why not do something to teach the women or the children of the group? It would help immensely, and it might make you feel better, too."

Lucy's heart warmed to the idea. The little children who darted in and out of the pews at Saint Swithin's were so adorable. How delightful it would be to sit with them, and read to them and instruct them. It would be as close to her dream of her own school as she could get. And when Louisa made her debut, and Lucy had to search for a new position, having some experience with small children might make it easier to find a new job.

"That's a brilliant idea, Sophie." She twirled a dark lock of hair around her forefinger. "I shall start making plans right now since we have the rest of the day off. And you? I suppose you'll start packing for Brightgate. How I shall miss you when you are gone, my dear."

Sophie rose, giving Lucy a deeply dimpled smile. "I love being called brilliant," she said with a laugh. "But don't worry. I'll be gone to Brightgate and home before you can say Jack Robinson. I am sure by then you'll have taught all the small urchins of the veterans' group their Latin declensions."

"Hardly." Lucy smiled. "But you've given me a sense of purpose and direction, and for that I am so thankful."

"You are welcome." Sophie started for the door, then paused, her hand on the latch. "Just promise me one thing, Lucy. Don't give up on love altogether. It's… wonderful."

Lucy gave a rueful grin. Sophie was such a romantic. She had no idea of the hard realities of life. 'Twould be a pity to squash her girlish dreams, even if they held no meaning for a spinster governess. "All right." She sighed. "I promise."

After Sophie had gone, Lucy settled at her little white desk with a sheet of foolscap. Time to plan a bright future for the lads and lasses who clustered at the meetings on Thursdays. There was no need to waste another thought on Ensign Rowland. She'd made a dreadful blunder, but she'd apologized for it. If she lingered too long, she ran the risk of being one of those obsessive old spinsters who pined after a lost love for decades. She wasn't like them. She was alive and full of purpose.

She might get lonely at times. But that was to be expected. The only way to stop those feelings was to live a life devoted to others. That was her true purpose in life. She was a mere background character in other people's lives.

"I want to go to the Assembly Rooms for our first outing," Louisa announced calmly the next morning at breakfast.

"The Assembly Rooms, Louisa? That's hardly the educational outing I had thought of," Lucy replied in her best governess tone of voice. And the Assembly Rooms were far too close to Felton's shop. Though she had resolved never to think of Ensign Rowland again, she wasn't yet ready to run the risk of seeing him so soon. "Why not something more educational in nature?"

"Because. Papa wouldn't take us to the Rooms yesterday." Louisa spread a thick layer of strawberry jam on her toast. "He said that we'd be seeing the interior of them all too soon. But that's not true for me, Lucy. It will be years and years before I get to see them." She took a bite out of her toast and chewed thoughtfully.

Lucy toyed with the eggs on her plate. Amelia was due for a series of last-minute fittings before the Assembly Rooms ball; Sophie had moved up the fittings just in case she would be departing for Brightgate within the week. So she and Louisa had the entire day alone together. "Why not the Circus?" she asked, a hopeful note creeping into her tone.

"The Circus? I've been there already. Please, Lucy? I shan't ask for another frivolous outing again. Cross my heart." Louisa made a solemn *X* across her bodice. "I just want to peek in the doorway. Such an outing would give me hope—something to think of in the coming years as I await my dazzling debut…" She trailed off, fixing her governess with a mournful gaze.

Thus conquered, Lucy couldn't suppress a laugh. Louisa was so funny. She couldn't help loving her charge. "Oh, very well. After breakfast, we'll stroll to the Assembly Rooms. And then, afterward, we'll come home. You shall spend the rest of the day in the schoolroom to give your poor governess some hope." It was quite likely that they wouldn't run into the ensign. After all, she'd had to wind her way back into the shop to even encounter Mr. Felton. 'Twould be highly unlikely that the ensign would be lolling around by the entrance to the Assembly Rooms.

That's what she told herself, but her hands began perspiring mightily, and her heart beat like a heavy drum in her chest as they drew closer. Thank goodness for her gloves. She was holding Louisa's hand, and it would never do for her charge to realize from her damp palms just how nervous she was. She must remain calm and practical, because pretending that she meant anything more to Ensign Rowland than a temporary annoyance was the height of pretentiousness and vanity.

"Do you think the doors are locked?" Louisa whispered as they stepped up to the entryway.

"Why are you whispering?" Lucy chuckled. Louisa spoke as though they were entering a sacred monument. "Just try the latch."

"No—I don't dare to try it. You try it, Lucy," Louisa murmured, tugging at Lucy's hand.

"Oh, for goodness' sake." Lucy grasped the latch and pulled, and the heavy door swung open with ease. "Come on, now. This was all at your bidding." She pulled Louisa inside.

The door swung shut behind them, the sound echoing through the empty room.

"Oh, my. How glorious." Louisa moved forward on tiptoe, extending her hands as though a phantom dance partner awaited. "Do you see the chandelier, Lucy? It's even bigger and grander than the one at home."

Yes, indeed it was. The morning sunlight streaming through the windows caught its innumerable prisms, sending little rainbows of light glinting around the pristine walls and polished dance floor. What would it be like, to be a young lady in a silk gown, waiting for a dance with a young man in this very room? She closed her eyes for a moment. What if a lanky young man with stormy green eyes walked up to her with a bow?

"Lucy, are you all right? You've got the strangest expression on your face." Louisa's voice snapped Lucy out of her reverie.

What a fool she must have looked. A right ninny in fact. She gave herself a shake. "I'm ready for something to eat. Shall we go home? Or shall we stop at Molland's?" The quicker they were out of this room, the better—and Louisa could hardly resist the temptation of a luncheon out.

Lucy's plan worked. "Oh! Let us go to Molland's," she gushed, grasping Lucy's hand once more. They turned to go, but their progress was halted as the door swung open and a group of workmen bustled in. "Come on, men, the work's being done in the back of the room," a familiar voice cried.

Lucy gasped as she spied Mr. Felton and behind him, a load of wood in his hands, Ensign Rowland.

Mr. Felton smiled and came toward her with his hand extended. "Miss? How do you do?"

Lucy grasped his hand and gave a quick curtsy. "Mr. Felton, this is my charge, the Honorable Louisa Bradbury. Louisa, this is Mr. Felton. He runs a cabinetry shop next door."

Mr. Felton bowed at Louisa. "That I do, Miss. Now, if you'll excuse me, I must put these men to work. We're repairing some woodwork for the ball next week." He turned to the ensign and relieved him of his burden of wood. "Rowland. You can join us in a bit. Make sure these ladies get out onto the street safely."

Lucy opened her mouth to protest, but Mr. Felton cut her off with a quick wink of his eye. Then he strode off, whistling gaily.

She steeled herself and assumed control of the situation. 'Twould serve no purpose if she melted into a puddle before the ensign, with her charge watching in infatuated interest.

"Ensign Rowland, may I present the Honorable Louisa Bradbury? Louisa is my youngest charge. Louisa, this is Ensign Rowland, a friend of Lieutenant Cantrill's."

Sudden interest gleamed in Louisa's brown eyes, but she was too well bred to say anything. And for that, Lucy said a small, silent prayer of thanks.

Ensign Rowland bowed dutifully toward them both, the stubborn lock of hair on his forehead falling forward as he did so. Lucy's hand itched to smooth it back, but she suppressed the urge. He stole a glance at Lucy, a searching glance that left her knees weak and trembling. What was he thinking? Would he speak to them at all?

"M-Miss Williams," he finally said in that rusty, cracked voice that never failed to cause her heart to lurch. "M-Miss Louisa." He took Lucy's arm and led her toward the door, Louisa still clinging to her hand. "Forgive our intrusion, b-but we have work we must do."

"Of course," Lucy replied in a businesslike tone. "We were planning to leave anyway. Thank you, Ensign."

"Ensign Rowland," Louisa piped up, a wheedling expression on her young face, "we were just going to Molland's for something to eat. Would you like to join us?"

Lucy shot her a look that would have wilted grass, but Louisa smiled serenely.

"N-no thank you, M-Miss," Rowland replied, his tone surprised but still polite. "I—I m-must get to work. B-but I thank you for the offer."

"Of course, Ensign Rowland. But I hope you shall join Lucy and me for tea some day," Louisa persisted. "We should love to have you."

Rowland bowed once more. Was he actually blushing? Lucy would have to give Louisa a talking-to once they finally left. Molland's was definitely out. Louisa had lost the privilege after pushing matters too far. With a final curtsy to the ensign, Lucy hustled her charge out the door and into the street as though hounds nipped at their heels.

Chapter Eight

"Don't be angry with me, Lucy. I was only trying to help," Louisa wailed as they bustled along the sidewalk. "I don't see how I did anything wrong. I was terribly polite. And you never mentioned that the ensign was working. Why didn't you say anything about that?"

Lucy halted abruptly, her skirts swirling about her ankles. How on earth could she explain? "Because it's none of our affair. None whatsoever."

Louisa looked up at her with a searching glance. "Why are you so angry? It's not like you to take on about anything in this fashion. Has something happened?"

Lucy gave a deep, shuddering sigh. It wasn't proper to confide in one's fourteen-year-old charge. She should keep her argument with the ensign absolutely quiet. Confiding in Sophie was one thing. Sophie was a dear friend. But she must keep some distance between Louisa and herself for propriety's sake. "Nothing happened. I knew that the ensign had started working for Mr. Felton. It surprised me to see him at the Assembly Rooms. That is all. I suppose I let my surprise show too much."

Louisa's eyebrows drew together skeptically. "You seemed a bit more than surprised. You seemed distracted."

"Well, that's really neither here nor there," Lucy replied crisply. She must divert Louisa. "I've changed my mind. I'm in need of refreshment and a rest. We shall go to Molland's after all." She took her charge's arm and steered her back down the street.

They walked in silence for a bit. The breeze ruffled Lucy's bonnet strings. Ah, how peaceful. The matter was all settled. That was easier than she had anticipated. And then—

"I didn't think the ensign's speech was that bad, Lucy." Louisa glanced up from under her bonnet brim. "Does he always manage so well?"

"Not always." Goodness, would the child ever let the matter drop? Couldn't she find some way to change the direction of her runaway thoughts? This was becoming interminable. "I suppose he speaks more fluently in some situations than others."

"Well, when you see him at the veterans' meeting next week, you can tell him that Dr. Phillips wants to see him," Louisa replied in a confident tone. "If he were cured of his speech defect, I am sure he'd go even further in life than he already has."

"Well, I shan't be seeing him for the time being. He's busy working with Mr. Felton and has no time for our meetings or for seeing Dr. Phillips. So you see, Louisa? Our offer to help, though kindly made, is not really necessary for Ensign Rowland." Time to put an end to this. Louisa was far too interested in the whole matter. Lucy rued the day she'd ever brought that medical text into her room. She should have hidden the book better, somewhere safe from her charge's prying eyes.

But no, she'd rushed and hurried and Louisa had found the text anyway. Now she'd have a time of it, trying to dissuade Louisa from continuing her interest in the matter. She glanced over her Louisa, who was pursing her lips in a pout.

"So...no more meetings? He won't need your help? And I can't help either? That's terrible." Louisa heaved a gusty sigh.

"Why no, Louisa, it's wonderful." Lucy injected a brisk, cheerful tone into her voice. "The ensign is going to find his own way in the world. And his speech impediment is no longer an obstacle. We should thank the Lord that He has been so good to the ensign." She gave Louisa's hand a quick squeeze. "Come now, let's speak of this no more. I see Molland's up ahead. Shall we completely spoil our lunch and partake of their famous marzipan?"

Louisa gave a brief smile, turning her attention toward Molland's, with its pretty window boxes of flowers giving a bright splash of color against the dun-colored stone façade. "Yes, let's." But even as her charge seemed absorbed in luncheon preparations, something about her expression made Lucy uneasy. She had the distinct impression that Louisa hadn't relinquished her interest in the ensign.

'Twas going to be a very long Season if that were indeed the case.

Rowland put the finishing touches onto a piece of mahogany he had carved. 'Twas to be a leg for a chair. Beneath his fingertips, the reddish-brown wood was as smooth as a satin ribbon. As he worked, curling a bit of the wood back from his knife blade, his thoughts wandered. His mind had been straying ever since he ran into Lucy a few days ago. There were so many things he had wanted to say to her, but he didn't have the nerve. Not in front of the Honorable Miss Louisa Bradbury, at any rate.

What would he have said, if Lucy had been alone? He flicked a scrap of wood off his blade and continued slowly carving, the scratching sound echoing through his workroom.

Well, he would have apologized for behaving like such a boor, first of all. He would have told her that her friendship still meant the world to him. What an idiot he'd been, throwing a temper tantrum like a five-year-old when all she did was try to help. His behavior must have seemed ridiculously overblown to someone like Lucy. She seemed so steady, so immovable. It wasn't her fault, of course. He just could never shake the feeling that, in some ways, his speech impediment was his cross to bear. It was his punishment—a lasting legacy of his cowardice on the battlefield.

How could a fellow say anything like that to anyone? He had a hard enough time speaking of it to his brothers in arms. But how could he admit to a pretty little slip of a governess the horror of men dying all around him? She would be aghast. And, knowing of his cowardice compared to the bravery of his dying comrades, she'd never speak to him again in all likelihood. A soldier was supposed to be stoic. And he most certainly wasn't. Youth and inexperience had nothing to do with it. He was simply, at heart, less than a man.

He finished the carving and turned it around in

the late afternoon sunlight that streamed through the window. Not bad. Not bad at all. He really liked making furniture and cabinets. It was altogether unlike the soldier's life. With woodworking, it was so easy to see your progress. Even the smells of the workshop and the soothing feeling of the wood beneath his fingertips—why, everything about his new job was restful, cathartic even.

"Looks splendid." Felton paused in the doorway, bracing his shoulder against the door jamb. "That's going to make a fine parlor chair. I'll have to watch myself. In no time, you'll leave me and go into trade for yourself."

Rowland grinned and gave his head a rueful shake. "N-no one will hire a c-cripple," he jested.

"Ah, I don't agree. Not at all. In fact, I had a message this morning from Lord Bradbury." He unfolded a piece of foolscap with a flourish. "His lordship has a townhome in the Crescent and his library is in rather shabby shape. He has requested a complete rebuilding of the library from the shelves to the desks and chairs. He has specifically asked for my recommendation. And I think you are just the man for the job."

Lord Bradbury? That was Lucy's employer. Surely she hadn't put him up to this. A governess would have very little sway over such a matter—wouldn't she? Even so, this was all rather curious. "Why not you, F-Felton?"

"A few reasons. First, I am far too busy overseeing the operations of this business to be at his lordship's beck and call. I'd much rather put you on the job, collect my part of the fee and continue going about my own business. And, to be honest, this is a reputation-making job. If his lordship likes your work, then he'll make sure to tell others in the *ton* about it. And you'll have commission after commission soon enough." He shrugged, folding up the foolscap. "I've already built my reputation. That's why his lordship sought out our shop. I don't need any further laurels."

"B-but I've only been here for a fortnight," Rowland protested. Was this charity? He would never accept charity, no matter how kindly it was meant.

"Oh, stop scowling, lad. You're the one person I know who would take a sure thing like this commission and then argue about it. His lordship asked me to put the right man on the job. I've been in this business long enough to know what makes or breaks a good carpenter. You're good at it. And with a challenging commission like this, you could be great." He pointed the folded-up scrap of foolscap at Rowland, lecturing him like a schoolmaster. "Prove to me that you can do this, Rowland. I think you can—but I want to make sure my instincts haven't become too aged."

Rowland squared his jaw. Felton had hired him without knowing whether or not Rowland could even speak, much less whittle a matchstick. He owed Felton a great deal. He could repay the favor by doing an incredible job for his lordship, no matter what it took. "When d-do I go to see his lordship?"

"I sent a message 'round this morning. Told him to expect you after luncheon." Felton grinned. "His lordship's a good sort for *ton* folk. Rich as Croesus but sensible for all that. He has a fine townhome in the Crescent."

Yes, Rowland knew that townhome. His mind flashed back to the day he walked Lucy home. Would she be there this afternoon? Would he have a chance to see her—just to catch a glimpse of her?

After luncheon, he took a hackney up to the Crescent, a box of pencils, foolscap and measuring devices tucked under his arm. As he approached his lordship's palatial townhome, he cast his glance at the upstairs windows, but Lucy wasn't there. At least, she wasn't looking outside the windows as he approached.

She was probably busy with her charges and might not even know he was there. He didn't know whether to be disappointed or grateful.

The butler showed him into the library, which was surprisingly shabby. Rowland walked over to the rows of shelves that stretched from the floor to the ceiling. He smoothed one of them with his fingertips. It wobbled slightly under his touch, and his forefinger, when he pulled it back, was streaked with dust. How very odd that such an immaculate home should have a library in such disrepair.

He turned as the door opened, admitting his lordship and a young lady he recognized as Louisa, Lucy's charge.

"Ah, Rowland," his lordship said in a hearty tone of voice. "So glad to meet you. Felton speaks highly of your talents. Hoping you can make something of all this." He waved his hand around the room with a listless gesture.

Rowland's nerves seized hold of him, and his throat worked mightily. "O-o-of c-c-c-ourse," he finally managed, his cheeks burning with shame. Why did he have to lose his power of speech now in front of his lordship? 'Twas wretchedly humiliating, especially when he was striving to appear professional.

Louisa stepped forward, tugging her papa's arm. "Papa neglected this room shamefully for years, because it was my mama's favorite room—"

"Louisa," her father broke in sternly. "Mr. Rowland does not care about the circumstances of this library's decline."

"But we need to tell him what we want done. He will understand better if he knows why. Mama is why I think we should redo everything," Louisa responded, turning to face her father. "We'll make it a new room, one that won't remind you so sharply of her. That's all I wanted to tell Mr. Rowland. That we want to have everything done—chairs, tables and all the shelves."

"S-s-s-so Mr. F-F-Felton told me," Rowland broke in. He didn't want to stand there helpless as father and daughter relived their grief. 'Twas a private affair and none of his business.

"Yes, so, Rowland, a complete overhaul, I think. New furniture, new shelves. I rather like those bookcases with glass fronts on them. Do you think you could fit us out in something like that?"

Rowland nodded. 'Twould be easy enough to do and would look quite sharp. He pulled out his box of tools and set about measuring as father and daughter continued to natter on about the details.

"Well, darling, you shall have your new library. But I confess, I can't attend to the details," Lord Bradbury was saying. "You know how Amelia's debut is consuming all of our time."

"Then I shall oversee it, Papa. I'll get Lucy to help me."

Rowland paused his measuring, keeping his face turned toward the bookshelf. Lucy Williams? Was she really going to help in this project? If so, 'twould be impossible to avoid her. Again—was that good or bad?

"Ah, splendid thinking. But I must say, I will put Miss Williams in charge of the project, and you may help her." At Louisa's good-natured groan, her father gave a short bark of laughter. "If you have your way, everything will be upholstered in ermine and studded with diamonds," he teased. "Miss Williams is quite organized and has good sense. Go and fetch her, Louisa. We'll talk about the matter now, while Rowland is here."

A scuffling of slippers and the door banging shut announced Louisa's departure. Rowland schooled his features to an outward semblance of calm as he continued measuring the shelves and walls of the library. His hands shook, and he had to redo one set of measurements three times until they finally made sense. But surely his lordship, who kept up a stream of polite chatter, did not notice.

The door to the library swung open again, and Louisa entered the room with Lucy.

His heart leaped in his chest as he turned around to bow to her, but he was determined to remain aloof and professional. He'd made such a fool of himself over and over again that he must have at least one meeting with Lucy that did not end in disaster. So he would force himself to remain calm and practical no matter what happened.

For her part, Lucy appeared a little pale, but that could be anything. Surely it wasn't his presence causing her pallor.

"Ah, Miss Williams," Lord Bradbury said, nodding to her as she entered the room. "We're going to completely redo this library. Floor to ceiling. Furniture to shelves. It's a project dear to Louisa's heart—" he paused to pat his daughter's curly brown hair "—but I want you to oversee it with a practical eye. You'll work with Rowland, here. He's a carpenter in Felton's shop, and I'm giving him free rein."

"They already know each other, Papa," Louisa hissed. Lucy fixed her charge with a glare that would curdle milk.

Rowland couldn't suppress a grin at Louisa's cheekiness. "Y-yes we d-do. Miss Williams." He gave her a brief bow, allowing his amusement to shine through his eyes.

She raised her chin and curtsied but did not smile. "Ensign Rowland."

"Ensign? A military man? Excellent. Then you know about discipline and whatnot." Lord Bradbury clapped his hands. "Louisa may pick out the colors and the materials, but I want you to keep her in line when it comes to spending, Miss Williams. I'm depending on the three of you to handle this project—for I am far too worried to pay any attention to it. Louisa knows my tastes, Rowland knows carpentry and Miss Williams knows the value of a penny. I'm leaving it up to you three to finish this project and make me a happy man."

Lord Bradbury gave a general bow to the room and left. Rowland was sorry to see him go. Now he was left with two females who were obviously not in great accord with each other about something—either this project, or possibly—just possibly—his presence.

He was never much of a commander, but he had to seize control of the situation. 'Twas the only way to remain in a professional frame of mind in Lucy's presence. "M-Miss W-Williams, I shall draw up a few plans for your approval this afternoon. His l-lordship has already m-mentioned g-glass fronted b-b-bookcases. M-M-Miss L-Louisa, do you have any s-suggestions?"

"I shall have to give the matter quite a bit of thought," Miss Louisa responded, giving him a grin. Her eyes sparkled with mischief. "I'll leave you two here to work out the details and go mull it over in my room."

"I'll come with you," Lucy responded. "Ensign, if you will send the plans to me when you are done, I shall be happy to look them over. And take your time with the measurements as well as the planning. I shall send Roberts, Lord Bradbury's butler, in to assist you with anything you might require."

She curtsied deeply, keeping her eyes cast down, and turned to follow her charge without a backward glance. As the door clicked shut behind them, Rowland grasped the edge of a table, holding on until his knuckles turned white.

He must remain master of his emotions. He'd be working with Lucy for the foreseeable future, and it would do no one any good if he thought of her as anything other than a partner in this project. After all, it was hardly likely that she could care for a worthless cripple like himself.

Chapter Nine

"Oh, Lucy, don't be angry," Louisa pleaded as they headed upstairs to the schoolroom. "After all, Papa's library *does* need work. Even you noticed how shabby it has gotten over the years."

Lucy wasn't angry. She had had ample time to prepare herself for the inevitable confrontation with her charge from the moment Louisa ran upstairs to fetch her to the moment they both curtsied and left the room. The entire time she'd been coolly polite to the ensign, she'd been formulating just how to handle the matter of Louisa's matchmaking in the back of her mind. And the solution dawned on her in that moment, like the sun breaking through the clouds.

She would do nothing. Nothing at all.

After all, anything she did would only fuel the fire of Louisa's romantic daydreaming. If she allowed herself to show that Louisa's actions in bringing the ensign to their home and having her work on a project with him threw her into a tizzy, Louisa would only continue to meddle. Louisa was determined to prove that the ensign and Lucy would fall in love like a couple in one of her romantic novels. But if Lucy grew nonchalant about the entire matter, then Louisa would lose interest and move on to something else, leaving her governess in peace. And perhaps Lucy could convince herself to truly be indifferent, as well. It was worth a try at any rate.

"Don't be ridiculous," Lucy mustered in her heartiest, snippiest governess tone of voice. "If his lordship wants me to assist in this project, I should be happy to oblige. Don't take on so, Louisa."

Louisa paused on the landing and turned to face her teacher. Confusion quirked her eyebrows. "You—you mean you aren't angry?"

"On the contrary," she replied briskly. Her plan seemed to be working—no need to stop it now. "I shall do whatever his lordship bids me to do. It's my job to do so after all."

"Oh." Louisa looked distinctly crestfallen, her shoulders sloping in disappointment. "I thought I would get a tongue-lashing."

Lucy managed a bright laugh and continued her progress up the stairs. This was going better than she had thought. "Not at all. Now, this afternoon I should like it if you would spend some time working on your father's library. Sketch out a few designs for furniture, if you like, and jot down any thoughts you have for furnishings. I want to have something to share with the ensign once we begin going over his plans."

Louisa grumbled her reply, and Lucy was hard put to smother her grin. Served the little meddler right. She loved Louisa, but she had to learn not to interfere in other people's affairs. Lucy would see to it that the girl spent as much time working on the library as the ensign. That would be her restitution for interfering in her instructor's life. And by the time the library was refurbished and life returned to normal, 'twas quite likely that Miss Louisa Bradbury would be sick of the sight of libraries, blueprints and architectural renderings.

They worked in the schoolroom side by side until the shadows began to lengthen on the wall. 'Twas late afternoon—time to bring an end to the school day. As Lucy and Louisa began packing away their things, Sophie and Amelia bounded into the schoolroom—Sophie's rosy cheeks and starry eyes indicating a high level of excitement.

"I leave tomorrow for Brightgate," she announced breathlessly, grasping Lucy's hands. "It's all arranged. Aunt Katherine is taking me."

"That's wonderful." Lucy squeezed Sophie's hands. Though Sophie wouldn't admit her feelings for Lieutenant Cantrill, they were as obvious as the dimples in her cheeks. This trip would likely wind up with their faux engagement becoming a reality. Which was wonderful, only—Lucy's heart gave a little lurch. Then Sophie would go, and she'd be on her own again. She'd come to rely so heavily on Sophie's friendship. She took the loneliness out of life.

"I think it's horrid," Amelia scoffed, flouncing over to a nearby chair with a huff. "For now I have no one to chaperone me next week. Papa won't do it, you know. He's always too busy with his own affairs once we arrive at a ball."

Sophie and Lucy exchanged a mutually understanding glance. Lord Bradbury's reputation, particularly as a wealthy and sportive widower, was well established amongst the *ton.* More than one highborn widow or captivating soubrette had been linked to his lordship since his wife's passing. And while he was a dedicated father, he also put a lot of thought and emphasis into his *affaires de coeur.*

"I think Lucy should escort you," Sophie replied, casting a pleading glance in Lucy's direction. Lucy understood the look. If they placated Amelia, then Sophie could go in peace. "Lucy is your governess after all. She understands all the rules of deportment just as well as I do."

Amelia toed the rug with her slipper, her eyes stubbornly downcast. "Papa says that because Lucy isn't of the gentry—"

Sophie cut her off with a snap of her fingers. "You shouldn't repeat such nonsense, Amelia." Her voice was so stern that Lucy eyed her curiously. Why would Sophie say such a thing? Whatever was the matter?

"Amelia, Louisa, we shall settle this matter later. Sophie has a chance to take a trip with her aunt, and we will not begrudge her the opportunity. Now, shoo." Lucy flicked her hands at both girls, flushing them toward the doorway. "Your dancing master awaits your presence down in the ballroom."

As both girls retreated, Lucy shut the door behind them. Now she would have an opportunity to get to the heart of the matter. Taking a deep breath, she turned to face Sophie. "Why did you shush Amelia so sharply?"

Sophie colored to the roots of her golden hair. "She was about to say something rather rude—or so I feared."

"Rude? In what way? I know full well that I am not of the gentry." Lucy sank onto the chair opposite Sophie and cocked her head to one side. Both girls were a little spirited, to be sure—but hardly ever outright offensive. They were too well bred for that.

"I know, but what she was going to say was far too impolite toward you." Sophie pursed her lips, her brilliant blue eyes clouding a bit. "You see, his lordship has a silly notion that because you grew up in an orphanage you don't know the finer points of etiquette or how to move in society. That is why, even though I am a seamstress, he placed me in charge of Amelia's debut."

Lucy's stomach sank like a stone. Of course his lordship felt that way. After all, Sophie's father was Sir Hugh Handley, and they had a grand family home before they fell prey to bankruptcy. Even though Sophie had no money, she was of gentle birth and breeding. But even before Lucy lost both of her parents to gaol fever, she had no grand roots. Her father was nought but a humble preacher. And he preached to the least of them—prison inmates.

'Twas a background that hardly qualified her for socializing with the *ton*.

Some of her conflicting emotions must have showed on her face, for Sophie leaned forward and hugged her. "Don't worry, Lucy," she soothed. "I've told his lordship that you are more than qualified to take over. And I insisted that you, and no one else, escort Amelia to the Assembly Rooms ball next week."

"I am not angry or upset." Lucy extricated herself from Sophie's embrace, a cold feeling settling at the pit of her stomach. She could well understand why her employer would hold those beliefs about her, even if they weren't true. It hurt, of course, to have Lord Bradbury say such things about her, but what could she do? That was how their world worked. And though she might be clever enough to teach his children, his lordship would never think of her as a gentlewoman.

Unbidden, an image of Ensign Rowland flashed across her mind. He was of impoverished nobility, much like Sophie. To his family, just like Lord Bradbury's family, she would be labeled an outcast. No matter how clever she was, how hard she worked or even how genteel her deportment might be, their perceptions of her would hardly change.

Whatever did that matter? She had no designs on Ensign Rowland, nor had he designs on her. His family, wherever they were, could rest easily.

Taking a deep breath, she looked Sophie squarely in the eye. "I shall be happy to take Amelia to the Assembly Rooms ball if his lordship will consent to me acting as a chaperone. I daresay I can be trusted not to spit on the floor, nor chew on straw whilst we are there." A thread of bitterness ran through her tone, and she masked it with a little laugh.

"I appreciate your help, Lucy. And I told his lordship on no uncertain terms that you are far more to be praised for how well his daughters have turned out as I am. After all, you've been with them for years. I've only been working with Amelia for a few months." Sophie rose. "Excuse me, dear. I must begin packing."

Lucy held herself together until the door clicked shut behind Sophie. Then, pillowing her head on her arm, she allowed herself one good cry. It had been a difficult day after all. The way in which the Bradburys interfered with her life, and judged her past, made matters worse. What would Ensign Rowland think of all this? She blew her nose on her embroidered handkerchief.

And why did she keep thinking about the ensign and

what his thoughts would be? She was as insignificant to him as a dust mote on a bookshelf. Now, more than ever, she understood her place in this world. She must continue to take care of herself and to make her own way in the world.

With both parents dead and no family to speak of—not to mention her background in the orphanage—she could rely on no one but herself.

Ensign Rowland let himself into the humble flat he shared with Macready. He paused in the doorway, hanging his hat on the nearby wall hook and removed his gloves. He'd spent all day working on his lordship's library. This one commission could make his career. As it was, he'd be earning enough money that he could, if he wanted, move into his own flat. He could hire his own housekeeper. For the first time in his life, he would be completely independent.

He tossed his gloves into a little wicker basket Mrs. Pierce kept by the door. It could actually be nice to have a home of one's own. Nothing grand, of course. Just something modest and cozy that he could kit out with furniture he made by his own hand. A sudden image of Miss Lucy Williams flitted across his mind. It could be more like a home than just a bachelor's quarters. And in time, maybe he could share it with….

Enough of this nonsense. He ran his hand through his hair, tousling it as though the gesture could drive Lucy from his mind forever. She didn't care a whit about him. Why, in the library today, she'd been as frosty as a snowflake. When would he accept that she had no personal feelings for him and that she'd only wanted to help him, as a Good Samaritan would help anyone?

"What ho, Rowland," Macready called from the kitchen. "Mrs. Pierce was here. Chicken and pastry for dinner, my good fellow. You'd better come quickly before I devour the whole thing."

And he would, too. Rowland rolled his eyes and ducked into the kitchen. "G-good thing I g-got here in time. Otherwise, t-t-t'would be bread and butter for me t-tonight."

Macready grinned and retrieved a plate from the cabinet, holding it out to Rowland. "Here you go. Tuck in."

Rowland spooned the rich mixture of chicken, gravy and delectable pastry bits onto his plate, breathing deeply. By Jove, but he was famished. This was just what he needed. Surely he had begun thinking about Lucy because hunger and fatigue had addled his mind. This meal would soon put him to rights. How many fellows had fallen in love because of an empty stomach?

"So, how were things at Felton's today?" Macready asked around a mouthful of his dinner. Army manners. Good thing no ladies were present to witness the horror of their table etiquette.

"Interesting." He related the tale of his new commission to Macready, who, judging by the way he set aside his fork and leaned forward in his chair, was an interested audience.

"Miss Williams? Isn't she that pretty lass who was reading to you? And then came to see you at Felton's shop the other day? Well, I say, well done, old fellow. Now you have all the time in the world to get to know one another and see if you suit." Macready quirked his eyebrow at Rowland and refilled his plate for a third time.

"D-don't b-be ridiculous." Rowland's face grew hot as though he sat too close to a fire. "We mean nothing to each other. We're j-just working t-together."

"Do you mean to tell me that you aren't going to pursue Miss Williams? Good gracious, man, you *are* a fool. You have this opportunity—handed to you on a silver platter, I might add—to get to know a young lady who went out of her way to be kind to you. And you're going to do nothing?" Macready gave him a puzzled, rueful grin. "That's daft."

Rowland's anger surged to the surface. 'Twas intolerable to be called crazy just because he didn't wish to make himself even more ridiculous in Lucy's eyes. "You're b-being absurd," he countered, looking Macready squarely in the eyes. "She m-means nothing to me. And I m-mean nothing to her."

Macready sat back in his chair, still smirking a bit. His posture was the posture of a man accepting a challenge, even though he knew the consequences. "You're so worried about being a coward, aren't you? Isn't that why you're here in Bath? Why you stammer so?"

Rowland clenched his hands into fists, breathing slowly as he attempted to regain control of his temper. Macready was going to feel the force of his left if he wasn't careful.

"Whatever notion you've cooked up in your mind about Miss Williams should be thrown in the rubbish heap where it belongs," Macready continued. "She's a young lady, and a pretty one from all I've heard. She's a governess, which means she's clever—she knows black from white. She's not feeble-minded or plain, and she's making her own way in the world." Macready ticked off this laundry list of attributes on his fingers, the scars running across his hand just visible in the dim kitchen light. "And she's shown an interest in your welfare. Maybe you don't know much about women, but allow me to enlighten you. They don't, on average, offer to help and assist a fellow they don't like."

Rowland slung his fist across the table, sending his plate and cup smashing to the ground. "It's out of pity!" he roared, smacking the surface of the table so hard it jumped. "Would you have me court her now? What a buffoon I'd be, trading on her gentle nature, trying to ingratiate myself on her compassion. How dare you call me coward for refusing to do that, Macready! I'm more of a gentleman than you'll ever be."

Macready watched him coolly, his mocking, black eyes half closed. "I'd rather be a lesser gentleman than you and have a fine young lady to squire about. I'll say it again. You're a coward, and you're refusing to see the truth. If she pitied you, she wouldn't have come to the shop to see you. She'd have gone about her business and found some other poor fellow to assist. There are plenty of candidates at the veterans' group. Many of whom would be happy to have a lovely young lady to talk to."

For a moment, Rowland heard nothing but the buzz of anger in his own ears. He took several deep, calming breaths. As his sudden rage ebbed, he sank back onto his chair.

Macready spoke again. "Dare I hope that the kitchen table is no longer in danger of being abused?"

Rowland rubbed his hand across his brow. "You may."

Macready grinned. "Glad to hear it." He paused, as though unsure whether he should continue. "You know, Rowland, you don't stutter when you're angry."

Lucy had pointed that out, too. Not that it mattered. He couldn't go around roaring at people. He'd have to find a way to overcome the stammer, whatever mood he was in. "Do you think I'm a coward? Really?"

"I don't blame you or consider you a coward for what you did at La Sainte Haye. I think you reacted as most young men might, when entirely unprepared for battle, outranked and outflanked, with the cavalry charging down upon them." Macready paused, rubbing his scarred hands together slowly. "But to do penance for it the rest of your life—to shut out youth, beauty and kindness in its name—then yes. I would say that is cowardice."

Rowland nodded. He closed his eyes for a moment, allowing Macready's words to sink in. What if he did attempt to court Lucy? What would be the worst that could happen? She might reject him, surely. And a sizable part of himself still believed that she should—that she deserved better than he could offer. But…for a moment, the possibility of Lucy returning his affection flooded his being, leaving him breathless. Could such a chance be worth the risk?

Yes. A million times yes.

"Fine." Rowland tried to keep his tone light. "I accept your challenge. But if she throws me over, it's on your head."

Macready shrugged his shoulders. "So be it. But I imagine I shall be dancing at your wedding."

Chapter Ten

James took his seat in Lord Bradbury's library, awaiting Lucy's arrival. He'd pondered over Macready's words the entire night through. Upon arising, he vowed he'd be a coward no longer. Starting today, as a matter of fact. He wasn't well-versed in the art of flirtation, but he would find a way to show Lucy that he enjoyed her company. Women liked flowers, so he'd selected a few bright, cheery buds from a street vendor on the walk over. But now, sitting beside him on the library table, the small bouquet seemed a trifle too brash. Should he chuck them in the wastebasket? No, she might see them there and wonder what he was about.

He loosened his neckcloth. There was little ventilation in the room, which faced full east and caught glimmers of the morning sun. It was a room obviously designed for winter's enjoyment, when the pale sun would stream in and a great fire in the hearth would make things perfectly cozy for reading and reflection. But what about the other months of the year? What could be done to make it livable and pleasant when it was not cold and rainy outside?

He had an idea.

He stalked over to the nearby window and opened it as far as the sash would allow. A tepid breeze drifted in, fanning his papers and the petals of the flowers on the library table. He breathed deeply. The air smelled fresh, like mown hay. This was much, much better. He took another gulp of air—for it calmed his nerves.

"I agree. It's rather stuffy in here," a familiar, lilting voice chimed behind him.

He whirled around. Lucy was alone, her charge nowhere in sight. Oh, good. That made giving his gift of flowers easier without a young miss eyeing him and giggling boldly. He caught them up and extended the bouquet toward her. "F-for you. A p-peace offering."

"For me?" Her warm brown eyes widened. "How lovely they are. I do love peonies." She buried her nose in the bouquet and closed her eyes. "They smell of spring. Thank you, Ensign."

"I m-must ask your f-forgiveness," he began haltingly. "I have a d-dreadful t-temper. My worst f-flaw. And you've caught the wrong end of it l-lately. I am g-grateful for all you have d-done for m-me."

"A dreadful temper, eh? Well, then, I shall give you the same advice I give my charges. Count to ten and breathe deeply. It works wonders." She gave him a shy smile and began arranging the flowers in a china vase that rested atop a nearby plant stand, using a pitcher of water to fill it.

He smiled, too. At least she seemed amenable to reconciliation. "Where *is* your charge?" If Miss Louisa were to come bounding in at any moment, any attempts at flirtation would be sadly dashed.

"She's upstairs studying. I have her ideas for the

library, but I cannot spare her from the schoolroom today without risking running behind on her lessons. I shall be chaperoning her sister for the next fortnight, as Sophie is going into Brightgate to visit Lieutenant Cantrill's family. So we shall be rather busy, and even I can hardly spare the time to work on the library." She gave the flowers a final pat and put the vase back on the plant stand. "Don't they add a nice splash of color? Just what this room needs. Anyway, I'll give you our ideas and get you started, Ensign, and then I'll have to attend to Louisa."

"James," he insisted. That was a fair way to establish a friendship, wasn't it? First names? Of course, it was rather bold—

She glanced up at him, her cheeks turning a rosy shade. "Beg pardon?"

"You should c-call me James," he repeated. "W-we'll be w-w-working together after all."

"Certainly, James. And you must call me Lucy." She cast her eyes down to the table and began rifling through her papers.

His mind worked rapidly as she began arranging her papers on the library table. If she were chaperoning the elder Miss Bradbury, then she might be seen at social events. His mother had been after him to attend one of these functions since he moved to Bath, but he'd laughed off her pretensions. But now, the Rowland name—impoverished though it was—might come in handy.

"What will you be ch-chaperoning d-during this f-fortnight?" He schooled his features into nonchalance. He didn't want to seem like a predator going after prey. After all, he'd only just begun to apologize for his past rudeness.

"Oh, you know. The usual social functions. Amelia is quite excited about the Assembly Rooms ball, and I shall be accompanying her to that." Lucy's voice grew a trifle cold and distant. "She rather wanted Sophie there, but I shall do in a pinch."

"I am sure you and Miss Bradbury will have a g-good t-time," he added heartily. "L-let's see your p-plans."

Though he feigned interest in all of Miss Louisa's suggestions, he really only gave his undivided attention to Lucy. She had a habit of twirling a lock of hair around one slender finger whenever she was at a loss for words. The silken strand curled around her finger like a piece of mahogany, satiny-smooth to the touch. But he said nothing of these observations aloud. There was still too much doubt in his heart as to whether he could truly win her affection. There was every chance that Lucy was simply being kind. He needed to have more time with her, to get to know her better, to learn the truth of her feelings toward him and to show her that he wasn't an ill-bred cripple with a habit of estranging well-meaning governesses.

When the clock on the mantel began chiming the hour, Lucy stood up, uttering a little cry. "Oh, dear. I must get back to the schoolroom. Is this enough for you to get started with? I wish I could stay longer, but I need to work with Louisa on her penmanship."

He nodded and rose. "This will give me p-plenty to d-do. I shall return in a few days with a g-group of m-men to b-begin the w-work." If only he could detain her—but she was devoted to her work. She wouldn't be deterred from her charge, not even for a little harmless flirting.

"Oh, good. His lordship will be most pleased with how quickly you are progressing. He does love efficiency." She handed her papers over to him, brushing his hand with her own. A tingle shot up his arm, though he suppressed any expression of embarrassment or pleasure from showing in his expression. This one lesson he'd learned well while in the army—never show surprise to anyone.

If Lucy was surprised, she kept her countenance too, except perhaps for her cheeks turning a little brighter pink. But then, that could just be his imagination. She scooped up the vase from the plant stand. "Our schoolroom could do with some brightening up," she explained and bobbed a slight curtsy.

"I w-wish you well in all your upcoming s-social d-duties, especially the b-ball," he responded with a slight bow. "B-but knowing you—as I d-do—I am sure you w-will even outshine M-Miss B-Bradbury." That was nicely put—not too flowery yet genuine.

She glanced up at him with something like amazement kindled in the depths of her eyes. "Do you really think so?" she breathed.

"Yes, I d-do." Why was she so astonished? Surely she knew how very wonderful she was. Any man would be proud to call Lucy Williams his.

"Well, if that's true, then you're the only person in Bath who thinks so." Her tone was quiet, subdued even, and as she left the room, she tossed a little smile his way as though she tossed a blossom at his feet.

Ever since her meeting with the ensign—no, James—Lucy lived in a sort of daze. He was so charming, yet his kindness seemed genuine. So many other men allowed compliments to flow from their tongues like honey from the comb, and you couldn't believe a word they said. But James was different. His words were few and halting, and so when he spoke admiringly, you simply had to stop and listen.

'Twas silly, of course, to devote all her waking moments to wondering if James really thought well of her. But she couldn't shake free of the spell his words had woven over her world. The peonies did not grace the schoolroom after all. She placed them in her room, on the little white desk, and kept them until the petals faded and fell. Now bereft of those blossoms, all she had was the memory of his words, so she played them over and over in her mind until they wore a path through her very brain.

She sat in her room, a week after their conversation, dressing for the Assembly Rooms ball. His words bolstered her courage, for on this night of all nights, she felt distinctively plain and unremarkable. She stared into her looking glass. If only Sophie were here. She would arrange Lucy's dark hair to make it look passably pretty. But then, if Sophie were here, Lucy would have no need of attending the ball tonight. She could while away the evening reading a book and nibbling a bar of chocolate and wouldn't have to worry one whit about chaperoning Amelia through innumerable waltzes and quadrilles.

She smoothed the bodice of the purple gown she borrowed from Sophie. At least she had something nice to wear. Her serviceable black-and-gray gowns would look distinctly out of place in the ballroom, even for a chaperone. The purple was dignified enough that she didn't look like mutton dressed as lamb and festive enough that she would fit in well with the crowd. While Amelia would never want to become a wallflower, that title was precisely Lucy's goal for the evening.

Her bedroom door banged open, and Louisa bounded in. "Lucy, you look so pretty! I love that dress. It suits you so well." She kissed Lucy's cheek. "Why don't you wear colors more often?"

"Colors aren't suitable for a governess, Louisa." She jabbed one last hairpin into her coiffure in a last-minute attempt to make herself passable. "But for this event, I must look more elegant than I do in the schoolroom."

Louisa flung herself across Lucy's bed, causing the ropes under the mattress to squeak in protest. "Do you think someone will ask you to dance tonight?"

"Don't be absurd," Lucy replied with a snort. "I am there to chaperone your sister. *She* will probably have quite a few admirers. She is already considered a Diamond of the First Water."

"I suppose so." Louisa rolled over on her back. "Lucy, I have a question. What if someone asks Amelia to marry him this very night?"

"It isn't done that way—except in novels." Lucy rose and shook out her skirts. "But if anything is likely to happen, then perhaps your sister will find a young man who wishes to court her. And perhaps in time she will get married."

"No elopements to Gretna Green?" Louisa pressed on, her face a study in romantic disappointment.

"I should say not." Lucy walked over to the bed and captured Louisa's hands. Giving them a tug, she pulled Louisa upright. "Remind me to go through your book collection tomorrow. 'Tis in need of a severe pruning. Now, mind that you go to bed on time tonight. I won't have you loafing just because your sister is going to a ball."

"Are you still going to church in the morning?" Louisa released her hands and danced backward a few paces.

"Why wouldn't I?" Sometimes Louisa asked the strangest questions.

"Well, can I come, too? Papa and Amelia will likely sleep through the morning, and I shall be hopelessly bored. I'd much rather go to services with you."

"Very well." She'd overlook the fact that her charge was going to church as a means to avoid boredom. After all, Louisa would be setting foot in Saint Swithin's of her own accord, and that was all that mattered at the tender age of fourteen. A deeper spirituality would have to be nurtured over time.

She gave Louisa a peck on the cheek. "I'm going to Amelia's room to see if she's ready. Want to come?"

"No." Louisa lolled on the bed. "May I stay here? As long as I don't disturb anything? Your room is nicer than mine."

Lucy gave an inward roll of her eyes. It was hardly likely that her modest room was anything to compare with the Honorable Miss Louisa Bradbury's quarters, but it did no harm for the girl to stay. And if it had the added benefit of appeasing any of Louisa's lingering jealousy toward her sister then so much the better. "You may stay but mind you keep everything neat."

She blew a final kiss at Louisa, who lay huddled on her quilt, and walked down the hallway to Amelia's room. She knocked on the door. "Are you ready, my dear?" she called.

"Yes. No. I don't know," was the reassuring answer.

Lucy cautiously opened the door. Amelia slumped in front of her vanity mirror, her chin in her hands.

"Hello, Lucy," she murmured as Lucy tiptoed in and closed the door behind her.

"You look lovely, my dear." Lucy smiled in encouragement. And it was true. Amelia looked quite pretty in her buttercup-tinted gown, created expressly for this occasion by Sophie. Her lady's maid had arranged her dark, curly hair in the Grecian fashion, and the hue of the dress brought out the creamy tint of her skin.

"Thank you." Amelia managed a faint smile but did not change her position in front of the mirror.

Lucy laid her hands on Amelia's shoulders. "What's troubling you, my dear?" For something must be wrong. Amelia was usually so effervescent, so confident. 'Twas strange to see her looking so upset. And before a ball, too.

"Well, I miss Sophie. I wish she were here. She's been guiding me through my debut from making my gowns to helping me with my dinner party. It just feels wrong that she's not here—on this night of all nights." Amelia heaved a gusty sigh.

"Well, that's understandable." Lucy drew a chair close to the vanity table and sat, looking at her eldest charge. "Sophie would be here if she could. But she had to make this trip to Brightgate—"

"Do you think she's going to marry Lieutenant Cantrill?" Amelia began playing with the bristles of her hairbrush, keeping her eyes cast down.

Good gracious, the Bradbury girls were all atwitter

about marriage tonight. 'Twas rather irksome. "That's none of your affair," she chided gently, using her best governess-in-charge tone of voice. "Now, stand up and shake out your skirts. The carriage is waiting. I am sure your papa has been waiting for us for an eternity."

Amelia nodded and did as Lucy bade her. Lucy draped a pearl-adorned shawl about Amelia's shoulders and drew on her own gloves.

"Lucy?"

"Yes?" Oh, they must hurry. His lordship would be furious if they were late.

"I am glad you are coming with me. I shan't feel half so out of place with you there." Amelia slipped her hand into Lucy's and gave it a squeeze.

"Oh, my dear. It's my pleasure." Lucy smiled and squeezed Amelia's hand in return. Then she led her charge through the doorway and down the grand staircase. His lordship's carriage would be waiting around the front.

Amelia drew closer to Lucy's side as they descended the stairs. "Dear Lucy." She sighed. "You'll never leave us. You wouldn't be like Sophie and run away and get married. We can depend on you." Lucy stiffened but ultimately decided not to reply.

Amelia was just nervous, that was all. There was no sense in saying anything that might disturb her young charge—at least not tonight as they were headed straight to a ball. Lucy patted Amelia's shoulder and murmured a few comforting words, but as they settled in the carriage, her mind whirled in tumult.

The implication was, of course, that Lucy would be around forever because she would never marry, would never leave the Bradbury girls until they needed her no longer. And then, she would move on to another family and another until she finally got so old and worn out that she could no longer teach.

And what was wrong with that picture? Hadn't she admitted to herself that her future lay precisely down that path? Hadn't she acknowledged as much just a few short days ago?

Why, then, did it make her sick, sick to the very core of her being, to have Amelia say just the same thing aloud? She caught a glimpse of her reflection in the coach window. She looked—young. And in that gown, passably attractive. Not pretty. Never pretty like Sophie. But still—less plain than she'd always imagined she looked.

What if she didn't want to be a governess forever? What if she wanted something more? More, even, than a school of her own?

But of course, that could not be. She had to make her own way. She was an orphan without family connections. Not precisely marriageable material.

'Twas the dress that caused that sudden, mad little inward rebellion. She gave herself a little shake.

One must beware of lovely lavender frocks.

Chapter Eleven

James sat alone in the darkened workshop, whittling a piece of oak. The wood was smooth as satin under his skilled fingers. This would make a splendid chair leg for the suite of furniture his lordship had commissioned. Really, Lucy had shown exquisite taste in her recommendations for the library furnishings, choosing this honey-colored oak over the usual mahogany. She was right—it would lighten the already dark room, where mahogany would have overwhelmed the space. As in everything he had seen of her up until this point, she'd shown outstanding judgment. If only she'd show the same discerning taste in men. But then, if she did, there'd be no chance of him attracting her attention. She'd want a good man: a whole one and a brave one.

A cacophony of noises, indistinct and muffled, droned through the wall of the workshop. James brought his candle closer as he worked, trying to shut out the sounds. Working with wood had become a source of solace, a moment free of distractions akin to being in prayer. He sought out the workshop after the other men left for the day and had gone home to their families, simply because those moments of peace helped, in some strange way, to heal his soul.

The noise outside grew louder. His concentration was broken for certain now. Whatever was going on? He laid the oak aside and walked over to the window. The street outside, illuminated by guttering torch lamps, was filled with men and women in fine clothing, carriages and horses of every description clogging the path in front of the Assembly Rooms.

The Assembly Rooms ball. Tonight, Lucy would be escorting her young charge to the most sought-after social event of the season. His meager social connections might have been enough to secure him entrance to the ball, but he hadn't pursued it. Was his resolution forgotten under a barrage of work for his lordship? On the surface, yes. But as James watched the fashionable throng outside, a feeling of bitter disgust flooded his being. Once again, he'd been a coward.

He leaned against the window, straining to see a familiar face. A pretty face, with large brown eyes and lips that always held a tender, humorous quirk. But the sea of humanity remained featureless in the torches' dim light. He'd do better to get back to work. At least he could show something for this evening if he finished the chair leg.

With a sinking feeling in the pit of his stomach, he moved from his comfortable position in the workshop to a lesser room in the back. Perhaps if he stayed away from the street he wouldn't hear the noise. The muffled sounds from the crowd only mocked him, as though everyone in Bath had gathered outside to jeer at his fearfulness.

The back room had but one window. It opened up

onto the Assembly Rooms building but not in a place, apparently, that drew a lot of lingering dancers. He spied the rainbow glimmers of a magnificent crystal chandelier, but no figures appeared behind the panes, and the orchestra as it struck up the opening chords of a quadrille was faint enough to resemble a child's music box. Well and good. He could hide out back here, and no one need know what a fool he'd been. Fool and a coward.

He settled onto a nearby stool and by the aid of his candle, finished working on the chair leg. As he put the finishing touch onto a bit of scrollwork, he glanced over at the nearby clock. 'Twas nearly ten. He'd better walk home and get a bit of supper and go on to bed. Though tomorrow was Sunday, he still planned to come in and work on more pieces of the furniture. It would do him no good if he were too exhausted to finish the job as he should.

James rose, dusting the sawdust from his hands, his shirtfront and his trousers. He was a mess. He'd do well to go home and take a bath while he was at it. He drifted over to the window, eager for a breath of fresh night air. He brushed at the dust covering his clothing. He'd been breathing sawdust too long.

He stuck his head out through the open window-pane, and as he ducked out, something caught his glance in the Assembly Rooms window across the way. A young woman in a pretty gown, her dark hair twisted and looped on top of her head, sat framed by the curtains on either side. As he watched, she gathered her knees to her chin, carefully arranging her skirts, and then leaned her head against the windowpane.

The girl in the window was Lucy Williams.

He'd know her anywhere, even though the finery she currently wore was a far cry from the practical, simple gowns she favored as a governess. He studied her more closely, his breath catching in his throat. She looked beautiful. Beautiful…but terribly sad.

She was close enough that, if he stood outside the window and yelled up at her, she'd see him in an instant. He leaned out a bit farther, hoping the darkness would continue to cloak him. He wasn't ready to make his presence known. There was a reason she sat, so silently and so still, in that window seat. From the tilt of her head and her downcast eyes, anyone could see that she was hardly enjoying her role as duenna for Amelia.

And no one was near to her, either. She must have sought out that isolated spot just to have a few moments to herself.

On the battlefield, he hadn't thought. He'd acted on pure instinct. And instinct had led him down the cowardly path. But now—

What if he obeyed his instinct?

He ducked back into the workshop and closed the window. Then he slipped out the back door, following a darkened path behind the Assembly Rooms. His heart hammered painfully against his rib cage. It was far too much like going into battle. Even his senses grew sharper: the sound of distant laughter echoed in his ears and the scent of smoke from the torches made his nose burn. The *haute monde* was not crowding around these doors; in fact, aside from a stray servant, he encountered no one.

Which was just as well. He was tidy enough, despite the wood shavings gracing his trousers but certainly not dressed for a ball.

He took the steps two at a time and gained entrance through an opened back door. Ah, yes. He knew this part of the building well; they had repaired several pieces of woodwork in this area just the week before. Just the week before—when he saw Lucy....

Judging from her position at the window, she would be well in the back of the ballroom. James rushed as best as he could without drawing attention to himself. What if Amelia had claimed her once more? The orchestra was playing a lilting song, a country dance of some kind. Good. Then perhaps Amelia would be occupied for another quarter of an hour or so.

He turned sharply to the right. Here was the ballroom, the dazzling light and cheerful bouncing strains of the music and pats of hundreds of feet forming a disconcerting kaleidoscope of sound and color. He paused, seeking Lucy, and the sounds grew muted and the light grew softer as he caught the outline of her form in the window seat. She was still there, and still alone.

Surely she could hear his heart beating as he drew close. But she stayed rooted to her spot, as though nothing profound were happening.

What if he couldn't speak once he caught her attention? What if he stood there before her, stammering like an idiot covered in wood shavings?

He approached the window seat, and strangely, his worries, his insecurities vanished. This was the right thing to do.

She still had her face pressed against the glass, and as he stopped beside her, his form was reflected in the window beside her. Lucy sat up, her lovely eyes opening wide, a shy smile bowing her lips.

He offered her his arm and bowed. “M-Miss L-Lucy, would you d-do m-me the honor?”

James was here before her, his clothing speckled with a fine dust. What on earth was he doing at an Assembly Rooms ball? She swallowed nervously. The ball, which was so dull and dreary for one who had no one to dance with, pulsed with new life as he stood before her, extending his arm.

She rose, taking hold of his elbow. “I’d love to dance,” she admitted, “but his lordship might not like to see me standing up with someone. I’m just here to chaperone Amelia after all.”

James peered around the ballroom. “W-where is Amelia? W-why are you t-t-tucked back into this c-corner?”

“Amelia is dancing with his lordship. A father and daughter moment before he leaves the ball for the evening.” She hesitated, biting her lip. Should she admit to how much she hated the ball? How lonely she’d been, hugging the wall all night? “The noise and the lights were giving me a bit of a headache. So, I sought this window seat out so I could rest a bit before his lordship left for the evening. When he departs, I must return to my post.”

“I see.” James turned toward her, his green eyes dancing with mischief in the dim light. “Well, I am hardly attired for a ball myself.” He dusted his trousers with his hand and grinned, sending her heart leaping into her throat. He was so attractive and so fun when he didn’t allow his speech impediment to overtake his life. Did he have any idea of the power of his attraction? Even in his dusty work clothes, none of the other men here could hold a candle to him.

He leaned forward and began to lead her through the figures of the country dance. After a moment's pause, she followed his movements, rising and falling and joining and parting with the rhythm of the music. She hadn't danced since she was at school, and even then she was only taught the rudiments. Fortunately, James was a superb dancer and a strong leader; once she gave up her embarrassment and allowed him to lead her through the dance, she found herself light-footed and sure in her movements.

And once she gave up thinking about the steps and instead simply followed his lead, an extraordinary thing happened. Warmth radiated from her being, and she could not stop smiling. This was how many of those girls felt right now. This was, in fact, how many such girls had felt for generations. And this is why so many of them adored stuffy old ballrooms.

"May I ask how exactly you managed to sneak into the Assembly Rooms dressed in your work clothes?" She chuckled a little breathlessly. "I can't imagine the circumstances."

He grinned and ducked his head a bit. "I was w-working in the shop n-n-next d-door. Heard all the n-noise and s-suddenly remembered that t-t-tonight is quite a big n-n-night not just for Miss B-B-Bradbury but f-for you as w-well." He fell silent as he led them through an intricate step. Then, he gazed down at her with an intensity that made her catch her breath. "I s-saw you s-sitting there in the w-window. And I d-decided I would be a c-c-coward n-no longer."

"A coward?" Her voice sounded squeaky to her own

ears. She cleared her throat and tried again. "Pray, why do you call yourself a coward?"

He halted midstep and turned to face her, grasping her other hand tightly in his. "Because I am. I—I've been a c-c-coward for years, since W-W-Waterloo. N-not speaking up when I should. N-not speaking at all. And I've led a m-m-miserable l-life b-because of it."

She nodded, returning his gaze boldly. He was willing her to understand. It was an unspoken plea between the two of them. "But why did you come here? How does this help you overcome any perceived cowardice on your part?" He wasn't telling her the whole story. He was holding something back.

He stared down at her a moment longer, and his throat worked as if he were stammering over a word. Odd, he didn't stammer when they were dancing together. And he didn't stammer when he was angry. But certain words or emotions triggered a tremendous obstacle to his speech, and his frustration would become palpable. She gave him a tentative smile. "No need to answer that," she said in a soft voice. "It was an impertinent question, after all."

The dance master called out the final steps for the longways country dance. Lucy spun around and faced the crowded ballroom. She could just make out the leading couple going down the dance. 'Twould be over in moments.

She must come back to earth. Amelia would be looking for her. And Lord Bradbury would not be pleased if he caught his daughter's chaperone dancing in a quiet corner with a young man. She tugged her hands away from James's grasp. "I should go," she murmured. "They'll send out a search party for me."

"D-don't g-go." James's voice, normally so hesitant when he stammered, now sounded strong and firm. She turned back to him, trying to read from his expression just what was causing the mighty war within him. She had upset him by repeating his silly self-accusations of cowardice. Perhaps if she apologized, then this whole matter could be dropped.

She took his hand in hers, ignoring the shock of warmth that shot up her arm as she did so. "I apologize, James, for repeating your nonsense about being cowardly. I don't think you are a coward. And I never have."

"I'll b-be a c-coward forever if I d-don't t-tell the t-truth," he stammered. "I c-came here because I saw you in the w-window..."

"Yes?" Oh, goodness, the final strains of the music lilted through the room. At any moment, the crowd would applaud and then part. And she'd have to go back to being a governess. 'Twas difficult indeed to make the shift from lighthearted, desirable young woman to governess and chaperone, but it was her lot in life.

"I s-saw you in the w-window." Whatever battle transpired was now over. The fire in his eyes was quenched, and his face settled into blank lines, as though he anticipated a blow. "And I d-didn't w-want you to f-feel unhappy any l-longer."

Her heart surged. Someone cared about her. Cared enough about her loneliness and her gloominess that he came in the back door of the Assembly Rooms, covered in dust, just to dance with her. "James, that's the sweetest thing anyone's ever done for me." Impulsively, she stood on tiptoe and touched his cheek with her lips. "Until you came, I was so terribly despondent. You've made my evening."

The stubble of his chin felt rough against her lips, and her face heated to the roots of her hair. He must think her a terrible hoyden for kissing him. But he had been so kind at a moment when she'd felt so dejected. He was such a good man. To cover her embarrassment, she rambled on. "My father was a preacher. He ministered to the poor and to men in gaol. I often read the Bible and think on the work he did. And I think if my Papa were here to meet you, he would quote from Proverbs, 'A man of knowledge uses words with restraint.'"

His brow furrowed as though her words confused him. Oh, bother, what a hash she was making of his perfectly wonderful gesture. She caught his arm in her hands, willing him to understand. "I mean to say, I like you—oh, I mean, your way with words," she hastily amended. Goodness, whatever would she say next? She was making an idiot of herself. She could only hope that James would take pity on her poor attempt at a compliment.

He lifted her gloved hands to his lips for a brief kiss. "Lucy, thank you for that."

She spun around to face the dance floor as a ruse to hide the expression on her face from James. He was being eloquent. He was being polite. A gentleman, through and through. And here she was in rapt adoration when he was merely being kind. She had to gain control of herself. He didn't really care for her—and she was here merely to serve as a duenna for her charge. There was no need to continue making a cake of herself.

She broke from his grasp. "I'd really better go. Amelia will be looking for me." And without a backward glance, she lost herself in the fashionable throng, eager to become, once more, just a governess. 'Twas the only role at which she excelled.

Chapter Twelve

"You're awfully cheerful this morning," Macready grumbled as James entered the kitchen, ravenous for his breakfast. "I don't think I've heard you whistle since the earliest days of the war. I'm happy for you and all that, old fellow, but could you tone it down a bit?"

"You n-need m-more t-tea," James rejoined. "Something t-to waken you." An inexplicable lightness soared through him this morn, as though he could spread his arms and float to the ceiling. Could one dance with Lucy cause all this transformation? She had such a profound effect on him. He sat at the table, eagerly grabbing the toast rack. Good grief, he was famished.

"Why all these good spirits?" Macready, his eyes half closed, sloshed more tea in his cup. Even when they were in the army together, Macready wasn't precisely a morning person. Half the time James would have to give him a good stout kick to waken him, and even then the fellow was usually late to mess. Now, as he adjusted to civilian life, James noted that Macready was becoming even grumpier in the mornings. He grinned cheekily, just to annoy Macready further.

"None of your b-business. I'm off to church. C-coming?" James spooned another egg onto his toast and took a hearty bite.

"I'll go to chapel this evening. I don't think I can make it yet. Need another pot of tea and another full hour to really waken. It's hard to get moving in the morning. My very bones seem to ache. My skin feels two sizes too small."

James swallowed and glanced at Macready, whose scars were visible beneath his rolled-up shirtsleeves. A wave of guilt washed over him. He had no right to be so joyful this morning. Not when others had suffered much more than he had. He'd go to church and spend his time there praying for forgiveness. Praying to become a better man. He finished the rest of his breakfast in silence. Words eluded him whenever his cowardice was brought to mind. As often as he tried to forget, to tamp it down as though it could be hidden, it would spring up at any opportunity. There was nothing he could do but go to church and pray.

The walk to Saint Swithin's did much to calm his spirits. The day was dawning quite fine. The gardens were now in full, lush bloom, boasting rosebushes so heavy with blossoms that they drooped toward the ground. He snapped off a vibrant blush pink bud as he walked by the public gardens. Its scent lifted his spirits, and its tint reminded him of Lucy's rosy cheeks after she'd kissed him the night before.

Lucy deserved better. If he were to be worthy of her, he'd have to make amends for his past, and strike forth as a better man. One capable of earning his own way. And he was working on that part of things. Felton approved of his plans for Lord Bradbury's library. He was becoming his own man, as long as he could find a way to release the ghosts of the past.

The bells of Saint Swithin's pealed jubilant notes that reverberated on the morning breeze. *Jesu, Joy of Man's Desiring.* A fellow couldn't help but feel transformed—transfigured, even—hearing those soaring notes. He paused at the foot of the stone steps that led up to the church, as the bells continued to ring out each note of the cantata. Passersby filed past him, calling out to one another, but their polite chatter did not deter him. He remained fixed in his place, staring up at the impressive stone façade of Saint Swithin's until the last peal rang out, echoing over the rapidly emptying churchyard.

"Ensign Rowland? How do you do?"

James spun around and spotted Reverend Stephens as he came walking up the steps. "Reverend, how d-do you d-do? Aren't you r-rather late for s-services?"

"Ah, yes." The reverend nodded and shook hands with James, his kindly expression never wavering. "Well, there was some business with the veterans' group—one of the men needing help with his family—and since Lieutenant Cantrill is still in Brightgate, I thought I should see to it." He indicated the chapel with a sweep of his arm. "Shall we?"

"Yes, of c-course." James followed the reverend as he began ascending the stone steps.

"Come to think of it, I haven't seen you at the veterans' group of late," Reverend Stephens continued jovially. "We do miss you, Ensign. All of the veterans are so closely knit."

"I've b-been b-busy," James stammered. "W-w-working for F-F-Felton's shop." He hated to miss out on the veterans' group, but it was a matter of business after all. And those fellows deserved the help more than he did. Most of them had wives and children, whereas he merely needed to support himself. Now that he was earning a good wage, he'd been able to send some home to Mother and Mary. Supplementing the tiny income that was left from Father's estate could make all the difference in the world to his family. And that gesture made him feel like a bit more of his own man.

"A new position? Excellent news. Felton's always been looking for someone within the veterans' group, but he needed a fellow with a genteel background." Reverend Stephens beamed as he continued up the steps. "Woodworking is considered a gentleman's art after all. And since you'd be working quite a bit with the gentry, well—he needed someone like you, with a bit of polish." Reverend Stephens clapped James on the back. "Well done, Ensign."

They approached the side door that led into the narthex. The choir had already begun the opening hymn, their blended voices spilling out onto the stone walkway that led around the building. A feeling of panic seized hold of James. What if he could never be forgiven his cowardice? His fellow men had forgiven him, but what of his Maker?

He seized hold of the reverend's flowing sleeve and gave it an urgent tug. "Reverend, I must ask you something. It's preying upon my mind. I cannot move forward until I have an answer." The words poured out of him, tumbling over each other in his haste.

"Of course." Reverend turned to James, his brows drawn together with concern. "What is troubling you, Ensign?"

"I know you must get on to services—" James waved toward the door, where the choir's chorus still echoed.

The reverend patted James's shoulder. "They can start without me. As long as I am there for the sermon."

"The battle at Waterloo was dreadful, chaotic—as tumultuous as you can imagine." Better to dive in to the middle of the tale before he lost courage and started stammering like an idiot again. "My group broke formation, scattered. The cavalry rode us down, chasing us into a rye field. Many men around me were hit. I was hit too, but it was just a scratch. The force of it stunned me, though. And I laid down as though dead. I—I remained there, pretending to be dead until night fell."

The reverend merely nodded, his expression open, his eyes still warm. At least he was not disgusted yet.

"I stayed there while the men around me called out for help. And I could not call out. I could not speak. I j-j-just laid there." His power of speech was failing; the emotions so long bottled were forcing their way up his very throat. Surely the reverend would cut him off with a mere look or a curt comment. He could never be forgiven this transgression.

Never.

The reverend nodded once more, his countenance unchanged. "I believe that has happened to others, countless others, in the heat of battle." He patted James's shoulder. "Not all wounds are physical in nature. What you suffered was as much of a torment as a cut from a saber blade. And you bear the scars to this day."

"M-my friends have forgiven me." He pushed the words out. "B-but can God?"

"My son, He already has." The reverend shook his head ruefully, giving James a gentle smile. "You veterans are so hard on yourselves. So quick to condemn your own actions, your own imperfections. Need I remind you that though we are made in His image, only He is perfect?"

James nodded, looking down at the ground. There was so much faith in the reverend. So much goodness.

"You may bear the scars of your ordeal for the rest of your life, simply because scars take a long time to heal," the reverend continued. "But you should not wear them as a hair shirt. You are forgiven. And the way you choose to live your life now should reflect His glory."

James glanced up. The reverend's words were, in a way, quite similar to what Macready had said. The past was over. And he should wallow in shame and cowardice no longer.

"Come back to the veterans' group when you can, Ensign. I think it would do you a great deal of good. Now, I must go—they'll need me soon—but I want you to think on this and to allow yourself the grace to grow from this experience." He shook James's hand warmly. "Good day, Ensign."

The reverend disappeared through the heavy wooden door, leaving James alone in the courtyard. Distracted, he wandered over to a shady spot and sat, breathing deeply of the scents of earth and grass. This was the tree he'd sat under with Lucy when she read to him so long ago.

He was still holding the rose he'd picked on the walk to church. Now he twisted and twirled it in his fingers as he allowed the reverend's words to sink into his very being. A life of grace, a life free of cowardice. What if he were to throw off the last bits of cotton wool that dulled his senses? What if he were to go free of the lingering shame of the battlefield?

Lucy began to remove those defenses, bit by bit, as they sat reading together under this tree. Time and time again, she'd responded to his temper with grace. She'd tried to help him. She'd given him such a sweet compliment last night. She was the first person who didn't look upon his speech defect as an impediment. And last night, she'd even kissed him. He'd be a fool to let her go. He'd be a coward if he continued to drive her away.

He stared up at the church, a prayer of thanksgiving flowing through him. He was starting afresh as of this moment. He would live a life of grace—with Lucy by his side. If she would have him. Despite his many, many flaws.

He said a little extra prayer at that thought.

Lucy turned to smile at Louisa as Reverend Stephens said the benediction. It was nice to have her there after all. With Sophie away—and probably engaged by now—Lucy's life was growing lonelier. And Louisa was, despite her girlish meddling, quite a good companion. 'Twould be hard indeed to lose her to the social obligations of her debut, but then that was the way of things.

"Can we go home and have tea? I'm famished," Louisa whispered as the last notes of the final hymn rolled out over the congregation.

"You shouldn't be thinking of your stomach at a time like this," Lucy replied with a stern glare. Then she softened. "But—yes."

"Oh, good." Louisa gave a happy sigh as the congregation began breaking up. She scooped up their wraps and turned to Lucy. "If we go out the side, we'll get through the crush more quickly."

Lucy scanned the crowd. Louisa was right. The aisles were jammed with parishioners; it would take forever to get through the front doors. "Come, follow me," she murmured, taking Louisa's hand.

She navigated through the throng with expert precision, winding through the pews and aisles as though maneuvering the steps of the country dance once more. The country dance…dancing with James…she clamped down tight on her memories and shook her head. It would never do to continue mooning over one silly dance. It meant nothing, after all. He was an extraordinarily polite gentleman who had come to her rescue just when she was feeling low. That was all it was and nothing more.

Louisa let out a giggle as they neared the wooden side door that led out into the courtyard. "I say, that was well done. You are as nimble as a cat, Lucy," she exclaimed, admiration evident in her tone. "Come, let's hurry. I bet Cook has scones almost ready right now."

Lucy pushed open the door, and they stepped out into the dazzling sunlight. The sun had a way of reflecting off the native tan stone that most buildings in Bath were made of, gilding them in a way that was almost hypnotic. She paused for a moment, shielding her eyes beneath her bonnet with the palm of her hand. "It certainly is bright today," she murmured.

She sought something cool and dark to rest her eyes, settling on a patch of green next to the courtyard. A figure that had been sitting beneath the willow tree stood. Her heart lurched. She'd know that tall, slightly stooped frame anywhere.

James.

He started toward them both, his hand extended in greeting.

Louisa elbowed Lucy sharply in the ribs. Lucy shot a quelling look at her young charge. "That's quite enough," she hissed. She had enough trouble keeping her emotions in check around James without Louisa adding fuel to the fire.

"Miss L-Lucy, Miss L-Louisa," he stammered, bowing before them both. "I'm g-g-glad to s-see you b-both."

Lucy murmured politely in return, but her heart refused to resume its normal beat. Something about James had changed. His eyes, normally a hazel shade of green, were darker now—almost emerald. And he seemed more assertive, more emphatic. Of course, he'd always had a soldier's bearing, but now he seemed—well, he seemed in command. These changes were quite compelling. Attractive, even, if one allowed herself to succumb. Not that she would, or even could.

Louisa spoke, too. "Ensign Rowland, I am so glad to see you. We were about to go home for tea. Would you like to join us?"

He shook his head. "N-no thank you, Miss L-Louisa. It's a k-kind offer. B-but I have some m-matters I m-must attend to this afternoon." He looked over at Lucy, his dark eyes holding her captive, as though there were a secret between the two of them. "I'll s-see you b-both t-tomorrow."

She was staring at him, as silly and enthralled as a schoolgirl. She snapped back to attention. It would never do to allow herself to fall all over a handsome man—in front of her charge, no less. "Of course, Ensign." She would maintain formalities in front of Louisa. No given names would cross her lips. "I look forward to seeing you and to seeing your progress."

He smiled then. How rare his smiles were. And how they transformed him. He was no longer a careworn soldier when he grinned but a playful, mischievous young man. Really, she must be careful. She must guard her heart. It would be all too easy to become enchanted with James, as charming as he could be.

He gave a tip of his hat to both of them and then strolled off with that new assured gait that was so striking. As they both watched his retreating back, Louisa burst into a vale of giggles.

"Oh, Lucy! I do believe he has designs on you."

"Don't be absurd," Lucy admonished. "He's a gentleman. That is all."

"I've read plenty of novels," Louisa continued in a knowing tone. "And the hero always looks at the heroine the way Ensign Rowland just looked at you."

"Remind me to clear out your bookshelf when we get home," Lucy replied crisply. "You're filling your head with nonsense."

Louisa merely smiled and tucked her arm into Lucy's as they headed down the stone steps. "Mark my words, Lucy. A marriage proposal can't be far from his mind."

Chapter Thirteen

Working with Louisa today was nigh on impossible. Lucy shook her head in playful despair. Louisa's concentration lagged during her Latin; she fumbled with her French, and even history—at which she normally excelled—had become a slog. Lucy turned away from Louisa's desk and walked over to the schoolroom window. The weather was still fine this morning. Perhaps that's why Louisa was having such trouble? They should go for an outing this afternoon. After all, she had promised her charge many outings over the coming weeks, and perhaps a trip to see some of the antiquities of Bath would renew Louisa's interest in her studies.

"Well, Louisa, since you have had so much difficulty this morning, I feel we should move outdoors this afternoon." Lucy turned from the window and smiled. "Perhaps a little fresh air would do you some good."

"Well, that would be nice." Louisa hesitated. How very odd—usually the thought of an outing would send her charge catapulting out of her chair. "But don't you want to work with Ensign Rowland in the library?"

"Of course," Lucy responded rapidly—too rapidly.

It made her sound eager and foolish. She took a deep breath and attempted to repair the damage. "What I mean is I will be happy to work with the ensign when he arrives. But he won't be here for another quarter of an hour or so." 'Twas really thirteen minutes until James was scheduled to arrive, but who was counting? Certainly not she.

Louisa rose from her desk and turned slow circles on the floor, tracing patterns in the rug with her slippered foot. "Lucy, do you think the ensign will ask you to marry him today?"

Lucy's heart leaped in her breast, but she schooled her features to spinsterly nonchalance. "Don't be absurd. The ensign has no designs on me." It was really time to put a stop to Louisa's romantic notions. For every time her charge mentioned any possible romantic connection between Lucy and James, it made her heart beat funny and her palms perspire. In short, it fueled a wild hope that someday James might want her.

But that was a ridiculous notion. And the more Louisa chattered on about it, the more Lucy began to believe it. Even though she kept her feelings tucked away, never letting on, it would do her no good to continue listening to Louisa. In fact, it could do real harm. It allowed Louisa to spin fantasies when she should be studying, and it made Lucy dream of marriage, a home, a family of her own—when she should be concentrating on her charge. In fact, she hadn't done a thing about creating a school for the young children of Bath. She should be working on that instead of daydreaming. A wave of guilt swept over her, and she turned sharply to Louisa.

"You must drop these silly notions about Ensign Rowland and myself." Her voice was nearing shrillness—she'd have to calm down before she continued. She took another fortifying deep breath. "Ensign Rowland comes of a noble family," she explained, noting Louisa's crestfallen expression. "He does not have any designs on me, and indeed he simply cannot. I have no family. Any possible connection between the two of us would be considered by his family a dreadful misalliance. Do you understand?"

"His family name is Rowland?" Louisa had stopped her dancing, and now she stared up at the ceiling, deep in thought. "Rowland. Rowland. I shall have to consult Papa's *DeBrett's.* I haven't heard of them."

"Minor nobility. Penniless, I suppose," Lucy hastily amended. Goodness, what if Lord Bradbury caught Louisa digging in his copy of the peerage for a connection for her governess? Oh, the madness that would then ensue. She closed her eyes for a moment, steadying herself.

"Well, if they are penniless, why do they care whom he marries? I mean, you are as wonderful as any titled lady in Bath." Louisa drew close and enveloped Lucy in a warm hug. "I can tell when I see you two together how very much you both like each other."

"Well, I suppose if they are penniless, they want their son to marry an heiress." Lucy returned the hug and then set Louisa away from her, looking into her charge's dark eyes. "You must listen to me, Louisa. There is no relationship between myself and Ensign Rowland, nor is there likely to be. We cannot talk about this any longer. It's a waste of breath and time."

Louisa shrugged, the corners of her lips pointing down. "Very well. I won't say anything about it anymore. But I think it's rotten that you can't marry the ensign just because of money and titles."

"Rotten? It's your world," Lucy replied, unable to suppress a laugh.

Louisa's face turned a shade paler, and her frown deepened. "I don't think that's funny."

A pang of remorse shot through Lucy. "I'm sorry, Louisa. I wasn't thinking." She looked at the little clock on the mantel as it began chiming the quarter hour. "I shall run downstairs and check in with the ensign about the library. While I am gone, I want you to continue your history lesson. And after lunch, we shall go for a walk. Would you like that?"

Louisa nodded and trudged over to her desk.

Oh, bother. She shouldn't have been so sarcastic with Louisa. But it was so difficult to make her young charges see the differences—not just in the classes of people one found in society but differences of situation and even differences of temper. Both Amelia and Louisa, coddled and pampered from birth, had enjoyed carefree, happy lives. They expected that everyone around them had, as well. She quit the schoolroom and closed the door gently behind her.

It was her nerves that had done it. She'd worked herself up over the ensign's impending arrival, she chided herself as she descended the main staircase. If she had been as calm as she should, then Louisa's silly expectations and notions would not have ruffled her feathers as they had. She must gain control of her emotions. She really must.

A cacophony of hammers and sawing greeted her as she neared the library. Workmen shuffled in and out of the room, carrying out crate after crate of books. These crates, she noted, were stacked neatly in the hallway or in the adjoining billiards room. Despite the racket, the entire operation looked calm and orderly. She was grateful for that. Though this plan carried with it some obvious need to cause disarray, it would please his lordship that the chaos was being kept to a minimum.

James would certainly earn his lordship's approval. But where was he? He was nowhere to be seen among the workmen bustling to and fro. So she must enter the hornet's nest, so to speak. Gathering her skirts along with her courage, she stepped over the threshold.

James glanced up from his station at a library table as she entered. His eyes glowed with an excited light. He beckoned her over with a wave of his hand. "C-c-come in," he shouted, his voice carrying over the noise. "As you see, we've s-s-started."

"So I can tell," she shouted, giving him a smile. Goodness, carrying on a conversation in this din would be a chore. "Do you need anything from me?" Perhaps making this brief appearance would be enough to satisfy everyone, and she could return to her schoolroom. Lingering too long with James was an invitation to heartbreak.

"Yes. B-but let's find someplace quieter." He laughed as his voice was drowned out by hammering. He grasped her arm above her elbow and steered her toward the doorway. She allowed herself to be carried along, enjoying the feeling of sure strength that came from being beside James. She would permit herself this morsel of enjoyment but no more than this.

They stepped out into the hallway, and James turned to her. "Where c-can we g-go for a few moments' p-p-peace?"

The workers, like industrious ants, continued filing in and out of the library, going back and forth between it and the billiards room. Well, perhaps they could have a moment in the music room. Louisa's practice would not take place until later in the day. "In here," she responded, crossing the hallway and opening the door. "We should have reasonable quiet to discuss our plans."

He nodded and followed her inside. She gave a sigh of satisfaction—this was the prettiest room in the house, in her opinion. The walls were a pale shade of almond green, very restful and serene to the senses, and the floor to ceiling windows offered a glimpse of the gardens outside. The pianoforte, a prized instrument that was well worth its weight in gold, anchored the room, providing a sense of purpose. And Amelia's golden harp glowed in the corner. Lucy smiled and sank onto the settee.

James remained standing, his hands clasped behind his back. This peaceful room seemed to have the opposite effect on him—for he began pacing back and forth. After a brief, tense moment, Lucy spoke. She had to break the strain. "Is something wrong with our plans for the library?"

"No, n-nothing is wrong with the l-library. It should b-b-be splendid, thanks t-to you." James glanced over at the open door. "D-do you mind if I c-close that?"

"No. Of course." It wasn't entirely proper to be alone in a room with a young man, but 'twas quite unlikely that someone as noble as James had dishonorable intentions. There was likely a practical explanation for their need of privacy. Perhaps there was a problem with the workmen, and he didn't want them to overhear as he explained the issue to her.

He shut the door with a quiet click and resumed his pacing before her.

"Oh, James, I wish you would say what's troubling you. I am quite in a swither, wondering what's causing you to march up and down on the rug." Perhaps a bit of humor would help ease the sudden nervous energy pulsating throughout the room.

He stopped and turned to face her. A brief grin flashed across his face. "M-my apologies. It's not the l-library. It's about y-you and m-me."

A knot worked its way up her throat, and in a moment, she would burst into tears or cry out. He knew that she fancied him, and he was going to let her down gently. She swallowed convulsively, but her mouth was dry as a desert.

"L-Lucy." He drew close and knelt on the floor before the settee, taking her hand in his. His hand was large and warm, whereas hers had grown cold. He chafed them, as though trying to thaw them. "I m-must speak frankly and quickly, for I—I—I lose m-my voice at t-times like these. B-but I m-must know the t-truth. C-c-can you—c-could you ever—c-care for m-me?"

She stared down into his face. Had she heard aright? Surely he'd said something else, and she misunderstood. Her silence grew long, and a bright flush stole over James's handsome features.

"I—I—I know I am a c-coward, and I s-s-stammer, but I'm m-m-making something of myself. And I am doing so b-because of you. I w-want to be a b-better m-man because of you."

Well, that couldn't have been her imagination. He had to be saying those words. She stared at his lips, her heart beating so that she had trouble catching her breath. Was he—did he—like her? Care for her?

James tightened his grasp on her hands. "P-p-please say something." His voice broke slightly, and he looked away.

She gasped, as though someone had thrown a bucket of ice water over her head, and leaned forward so that he had to turn back and look at her. At the very least, she owed him the truth. "I do care for you."

A rush of heady triumph surged through James. She cared for him. Despite his stammer, despite his cowardice, Lucy Williams cared. He made a motion as though to scoop her into his arms, but the expression on her face stopped him. This was not the way a woman joyfully in love should look. Her creamy cheeks were so pale they were almost translucent. The freckles sprinkled across the bridge of her nose stood out in bold relief.

And those eyes. Those rich brown eyes that haunted him night and day. All the spark was quenched from their depths.

She looked sick and terribly sad.

His heart dropped like a stone. "What's wrong?"

"We can never speak of this again," she whispered, trying to extricate her hands from his grasp. "I should go."

"You can't go. Not until you tell me what's wrong." If he let her leave now, she'd disappear from his life. He was certain of it. The mutinous tilt of her chin, the quenched fire in her eyes, all spelled a determination to leave him. "If you care for me as much as I do you, we should be the happiest creatures in all of Bath."

"We might be, perhaps," she admitted. "But what of your family? Surely they would be quite unhappy at our declarations."

"Mother? And Mary?" He was befuddled, he had to admit it. Why would his family object to Lucy? She was an extraordinary woman. Surely they would see it the moment they met her.

"James, please listen." She stopped trying to take her hands from his grasp, but she kept her eyes cast down. That was a good sign, wasn't it? "I am a penniless orphan. I have no family connections. Nothing to recommend me. Your mother and sister are relying upon you to marry well, I am sure."

"My family is not as snobbish as you think." Mother wanted him to marry well, of course, but once she met Lucy she'd know what a wonderful girl he'd found. He rose from his spot on the floor and sank beside her on the settee, moving as close to her as propriety would allow. "And I would never marry any woman for her money or her connections." His stammer had quite vanished under the emotion of the moment and he said a silent prayer of gratitude. 'Twas hard enough to say these things aloud without tripping over his words.

"Oh, I know you wouldn't, James." She gave a deep, shuddering sigh. "But I am a realist, and you must be, too. You must know that my lack of family, lack of breeding, lack of anything to recommend me makes me a very poor choice for you."

"I won't listen to this any longer." A spark of anger grew hot within him. "Your family—your father—were good people. I won't have you denigrate them. And I won't sit here like a fool and beg you." He let go of her hands and rose. "Perhaps these excuses are a ruse because you don't really like me and want to ease my hurt feelings."

"They aren't. And I do care for you very much." At length, she gave him one of her quick, darting glances, her eyes bright with unshed tears that extinguished his anger in an instant. "I have told myself time and again not to care, because I was certain there was no future in it."

"D-don't c-cry." His voice sounded ragged even to his own ears. He touched the side of her face with his hand, stroking his thumb along her jawline. "There is a future for us. I swear t-t-to it."

She closed her beautiful eyes, and tears spilled forth, tracing paths down her pale cheeks. "I wish I could believe it."

He was so close to happiness. It was like a leaf dancing on a chill autumn wind. He kept drawing closer, trying to grasp it, and another fickle breeze would blow it just out of reach. "Will you c-c-come home with m-me and m-meet m-my family?"

"I can't leave here. Not with Sophie gone to Brightgate." She gave a little hiccupping sob. "The girls are relying upon me."

"Then I shall write to Mother and Mary and ask them to join me here for a visit." He withdrew his handkerchief from his pocket and gently scrubbed away the paths of her tears. "Once they meet you I am certain they will adore you."

"I wish I could be so sure." Her lips trembled into a shadow of a smile.

"You c-c-can be." Again, happiness just flitted out of grasp. He was ready to seize it—to make it his. "L-Lucy, d-d-do you *want* to m-marry m-me?"

"I…I do. But I cannot make any promise to you. Not until I meet your family and gain their acceptance and approval." Her lovely face had settled into lines of determination. She was a stubborn one. He admired her for it, and at the same time, exasperation threatened to overtake him completely. He was ready to sweep her into his arms and kiss her until she consented to become his wife and gave up this silly nonsense about family connections.

But as a solider, he had to know when to make a strategic retreat. He had not given up, but he knew that victory would not be won today. At least he knew she cared. That little flicker of hope would keep him going. And once Mother and Mary came and met Lucy, the matter would be settled. They would be married, and he would have his adorable Lucy forevermore. He need only be patient a bit longer.

He stroked her soft cheek with the pad of his thumb. "B-but I shall ask again s-s-soon. I h-hope to hear a happier answer then. And in the m-meantime, I shall c-c-court you with a v-v-vengeance." When she opened her mouth to protest, he laid his finger across her lips. "Just s-s-say yes to that, L-Lucy," he breathed, willing her to understand the depths of his emotion.

Lucy looked at him, her dark eyes still bright with tears. She gave a trembling sigh. Then—"Yes."

Chapter Fourteen

Lucy stuffed another schoolbook into her bag. The children of the veterans' group would wait no longer. As of today, she would start spending her off days up at Saint Swithin's, holding an impromptu school. 'Twas something she'd meant to do for weeks, before Sophie's departure and Amelia's debut made it necessary for her to put it aside.

But if she were to be honest with herself, the idea of a school was a good distraction that she needed now more than ever. She had not seen James for three days now, not since the day he proposed to her in the music room. And she had not breathed a word of their conversation to anyone. When Sophie returned home the day before, Lucy kept her counsel, immersing herself into Sophie's problems with Lieutenant Cantrill. She'd certainly not said a word to Louisa. Besides being highly improper, such a course of action would open Lucy to an onslaught of Louisa's romantic notions, and she was not strong enough to endure more of that nonsense.

She laced up the leather satchel, which now bulged with books, slates and slate pencils. She'd done such a fine job of convincing herself that James's proposal was meaningless—hopeless, in fact—that sometimes she wondered if it had really transpired. Perhaps she'd dreamed the whole thing. And that thought made her heart ache. She wanted it to be true, even though the marriage he'd said he wanted could never, ever come to fruition.

She struck out for Saint Swithin's alone. Sophie had broken off her engagement with Lieutenant Cantrill and would no longer be attending any veterans' group meetings. The lieutenant was probably still home in Brightgate, so he wouldn't be there. It promised to be a rather small crowd with no familiar faces. She infinitely preferred the familiar. At the mere thought of confronting a lot of strangers, Lucy began twirling a lock of her dark hair with her fingers. But then, it was either this or sit at home where she would have the option of listening to Sophie wail or sitting at her window seat and stare at the walls, replaying her conversation with James in her mind over and over. Action was definitely preferable to moping about the house.

The weather was gray, and storm clouds gathered menacingly on the horizon. It was going to be a wet walk home, quite likely. She scanned the skies with an anxious glance. Perhaps she could stay in the church until the storm passed this afternoon. It would be horrid to get soaked to the bone, and the books would likely be ruined, as well.

She mounted the stone steps leading to Saint Swithin's as hastily as ladylike behavior would allow. Bother. The satchel with the books was so dreadfully heavy. Why had she brought so many? She'd have to start a lending library and leave the books in the chapel.

She'd ask Reverend Stephens if that would be a welcome thing. It would certainly save her back and shoulders to do so.

A familiar figure stood at the top of the stairs.

James.

Her heart leaped as he spied her and began descending the stairs, his face creased with a sudden smile of welcome. James grasped the satchel and lifted it onto his shoulders, stealing a quick peck on her cheek as he did so. She darted a warning glance at him as she surrendered her burden.

"What?" He laughed with triumph. "I p-promised you I would c-court you. You c-can't b-blame a fellow for t-trying." He tucked her arm into his elbow and led her up the rest of the stairs. "What's in the b-bag?"

"Books for the children," she murmured. "I want to start teaching here at the veterans' group meetings." She looked up at him, her brows drawing together in confusion. "Why are you here? Aren't you working most mornings now?"

"F-Felton has g-given me leave to attend the m-meetings. I've m-missed them. And it's a g-good opportunity to s-see you." He grinned like a mischievous boy, an endearing grin that made her smile back. "A school, you s-say? That's a g-good idea."

Warmth glowed through her at his approval. It was nice to be able to confide in him. Why, if they were married, they could meet just like this, walk home in the evenings, share their trials and troubles over dinner in a cozy flat. The mere thought of it filled her with longing. Perhaps—perhaps—he was right. Maybe everything could work out, and they could marry. She briefly explained her idea of a school to him, and he nodded in approval.

"I think it's s-something the children n-need. And what's m-more, you're a g-gifted t-teacher. You should use your g-gift to help others." Instead of leading her inside, however, he steered her over to the willow tree in the side courtyard. "We'll join them in a m-moment," he muttered, pulling her close. "B-but I wanted to let you know I wrote to my family. I am sure M-Mother and M-Mary will join me within a fortnight."

"A fortnight?" It seemed so soon and yet so long to endure. She allowed herself to rest her head on his shoulder, breathing deeply. The fine linen of his shirt-front rubbed against her cheek, and she closed her eyes. He smelled of shaving soap, a citrusy scent that made her think of the tartness of limeade. Sitting here like this, she could almost believe they would be wed.

"And I have m-more p-plans." He rubbed his chin against the crown of her hair. "Lord B-Bradbury's already recommended m-me to some of his c-cronies. I have garnered t-two more c-commissions in the past three days. F-Felton's given me his approval to keep going with these jobs. So I am m-making inquiries to find a home. Our home."

She drew back, staring up at him with widened eyes. "Our home?"

"I c-can't have M-Mother and M-Mary stay with me and Macready anyway," he teased in a light tone. "B-but it's something I've b-been thinking of for a long t-time. A nice little house of our own. W-will you help me choose one?"

"I don't know." She braced herself against his shoulder. First, she was allowing him to court her. Now, he was asking for her help in choosing a home? If she helped him to select a place to live, would she be opening herself up to more heartache later when his mother disapproved? Very likely so, no matter what James said. No, it was better not to even involve herself in the search for a new house.

She stole a glance up at James's strong profile. He was determined, and he was stubborn. If she said no, flatly, then it would anger him or even hurt him. So it was better to find a different, truthful answer to give him now until this inevitable farce played to the bitter end.

"I'd rather it be a surprise," she murmured.

He looked down at her, a flicker of amusement in his dark green eyes. She'd forgotten that James was also very, very smart. He said nothing, but a wry grin twisted the corner of his mouth.

"Very well, a s-surprise it shall b-be." He patted her shoulder. "We'd b-better go in. It looks like rain."

She pulled away from him and rose, shaking out her skirts. "I did want to say congratulations on your commissions," she admitted, tucking her hand into his elbow. "I knew you would do splendid work at Felton's. I peeked into the library yesterday, and I must say it's looking quite wonderful. Those barrister bookcases are so elegant."

James smiled. "I would never have g-gotten started without your help."

She said nothing, but it was hard to tamp down the happiness that welled within her. Even if they never married—even if she never saw him again—James was going to be fine. He had come so far from the lanky young man who couldn't speak two words to most people. Now, he spoke to almost everyone, with merely the hint of a stammer. He was gaining acclaim for his work with Felton. He was moving out of the flat he shared with Macready.

He was going to make some girl very happy some day. Even if the girl in question wasn't Lucy Williams.

It felt good to be part of the veterans' group again. James had never been active in the group and had kept to the outskirts of the meetings whenever he'd shown up before, certain that the other veterans scorned him for his lack of courage under fire. And yet, as he entered the narthex today, several of them called out to him in greeting. His work with Felton was the talk of the men, many of whom were looking for work themselves.

"It does me good to hear that another bloke is doing well," a grizzled old veteran laughed, slapping James on the back. "It gives me hope for the future."

Cantrill was nowhere to be found, which was too bad. He must be in Brightgate visiting his family still. James missed the lieutenant, who, along with Macready and Lucy, had been among the few who cared enough to help break down his defenses and try to help him.

He settled into a pew, giving a brief backward glance to the group of women and children settled near the back of the chapel. Lucy had gathered a group of children off to one side and was reading aloud to them. Judging by their rapt expressions, she had them completely enamored. He couldn't suppress a grin at the reminder of how smitten *he* had been when she met him under the willow tree and read from the book of poetry.

Macready limped in and settled onto the bench beside him. "Well, I found a place for you to let. Not that I'm eager to run you off. But as I was on my way over, I turned down a side street and there it was. A charming little house on York Street. The sign in the window read, 'to let.' So I knocked on the door and obtained the information for you in case you are interested."

"Well d-done." He unfolded the scrap of foolscap Macready handed him and scanned its contents. "S-sizable rooms, s-serviceable k-k-kitchen. D-does it have a g-garden?"

"Yes, a very pretty one in front with flowers and what looked to be a vegetable garden behind. I hate to lose you as a roommate, but I was tempted to take it myself. It's made of stone, nice sturdy slate roof, as pleasant a little home as you can imagine. I think even your mother would find it suitable." Macready laughed and waggled his eyebrows.

"You should just b-be happy that I am leaving so you d-don't have to endure my relatives," he rejoined crisply, mostly joking. True, Mother could be hard to take. But Mary? His sister was a sweet soul, always had been. "You will c-c-come and c-c-call while they're here, w-won't you? B-but you must p-p-promise you'll at least b-be kind to Mary. She's a g-good g-girl. Like m-me, she stammers. Her m-marriage p-p-prospects because of it aren't very h-hopeful."

"I promise not to be a bore," Macready replied, solemnly crossing his heart. "The place is furnished except for a few bits and pieces. I told the agent you'd probably stop by this afternoon."

Thunder rumbled, dulled by the thickness of the church walls, joined soon thereafter by the patter of raindrops against the windowpanes. "I'll g-go, but I must g-get a hackney. And we'll t-take Lucy home, t-too. She walked here with a satchel full of b-books. I don't want her to g-get soaked."

Macready nodded his assent, and they both turned their attention to the meeting. Reverend Stephens conducted the gathering, leading the men in prayer. When the meeting drew to a close, the reverend beckoned James over, a kind smile on his face.

"I am so glad to see you again, Ensign. Did Felton let you have the morning off?"

"He d-did. He feels the g-group d-does fine things for the c-community, and so he insisted I return to the m-meetings." James shook the reverend's hand. "And I owe you a d-debt of g-gratitude, as well. Our c-conversation the other d-day was a turning point for m-me. I am b-becoming a new m-man."

The reverend nodded. "Well, there was nothing wrong with the old one except a tendency not to forgive."

"Thank y-you again." With those words, James bowed to the reverend and went to the back of the church to collect Lucy. Perhaps the reverend would be officiating at their wedding before long.

Several of the children clustered around Lucy, pulling at her long skirts with grubby hands. She smiled at each one of them so lovingly, so patiently, where other women would have been politely horrified at the damage to their gowns. "I promise we will continue our lessons every week," she told them firmly in that musical voice of hers. "Now that I know how many of you there are and what you like to read and learn, next week will be even better. I promise."

She glanced up, her brown eyes twinkling as James approached.

"It l-looks like your s-s-school is a s-s-success," he stammered. How pretty Lucy was when she was confident and happy. When she wasn't deliberately walling herself off from other people. He would spend the rest of his life trying to keep that delighted expression on her face.

"Yes, it is." The children's parents clustered around, gathering up their progeny and thanking Lucy for her help. He helped her to gather her books in her worn leather satchel until the church was finally emptied of the families who ventured out into the pouring rain.

"Macready and I are r-renting a hackney. C-come, let us escort you home," he said when they finally had a moment to themselves.

"A hack? Oh, goodness, how kind you are. I did not relish the prospect of walking home in this downpour," she replied with a happy chuckle.

Macready joined them in the vestibule. "I've already called for the hack," he replied, indicating his damp clothes with a wave of his hand. "As you can see—even just waiting outside for one was a bit of a soak."

"M-Macready, d-don't think you've m-m-met Miss Williams." James set about making the introductions as calmly as he could. Macready and his gift of Irish gab—he'd have to be careful and not allow his comrade to say too much. Lucy was so easily embarrassed and so determined not to be thought of as anyone but a governess. Certainly not James's sweetheart.

"I apologize, I didn't catch your rank," Lucy replied sweetly, curtsying before Macready. "I want to make sure I address you correctly. I know how important that is to military men."

Macready's thin face broke into a wide grin. "Oh, tosh, Miss Williams. You may call me plain old Macready. It's how all of my friends address me."

"Very well then. How do you do, Macready?" Lucy smiled. A dart of jealousy shot through James. He wasn't entirely comfortable with the way Macready was looking at Lucy. As though she were a sweet, ripe apple and he was hungry for a bite. James offered her his elbow, asserting his place once more.

"Shall we g-go?" Blast his stammer. He was learning to live with it, but surely as the sun set in the west, it would pop up at the worst times. And standing next to Macready, with his fluent speech and his gift of complimenting the ladies, made James's deficiencies stand out in bold relief.

"Yes, of course." Lucy tucked her hand into the crook of his arm, her gentle brown eyes shining up at him.

They exited the side door and rushed down the steps. The hack stood patiently down at the foot of the stairs, but even with the carriage ready and waiting, the chilly rain drenched them all to the skin. He bundled Lucy inside and leaped in after her, Macready close on his heels. Macready slapped the side of the carriage before he shut the door, and the hack took off.

Lucy settled on the bench, laughing and wiping the raindrops off her cheeks with her gloved hands. "Oh, dear. I cannot tell you how thrilled I am that you gentlemen were willing to share this ride. I would have had to wait inside until a break in the storm."

"We're only too glad to help," Macready chimed

in, before James could say anything. "What do you do with the veterans' group, Miss Williams?"

"Well, I am a governess for Lord Bradbury's daughters, and I am assisting the group by reading to the children," she explained, peeling off her sodden gloves. "I hope someday to teach the children the rudiments of reading and writing. Perhaps a little basic arithmetic."

"Excellent. I know you'll do a superb job. Rowland here speaks quite highly of you."

James slanted a warning glance at his friend as the color rose in Lucy's cheeks. Macready turned to less potentially dangerous topics, maintaining a pleasant stream of chatter as they rolled toward the Crescent. Even James was able to dart in a comment here and there. As the carriage pulled up in front of his lordship's impressive townhome, James helped Lucy out and escorted her to the back door.

Rejoining his friend in the carriage, he noted Macready's pensive, almost meditative air. He rested, his chin in his hands, and stared out the window at the driving rain. "You know, Rowland, the bachelor life is quite losing its charm for me," he muttered after a long pause. "Like you, I think I am ready to settle down."

James clenched his jaw and said nothing. A suspicion, strong as black coffee, washed over him. Lucy made Macready doubt the bachelor lifestyle. He'd have to watch his comrade and his easy charm. Not that Lucy was the type of girl who was easily swayed—but still.

He was releasing most of his self-hatred. He was coming to accept his past and he now believed he could move on from his actions. But the old insecurities were slow to loosen their hold. Part of him still believed that Lucy could do better—that a stronger, braver man could make her happier. He would have to be wary lest some such man sought to steal her away. Caution was a virtue when happiness was so close.

Chapter Fifteen

Lucy hesitated before Sophie's door. Servants' gossip was just servants' gossip—but still. The house was abuzz with titillating details about what had transpired between Sophie and his lordship that morning. They'd been seen leaving the house together in his lordship's carriage; Sophie was wearing a prized pearl necklace that had last been seen in the window of a very exclusive jeweler in Bath. And the pair of them had just returned not two hours ago with Sophie swooning on his lordship's shoulder. Of course, the ready excuse was that Sophie was hungry and exhausted and had succumbed to a fainting fit. But everyone in the house, from the scullery maid to his lordship's impassive butler, knew the truth. His lordship had made a certain offer to Sophie—but not an offer of marriage.

Or at least, that was the gist of things. The cook had spilled all the details out to Lucy over luncheon preparations. And if all of this were true, it would explain why Sophie was holed up in her room, hiding from everyone. Lucy stole up the stairs, her mind whirling at the news. She'd suspected that his lordship harbored some kind of affection for Sophie—indeed, what man wouldn't? Sophie was so lovely. And Sophie had grown up in wealth and luxury, at least until her father's death. Would she be willing to bankrupt her very soul and become Lord Bradbury's mistress? Such an action would assuredly bring her the material comforts she'd been missing.

Lucy paused outside Sophie's door. Though they were close in age, Lucy felt older than Sophie by years. She had been awakened to the harsh realities of life much quicker than Sophie, and had no family to back her as Sophie had. She had a responsibility to nurture Sophie and direct her on the right path. And yet, if Sophie suspected that Lucy was acting as her elder sister, she might just as easily balk and agree to become Lord Bradbury's mistress out of pique. For there was nothing that Sophie disliked more than being told what to do.

No. She'd have to pretend to support Lord Bradbury. She'd have to show Sophie only the sensible aspects of becoming his mistress. And Sophie, who hated being preached to—rightly or wrongly—would then choose the right course of action.

Lucy knocked briefly and then let herself in. She squared her shoulders and assumed a look of practical nonchalance. "You look rather mutinous, Sophie. I fear that doesn't portend well for Lord Anthony."

"Would you have me stay in Bath and be his mistress?" Sophie snapped, sitting up sharply from her nest of pillows.

Lucy tilted her head to one side, considering Sophie's situation. Now was the time to dictate all the supposed benefits of mistresshood. After all, there might be some good to be had from that kind of security. "Well, he would protect you. And you would be set up for life. He's very generous—the way he treats his daughters, the high pay he lavishes on all the servants—he would never be stingy or mean."

"He offered to set me up as a modiste. With my own townhome," Sophie admitted, plucking at the fringe of her coverlet.

Lucy's heart lurched. Was Sophie actually considering it? Her plan was going awry—she must lay on the sensible aspects with a trowel. "You see? You would never have a care in the world. And just think, Sophie. After turning down two marriage proposals and losing out with Charlie Cantrill, this may well be the best offer you will ever have. So why do you look like a thundercloud? Surely this is a wonderful bit of luck. You have nothing to lose by becoming his mistress." Though the words choked her a bit, she steadied her voice and offered Sophie a brisk smile.

"I would lose my self-respect. I would lose everything. My life would be just like that vacant townhome he showed me today—beautiful but empty. I don't love him. And I won't debase myself by entering into a relationship with him that cannot be sanctified."

Ah, there it was. Sophie knew she'd lose any sense of self she had if she agreed to Lord Bradbury's terms. Lucy eyed her closely. Sophie's mind was set, surely. But just to be sure, Lucy fired her last set of arrows. "But what of Louisa and Amelia? You could become like a second mother to both of them. They both adore you so."

"I love them too, but I cannot be a second mother to those girls when I am a courtesan to their father."

Lucy sat back and suppressed a wide grin. What a

relief. Sophie had an honest and honorable heart, but she was also accustomed to a very different life than that of a seamstress. The temptations of a secure situation of greater luxury than she would ever be likely to earn on her own must have been powerful indeed. How good to know that Sophie's higher principles had held strong.

She glanced speculatively at her friend. "How are you going to tell his lordship no? I would never, ever want to defy that man. He's generous, but I think he would be a terrible adversary. Isn't he coming up to see you this evening? What do you propose to do?" She had a sneaking suspicion that her diplomacy and tact would be called upon in the near future.

"I'm leaving." Sophie threw off the coverlet and rose.

"Where are you going?" Lucy stared at her friend, her mouth dropping open.

"I'm going home to Tansley, where I belong. I'm leaving right now through the back door. And don't you breathe a word of this to Lord Anthony." Sophie scurried about, changing out of her chemise and into a dark wool riding habit. "I'll take one small bag with me so that I can travel quickly. You can have the rest of my clothes." Sophie opened a carpet bag and tossed a few garments inside.

Lucy leaped from the bed and knelt beside her on the floor. She was losing the only friend besides James that she had in Bath. That was deeply troubling on its own, but there was more at stake here than Lucy's comfort. Sophie's very safety could be at risk if she left without taking adequate preparations. "Sophie, are you mad? There is no way for you to travel alone. Have a little sense. At least stay the night and start fresh in the morning."

"I have my own money. I shall hire a yellow bounder and leave right away."

Sophie wasn't thinking clearly. There was no way that Lucy would allow Sophie to leave in this state of mind and on such a long journey alone. "If you do that, I shall tell Lord Anthony. Right now." Lucy stood and walked over to the door. "It's simply not safe for any young woman to travel alone."

"Botheration, are you on his side or mine?" Sophie snapped.

"Neither. But I would never forgive myself if you were harmed, Sophie." Lucy's hand rested on the doorknob. Her heart pounded in her chest. She'd never defied anyone this openly, but she couldn't stand aside and watch her friend get hurt.

Sophie sat back on her heels. "Stop. Don't tell him. I shall think of another way." She paused for a moment, her brows drawing together. "I shall leave right away and go see my aunt Katherine, and she and I will arrange my travel together."

Lucy removed her hand from the doorknob. If Sophie was traveling with family, then that would be all right. Certainly safer than going alone. "That's more sensible. She will travel with you or send a servant."

Sophie finished her packing and then turned to Lucy. "Will you find a way to tell Louisa and Amelia that I am all right and that I send my love? Without alerting Lord Anthony, of course."

Lucy nodded, her brows drawing together. That would not be an easy conversation. Sophie was so adored by both of the girls. "I don't relish the task, but I will."

Sophie opened the drawer of her dresser and withdrew a leather pouch. She weighed it in one hand and looked at Lucy.

"I pawned the bracelet Lord Anthony gave me."

Lucy nodded. "Yes, I know." The bracelet, like her pearl necklace, had been the talk of the servants' hall for many weeks.

"Do you think that the money I received from pawning the bracelet is mine? Or should I give it back to his lordship?"

Lucy paused for a moment, giving the matter some thought. It was a rather heavy moral issue. "Why did you sell the bracelet, Sophie? For material gain?"

"No. I sold it because it seemed like such a fetter. Even then I was being tied to Lord Anthony in a way I disliked. I was going to use the funds to make clothes for the widows and children of the veterans' fund. I never had a chance to do so."

"Oh, Sophie." Lucy came over and folded her in a warm embrace. "Of course, it's yours. I would keep it and do whatever I want with it. Lord Anthony has plenty of money, and besides, he gave that gift to you. It was yours to keep."

"Then this is what I want you to do. After I am gone—several days after I am gone, in fact—I want you to take the money to Charlie and say it is an anonymous gift for the widows. Then, if you don't mind, try working with the women to create a sort of sewing class or ladies' group—one that would allow its members to sew dresses for each other."

Lucy accepted the leather pouch from Sophie and

opened it. "My goodness, there is enough money in here to feed and clothe several families for a year or more. Sophie, are you sure you want me to do this without telling Charlie anything?"

"Do not tell him it came from me." Sophie hefted her valise in one hand. "When I came to Bath I had every intention of striking out on my own. And over these few months, I have failed at every turn. I failed with Charlie and now with Lord Anthony. I have barely begun to shepherd Amelia through the rigors of a London season. And I never had a chance to do anything for the widows." She patted Lucy on the shoulder and crossed to the door. "Perhaps if I stay far removed from it, the Widows of Waterloo will become a success."

"Sophie, don't feel that way. None of this is your fault." Lucy's eyes burned with unshed tears. It was so difficult to see Sophie leaving. But then, feeling as she did, there was no other choice.

Sophie blew her a kiss. "I shall write when I get settled at Brookes Park."

And then she was gone. Lucy blinked back the tears that pricked at her eyelids. There was nothing to do but allow Sophie to go back home. Perhaps in the comfort and security of her family, Sophie would find peace. She deserved it. She was such a sweet girl.

Lucy weighed the leather pouch full of coins in her hand. She certainly had her work cut out for her over the next few weeks. Telling the girls would be a stroll in the park compared to telling Lieutenant Cantrill that Sophie was gone. He likely wouldn't believe her unless she told him everything, which meant finding a way to inform him that Lord Bradbury had tried to make Sophie his mistress. Not to mention that Lord Bradbury would probably have her hide if he found that she'd helped Sophie leave without his knowledge. And then, sometime in the next few days, James's mother and sister would be arriving from their cottage in Essex.

Lucy trudged back over to Sophie's bed and sank down onto its plump, soft surface. However would she make it through? She bowed her head and prayed for the strength to carry herself with dignity. After all, if Papa could minister in prison wards, then she could face down a few aristocrats.

"So, have your mother and sister arrived yet?" Macready inquired as he entered the parlor of James's new home. "Have I missed anything important?"

"N-not yet." James waved Macready over to a chair. "G-good of you to c-come t-tonight. It makes things easier, having your support."

Macready sat and glanced at James with mirth twinkling in the depths of his black eyes. "So you think your mother won't create a scene whilst I am here? You have that much faith in her innate breeding and tact?" He chuckled, rubbing his hands together. "So what are you worried about?"

Everything. Nothing. It was all so complicated. "Mother won't like that I am w-working with my hands," he admitted. "She still c-clings to the n-notion that our family n-name m-means something. She probably d-daydreams that we should have a home of our own on the C-Crescent."

"And instead, her only son is building a library for a lord in a townhome on the Crescent," Macready finished. The corner of his mouth quirked ruefully. "I don't envy you that conversation."

"I haven't t-told her about L-Lucy either," he added. His nerves were so shot that he no longer cared if he kept his feelings about her a secret. Certainly it wouldn't hurt to tell Macready that they were, for all intents and purposes, engaged. After all, Macready had suspected something was afoot from the very first moment James laid eyes on Lucy.

"I am sure your mother will find her delightful—as we all do," Macready said gallantly—a trifle too heartily, as well. Again, jealousy pierced James like a particularly cunning arrow. After all, Macready was handsome and wellborn and quite jolly to be around—much more so than he. 'Twas entirely possible that someone as sweet and delightful as Lucy would prefer Macready over him.

A knock sounded on the door, sparing James the necessity of a response. His new housekeeper, Mrs. Peyton, would answer it. He was used to getting his own door, but now he could afford a servant or two. And having a few people in service would help show Mother that he was getting on in the world.

"That's probably your family." Macready ran a finger under his collar, loosening it a bit. "I'm already nervous for you, old fellow."

Nervous wasn't precisely the right word for how he felt. This was worse than getting a poor mark in school and having to show it to his parents when he got home. This was more like trying to put back something you'd taken and getting caught in the process. Just like when he was a boy and got caught replacing Father's pipe in the humidor after taking one sickening puff.

The parlor door opened, and Mrs. Peyton admitted his guests. Mother drifted in, pale and faded yet still lovely—rather like a worn lace curtain buffeted by a breeze. Mary followed behind, her bonnet completely obscuring her bowed head.

"M-M-M-M..." He hadn't stammered this badly in months. He couldn't even cease stammering long enough to try a new word. This was disastrous. His throat worked painfully, but only a series of gasps pushed their way out. He flicked a pained glance at Macready, who was staring openly at Mary. Perfect. Just when he needed help most, Macready's mind was obviously elsewhere.

"James, my son." Mother's aristocratic features registered resignation at his plight. "Don't try to speak. I know how difficult it is for you." She bestowed a kiss on his cheek, then turned to survey the room. "My, what a cozy place this is."

He knew that tone of voice. It was her "I am disappointed, but hiding it" tone of voice. His hackles began to rise, ever so slightly. The little cottage wasn't as big as his lordship's home in the Crescent, but it was certainly bigger than Mother's place in Essex.

Mary, blushing hotly under Macready's scrutiny, embraced her brother warmly. "J-James, d-darling, how g-good to see you again."

He nodded, the painful lump in his throat still rendering any attempt at speech impossible. It was good to see Mary again, too. She'd always softened Mother's sharp edges.

Mother turned to Macready. "How good to see you again, sir."

He bowed over her hand with extravagant courtesy. "It's my pleasure, Mrs. Rowland."

Mother laughed into her fine linen handkerchief,

which had been mended a few times over. "Do you know, sir, that you and I are the only ones here who can converse without stammering most dreadfully? I vow, it shall remain our duty to keep the flow of conversation from ebbing."

And there it was. The iron fist in the velvet glove. He had forgotten how Mother's barbed comments could flick on a raw wound. Mary uttered a pained little cry beside him, and the sound gave him the courage to speak.

"M-M-Mother." He stopped to clear his throat. "M-Mary and I shall d-do our p-part as w-well."

"I'm sure you will try, the pair of you. But honestly, it can take a very long time for you to finish the simplest utterance." Mother's voice was soft and her blue eyes grew wide and pleading. As though she were trying to calm a recalcitrant child. "Now, where should we lay our things?"

Frustration welled within him along with the old urge to chuck something breakable against the wall, but he quelled it with some effort. "M-M-Mrs. P-Peyton will show you t-to your rooms." He rang the bell.

"How fortunate that you have a servant, though it hardly seems necessary in a house as small as this." Mother waved her hand about the room with a languid smile.

"I think it's p-pretty," Mary rejoined stoutly, giving James the old "chin up" look they used to share.

"It's certainly better than my old flat." Macready joined in with a hearty laugh. "I don't even have my own servant. I share one with Lieutenant Cantrill."

"Ah! Lieutenant Cantrill." Mother dropped her hand and nodded at Macready. "Now there is a young man who came back from the war horribly disfigured and yet has made quite a bit out of his life despite the unfortunate circumstances." Mother shot a knowing look at James. "You should follow his example, my son."

"Well, I don't know that Cantrill's family would agree with you." Macready, always game for a fight, took up the reins with alacrity. "His own mother came here not long ago, begging him to live in a style more suitable to their family's standards."

"Well, we mothers worry," Mother simpered. "It's hard to understand you boys once you enter the military—how very fundamentally it changes you."

"And I am thankful for it." Hot anger singed through James, burning its way through his stammer.

"Why, James—" Mother began, but the door to the parlor creaked open, admitting Mrs. Peyton.

"P-p-please show my g-guests to their rooms," he murmured, running his hand through his hair. He was tired already, and Mother hadn't been here more than a few moments.

Mrs. Peyton nodded and beckoned to Mother and Mary to follow her. As the door clicked shut behind them, Macready turned to James, a rueful grin twisting his face. "It's going to be a long visit."

"Yes," James admitted with a sigh. "B-but Lucy is worth it."

Chapter Sixteen

"I cannot believe Sophie has gone. I refuse to believe it." Amelia jumped up from her spot on Lucy's bed and walked over to the window. "She would never leave without saying goodbye."

"I'm afraid she had to leave in rather a hurry." Lucy followed Amelia and laid her palm gently on her charge's shaking shoulders.

"Why?" Louisa piped up from her spot on Lucy's settee. "Why did she have to leave so quickly that she couldn't even say farewell?"

Lucy hesitated a moment. How could she tell Louisa and Amelia that their Sophie had left because their beloved father made an improper proposal to her? A proposal she rejected? No, it was impossible. She must spare their feelings—and their innocence—a bit longer.

"There was a personal emergency that required Sophie to leave at once. Because time was so urgent, she did not have a chance to stay and bid an adieu to you two. But she did beg me to tell you both how much she loves you."

Amelia turned from the window, wiping her eyes with her fingertips. "Of course. I know I shouldn't be so selfish, but I shall miss her dreadfully." Lucy handed her a handkerchief from the freshly laundered stack in her chest of drawers. "Thank you, Lucy." She blew her nose gustily.

Lucy was buffeted on a sea of emotions. Her stable world had changed so much in the past few months. Her days used to be so simple, so predictable. Schoolroom work in the mornings, afternoons for lesson plans, Thursdays and Sundays to herself for reading and sewing. She expected nothing more of the world—for the world had nothing more to offer her. And then, in the space of a few weeks, she'd made and lost a friend in Sophie. She'd started working with the poor children of the veterans' group. She'd met James and come to care for him more than she should ever allow herself to care for another human being.

"I wish everything weren't so topsy-turvy," she sighed and sank onto the settee beside Louisa.

"Are you quite all right, Lucy? It's not like you to speak so." Louisa's brows drew together with concern. "Usually you are so brisk and cheerful."

"I don't feel brisk and cheerful. Not anymore." She pursed her lips. She shouldn't speak so. The girls were not her confidantes, after all. Everything was just overwhelming at the moment. She'd never even had a chance to tell Sophie about James's proposal or his mother's impending visit. And now Sophie had gone home with rather dreadful problems of her own. To whom could she confide?

Never before, not even in the orphanage, had she felt so unbearably alone.

She must snap out of this.

"Shall we go for a walk? Perhaps a stroll near the Circus would help to revive our flagging spirits," she suggested, rising and stretching her arms.

"No, thank you. I shall stay and write a letter to Sophie," Amelia demurred. "Will you post it? Do you know her address?"

"She promised to write when she is settled," Lucy said, opening her closet and rummaging for her bonnet. "But I am sure we can just direct it to her in Tansley village. It's a small place, and I daresay there's only one Sophie Handley living there." She tied her bonnet strings under her chin and drew on her gloves. "Louisa? Are you coming?"

"Yes, I will come with you." Louisa rose from the settee and walked over to the door. "I'll meet you outside, Lucy. I need to find my bonnet and pelisse."

Lucy nodded. After Louisa and Amelia left her room, she hastened downstairs and out the front door. The cool breeze caressed her skin and caused her bonnet strings to dance. The leaves on the trees were beginning to fade from vibrant green to earthy oranges and yellows. Soon, fall would come. And what would it bring? Glad tidings or emptiness? She shivered a little. She should have brought her shawl.

The crunch of boot steps on the brick sidewalk made her glance up. James was fast approaching, his head down, his features obscured by the brim of his hat. Goodness, whatever was he doing here? They weren't supposed to work on the library until the morrow. She cast a hasty glance up at the house. Louisa had not descended yet.

Lucy scurried down the walkway to meet him. "James?"

He glanced up and halted when he spied her running his way. "Lucy." As she drew near, he grasped her arm and drew her close to his side, planting a kiss on her cheek that made her toes curl in her boots.

"Whatever's come over you?" She glanced over her shoulder. If Louisa saw that kiss—

"Mother's here," he announced, his emerald green eyes staring down at her with an intensity that made her catch her breath.

Well, of course she was there. She had been due to arrive any day now. After all, James had invited her. And yet, why did the news make Lucy feel as though she'd been knocked from her horse?

"I see," she gasped.

"I w-want you to d-dine with us. I came to see if you c-could join us. Tonight." His voice sounded care-worn, strained. She searched his face for clues as to his real feelings. His firm lips were tightly drawn, and the darkness under his eyes suggested he hadn't slept well.

"So soon? I don't know...." She glanced behind her once more. The girls would be dining with their father tonight. His lordship had canceled all his evening plans in the wake of Sophie's departure. So she would not be expected to dine *en famille*. There was no reason to say no. She'd have to face Charlotte Rowland sooner or later. 'Twould be better to have things done quickly than to prolong the inevitable.

"I'll come tonight," she agreed.

"Thank you," he replied and touched her cheek with his gloved hand. The softness of his touch was in direct contrast with the taut tone of his voice. "I know Mother and Mary will adore you. Is eight o'clock all right? I c-can c-come by and walk you to our new home."

Our new home. He was so certain, so absolutely sure that everything would work out all right. Her eyes welled with sudden tears and she blinked them back rapidly. He mustn't see how this affected her, for then they'd argue about it again…

Footsteps sounded behind Lucy, and she sprang away from James's touch.

"Lucy?" Louisa called as she bustled toward them.

"I must go," Lucy murmured, hastily wiping her eyes and composing her features into a semblance of blandness. For if Louisa knew that Lucy were about to meet her potential mother-in-law, there would be no end to the questions and suppositions.

James nodded and squeezed her hand. "Eight o' c-c-clock."

"I shall be ready."

Louisa drew near, and James touched the brim of his hat. "Miss L-Louisa, how g-good t-t-to see you again."

"Ensign Rowland," Louisa replied, a smile lighting her face. "Have you come to finish the library? I am so excited about it. Papa is anxious to see the final results of your hard work."

"We'll be finished within the f-fortnight. There are still a f-few m-minor d-details that the workmen must see t-t-to," James replied with a grin. He seemed to enjoy Louisa's company and never grew impatient or affronted with her many questions.

Lucy tilted her chin, slanting her gaze up at him. He would be a good father someday. Her cheeks grew hot at that thought—but it was true. Some men had the gifts of nurturing and patience; others did not.

"Oh, very well then." Louisa's wide brown eyes narrowed, and she shifted her gaze from Lucy to James as though sizing up just why the two of them had met on the sidewalk. "Papa will be that much more surprised when he does get to see it." She threaded her arm through Lucy's. "We were just going on a walk over to the Circus. Won't you join us?"

"No, thank you. I will go inside and m-make sure the w-workmen are fitting the m-moldings in as they should—it's a t-tricky b-business." James bowed to them both. "It was g-good to see you b-both again."

They made their curtsies and continued down the sidewalk toward the Circus. As soon as they were out of earshot, Louisa spoke up. "I saw him kiss you."

Lucy halted in her tracks. If Lord Bradbury found out that she had been kissed out in public, she'd lose her position for certain. Why, if he had even an inkling of a suspicion that Lucy was nearly engaged, he'd start looking for another governess. She turned to Louisa, her heart beating a rapid tattoo in her chest. "Please don't tell anyone. It was perfectly innocent, I assure you."

"Oh, Lucy, why must you keep pretending that I don't know about you and Ensign Rowland? I can tell he adores you just by the way he looks at you. And I can tell that you adore him, too." Louisa twirled her bonnet strings, a happy little smile quivering about her mouth. "Has he asked you to marry him?"

Lucy closed her eyes for a moment. Whatever should she do next? Louisa guessed at the truth, and she was becoming less and less adept at skirting the matter. "If your father finds out, I could well lose my position as governess in your house," Lucy finally admitted. Perhaps if Louisa knew the gravity of what Lucy faced, she would cease her teasing ways.

Louisa shook her head. "Papa would never sack you," she responded, "but I won't tell a soul. So he has proposed? And did you say yes?"

"James has proposed." Lucy sighed. "But I cannot say yes. Not until his mother and sister meet me and I earn their approval." She took Louisa's arm once more, and they continued their progress, dodging a flower cart that gave off a dizzying mélange of scents—roses, gardenias, violets.

"Well, of course they shall love you," Louisa avowed stoutly. "Everyone does."

"I wish I could be so certain," Lucy murmured. "Remember, the Rowland family is of a much better background than mine. Few mothers would welcome a penniless orphan for their son."

"Then we shall change their minds. When do you meet them?"

"Tonight. That's why James came to call. I am to have dinner with his family this evening. His mother and sister came from Essex just to meet me." Even saying the words was difficult. The thought of meeting Charlotte Rowland, of having to carry on an intelligent conversation with her, of having to eat with her—made her throat tighten. So much of her happiness lay in what James's mother thought of her.

"Goodness. That doesn't leave us much time to plan, but we shall persevere. Now, what did you plan to wear this evening?"

"I hadn't really thought about it. I only just learned about the dinner a few moments ago," Lucy admitted.

"But I suppose I shall wear my gray silk. It's the best dress I own."

"Gray silk? For dinner with your prospective mother-in-law? I should think not. We must find something more festive." Louisa paused at a milliner's shop window, staring with grave intensity at a bonnet festooned with ostrich plumes. "Haven't you anything more alluring than that gray silk?"

"Hardly." Lucy's defenses began to rise. It was never her place to look or be anything but serviceable and plain. She was a governess after all. Not a debutante... but then, there was that chest full of dresses that Sophie had left behind. "But Sophie left a few gowns for me. Perhaps I could rummage among them."

"Yes, that's much more what I was thinking of," Louisa pronounced, turning from the window. "We shall go through Sophie's things and find something elegant and beautiful. And we shall try a new way of dressing your hair. Perhaps in the Grecian manner, with part of it up, and the rest of it loose and flowing about your shoulders?"

"That's quite enough," Lucy interrupted crisply. "I'm just going for dinner with James's mother and sister. I am not going to doll myself up as though I am headed to Vauxhall Gardens. I'll find a suitably pretty gown, but I draw the line at fantastical hairstyles." She tilted her head, eyeing her charge closely. "And why, pray tell, are you so eager to marry me off? With Sophie gone, one would think you might be eager to keep me about. Do I mean so little to you and your sister?"

"Oh, Lucy. You mean the world to us both." Louisa flung her arms around Lucy and smothered her in a tight embrace. "But I cannot help myself. I am such a romantic. I want everyone to have a chance at their fairy-tale ending."

James sat in the rented hackney for a moment, breathing deeply. He must go in and announce himself to Lucy, but first he must prepare himself. This evening was, in many respects, the culmination of his life since leaving the army. He was hosting a dinner in his own home. His mother and sister were ready to meet the woman of his dreams. And the woman of his dreams had consented to marry him if his mother gave her approval. When he lay praying for death in the rye field at La Sainte Haye, the prospect of an evening such as this would have seemed the product of a fevered hallucination. He was now, after years of being a boy, a man in his own right.

He opened the door—and nearly tumbled over Lucy who stood waiting on the mounting block.

"Are you all right?" he gasped. What in the world was she doing out here?

"Yes, I am quite fine. Let's go now. Before his lordship can see." She grasped his hand and pulled herself into the carriage, landing on the squabs with a thud. He closed the door and rapped on the window, signaling to the coachman that they were ready to return home.

Lucy pulled herself into a sitting position, arranging her pale yellow skirts around her ankles. "Why did you bring a hack? It made things so much more difficult for me to sneak away. I thought you were walking up."

"Sneak away?" Something wasn't right. Was she trying to hide being seen with him? Was she ashamed of him? "I d-don't c-catch your meaning. I thought hiring a hack was the p-proper thing to do on a night like this. A sight better than w-walking."

"Oh, James, don't get angry. If his lordship realizes that I am meeting a young man, my very position as a governess in his home could be called into question." She sat back on the cushions and drew her wrap about her more tightly. "I had to creep out and wait for you in the shadows like a footpad."

"You cc-c-an t-tell his lordship t-tonight that we are t-t-to be m-married," he protested, wishing that the words rang true. But somehow, they felt hollow. A niggling feeling of anger and despair roiled within him. He was going to lose her, somehow. He couldn't hang on to her—she was too fine, too beautiful. She'd slip away like a leaf tossed on the wind.

"Don't count your chickens before they're hatched," Lucy retorted crisply. "I still haven't garnered your mother's approval."

He bit his tongue and fell silent for the rest of the short journey to their new home in York Street. He always thought of it as Lucy's home as well as his. It was meant for the two of them. Without her, there would be no need for a sweet, cozy home in his life. No, he'd still be rooming with Macready in their bachelor flat.

As the carriage slowed to a halt before the mounting block, Lucy glanced out the window. "Oh, my," she breathed. "It's so charming."

And it was. The last threads of daylight were fading from the sky, and a smoky twilight enveloped the little house, shrouding it in a blue glow. Candles twinkled from every window—even the tiny dormer window that dotted the attic. A low iron fence contained the flower garden, which gave off the dusky attar of late summer roses. The stone cottage with its slate roof was beckoning to its future mistress with all the allurement of a diamond winking in a jeweler's shop window. She had only to say one word and it could be hers.

He smothered a wry grin as he helped Lucy from the carriage. At least something was speaking in his favor to his beloved. Between his hot temper and his stammering tongue, he had very little to recommend himself. As they mounted the shallow steps that led to the front door, he bent low and whispered urgently in Lucy's ear, "Welcome home, dearest."

Chapter Seventeen

Lucy hardly had a moment to compose herself before being thrown into the social whirl of meeting Charlotte and Mary Rowland. Fortunately, Macready was there, so she wasn't the only guest. But she was the only guest with, perhaps, a deeper motive for her attendance. Though, judging by the way Macready gazed after Mary, perhaps he was there for another purpose, as well.

They gathered in a small dining room, where a rosy-cheeked, snowy-haired servant ladled out the soup course. It was a fine meal, and the dining room was everything that could be desired in a dining room. She'd always taken her meals dormitory-style at the orphanage; later on, after joining his lordship's employ, she dined in the schoolroom or on a tray in her room. She'd always wondered why people thought of meals as convivial events. They never had been in her experience. And yet, as they gathered together under the candlelight, with a superb chicken soup warming their souls and Macready and James cracking jokes, it was a little more apparent why some people thought of meals as gatherings.

Was this what having her home, her own family could be like?

Mary leaned over, her dark green eyes sparkling. "I'm s-so g-glad to m-meet you finally," she murmured. "James has certainly s-sung your p-praises to M-Mother and to m-me. And none of the p-praise was exaggerated."

"That's very kind of you." Lucy's heart warmed to Mary, whose stammer and whose wide, dark eyes were so like her brother's. "Have you ever come to Bath before?"

"No," Mary admitted, tucking a lock of honey-blond hair behind her ear. "We hardly ever t-travel outside of Essex. When James used to write t-to m-me from B-Belgium, it was such a thrill. T-to see those foreign m-markings on the envelope and to w-wonder what he was seeing." She dropped her eyes to the tablecloth. "Of c-course, I had no idea of the horrors he w-witnessed. He c-concealed those from me as long as he c-could."

Lucy nodded, slanting her gaze over at James. He was chatting with Macready about their youth. Charlotte Rowland occasionally interjected a languid comment. He really had pulled himself out of his self-contained misery. James was no longer a haunted, hunted shell of a soldier. He was back among the living.

She loved him for that. In fact, she loved James Rowland as she had loved no one before.

The clarity of her emotions startled her, like a beacon turned on the darkness, searing in its intensity. But there it was. She loved James. She always would, even decades from now when her memories had faded.

She tore her gaze away from James before he could look over at her. For if he did, the love she felt for him would be shining in her eyes, and he would see it—and all could be lost. Thus far, Charlotte Rowland had not given her any encouragement or sign that she was welcomed as a potential daughter-in-law. In fact, she'd hardly said anything beyond the usual expected *politesse.*

Mary smiled. "He's a g-good b-brother," she confided. "He'll m-make a g-good husband too, some d-day."

Lucy cleared her throat. "Yes, I am sure he will." Time to change the subject—move on to less contentious territory. "If you haven't been to Bath before, there must be some things you'd like to see. What is on your itinerary whilst you are here?"

"Oh, I'd love t-to see all the famous spots—the Assembly Rooms, the Roman B-Baths, the Circus." She plucked at the frayed collar of her dress with a rueful gesture. "I'd love a chance to p-peek into the windows of a real m-m-modiste."

Lucy eyed the worn dresses that Mary and Mrs. Rowland wore, which were in sharp contrast to her own gown of buttercup-yellow, the bodice ruched and embroidered to perfection. Sophie had even embroidered the sleeves. What use had a governess for such gowns? Sophie had left a dozen or so behind. Wouldn't it be lovely for Mary to have an entirely new wardrobe just for her trip to Bath?

"You know, I have just the thing for you, Mary. A friend of mine who is a modiste recently had to leave town and gifted me an entire wardrobe of gowns, such as the one I am wearing tonight." She took a small spoonful of soup. "But as a governess, I can't possibly make use of them all. They are far too pretty and impractical for a governess to wear. Would you like to have them?"

Mary gasped as though Lucy had offered her a treasure hoard. "Are you certain you can b-bear to p-part with them? If they are half as lovely as that g-gown, I can't imagine anyone g-giving them away."

"I would consider it a favor if you would take them and wear them until they fall to pieces," Lucy said with a chuckle. "Otherwise, I shall feel guilty for keeping them in a chest, hidden away while I wear my serviceable grays and blacks."

Mary's eyes grew brighter, and she cast a shy glance over at Macready, who happened to look up at the same moment. Lucy caught their joined glances and looked away. How sweet—Mary and Macready admired each other. If everything worked as one hoped, then Mary's first trip away from home could be everything a girl would want—a new wardrobe, amazing sights and a beau to call her own.

"I'd l-love the d-dresses if you really c-can't use them," Mary confided in an undertone. "B-but on one c-condition. You m-must k-keep the yellow one you're wearing. When my b-brother c-came in the d-door with you on his arm, he l-looked so p-proud. I'm surprised he didn't p-pop a waistcoat b-button, his chest was so p-puffed out."

Now it was Lucy's turn to blush, and her cheeks grew hot accordingly. "If you insist," she replied quietly and turned her attention back to her soup.

The rest of the dinner passed rather uneventfully, and for that, Lucy was grateful. She sank into the gentle hospitality of James's new home. Everything about it was so perfect. After dinner, as they gathered in the parlor, Lucy played the spinet while Mary sang. Her stammer disappeared entirely as she sang, and Macready watched her with rapt attention. James fixated on Lucy, his admiring glances and encouraging smiles combining to make her rather giddy. When the mantel clock chimed ten, she stood up with a regretful sigh.

"I really should go," she said. "I usually awaken early to prepare my lessons."

James stood with her and rang for his servant to order the hackney brought around. But his mother placed a retaining hand on his arm.

"James, dear," she said in that quiet, languid tone of voice, "I wish you would stay here whilst Miss Williams is driven home." She looked over at Lucy, her expression one of resignation. "I would like to speak with you before I retire."

As though sensing the awkwardness of the moment, Macready sprang into social action. "I'll escort Miss Williams home," he said with a jovial laugh. "I must take advantage of a hackney cab wherever I can get one."

Mary's eyes flashed with a protective light, and Lucy's stomach lurched with pity. Poor thing, to be so fearful of losing her sweetheart's regard. As if Macready ever had any real designs on someone like Lucy. He was so obviously besotted with Mary. As she embraced Mary, she whispered, "He's just being a gentleman. Good night."

Mary nodded. "I know," she whispered in return. "B-but—"

"Girls, that's quite enough secret-sharing for tonight," Mrs. Rowland broke in. "Good night, Miss Williams. It was a delight to meet you." She curtsied briefly to Lucy and then turned to Macready. "A pleasure to see you again, Lieutenant."

Lucy managed a curtsy for James but couldn't trust herself to meet his gaze. This cozy house, James's strength and gentleness, the warmth and conviviality of the company—why, for a moment she had almost believed they would all be hers. But his mother's pretty blue eyes held a distinctly steely light as she said goodnight. 'Twas quite likely that when she and Macready departed, all the talk would be about her and the reasons why she was a totally unsuitable match.

She took Macready's arm and allowed him to lead her down the front steps. He handed her up into the carriage. At no point did she permit herself a backward glance. Doing so would only cause unnecessary pain. She must focus on the future, and her future did not, in all likelihood, have anything to do with Ensign James Rowland.

"I say, Mary Rowland is the prettiest creature I ever laid eyes on," Macready pronounced as the carriage wheels rolled into motion. "Present company excluded, of course," he added with exaggerated courtesy.

She chuckled. "If we were playing at a farce, I should tap you lightly on the arm with my fan for that remark."

"Though your words are cheerful enough, your tone sounds rather wan," he rejoined. "Were you disappointed in the Rowland family?"

"Not at all. I liked them very much. I'm just afraid that they don't like me." She settled back on the cushions. If she pressed back far enough, the carriage lamps could not illuminate her face, and that suited her quite well. There was no reason for Macready to read the truth in her expression.

"Why would you think that? Mary seemed quite taken with you."

"Mary's a dear." Perhaps it was time to deflect the conversation from her feelings to Macready's. "In fact, I think you two would be a perfect match."

Macready gave an embarrassed cough. "You are a perceptive one, Miss Lucy."

"I think I would have to be blind to miss the sparks between the two of you. Why, it was tantamount to watching a fireworks display at Vauxhall." Macready spluttered, his cheeks flushing even in the dim carriage light, and she smiled at his discomfiture. "Don't worry, Lieutenant. I am rather certain your feelings are returned."

"I wish that were true." He sighed. "Her mother wants better things for her, though. I am quite certain that life with an invalid soldier is not high on Charlotte Rowland's list of priorities for her daughter."

"But Mary stammers most dreadfully," Lucy argued, tapping her finger on her knee. "And she has no dowry. The family is penniless. Despite their former noble status, Mary's chances in the marriage mart are slim. And I know you, Macready. You are a good man. Any woman worth her salt would be lucky indeed to catch you."

Macready regarded her quietly. "Why can't you say the same for yourself? We are in the same boat, are we not?"

She sat back abruptly, hiding herself in the shadows. "I have no idea what you mean."

"Come now, don't dissemble," Macready wheedled. "It's quite clear that you and Rowland have been enamored of each other for some time. Surely you see that you are the best thing that could possibly ever happen to him."

"I'm a penniless orphan. A spinster. A lifelong governess. There's no room in my life for love," she argued, and her voice shook with suppressed anger.

"Rubbish. Excuses, all of them," came the curt response from his corner of the carriage.

"What would you have me say? That I adore James? Well, I do. It's true. But I also guarantee that his mother is talking him out of any thought of marriage between us right now." She pressed her lips together, willing them to stop trembling.

"If that's true, then you and I should form an alliance against Mother Rowland. We must work together to secure our own ends. Just like in the army—not breaking formation, presenting a united front to the enemy. For if she is talking Rowland out of marriage now, you know very well that she will be telling Mary that I am an unsuitable match, as well."

She sighed. "What on earth can we do?"

"I shall prevail upon Rowland if you will do the same for Mary," he suggested. "They will be here for a fortnight. So we must dance attendance on them as much as we can. And at the end of the two weeks, I will propose to Mary. I know that Rowland will do the same for you," he reasoned.

Lucy's cheeks burned hotly. Thank goodness the dim carriage light hid her flush. "He already has. But I postponed making an answer until after his mother leaves."

"There you go." He smiled and rubbed his hands together with mock glee. "Within two weeks, I daresay we will both be planning our weddings."

The carriage lumbered to a halt, and Lucy gathered her skirts. What an odd evening it had been. And yet, it was good to have a friend and ally in Macready. He was rather like the elder brother she always wanted but never had.

He helped her out of the carriage and pressed her hand warmly. "Soldier on, Miss Lucy. All will be well."

"Thank you," she said with a smile. "It's good to have a fellow soldier in the fight."

Mother sank into the worn velvet chair she favored, reaching her hands toward the blaze kindled in the hearth. James watched her warily. All evening, he knew this moment would come. He'd felt it in his gut. And now that it was here, he was already anxious to have done with the conversation.

"Mother, I know what you want t-to t-talk about, and I want to let you know that I won't s-stand for any r-rude r-remarks about L-Lucy." Perhaps if he began the attack, she would fall back, and her arguments would dissolve before they even began.

"On the contrary, she's charming." Mother sat back in her chair and poured a cup of tea from the china teapot on the table beside her. "But you do understand your position in the family. Charming though she may be, she is not the wife for you."

"That's m-m-my choice to m-make." He leaned against the mantel, grasping it for support. The rough oak rubbed against his fingertips. He'd have to plane it and sand it down. There was no need for a mantelpiece to be so splintery.

"Of course." Mother's voice was so soft that he could barely register the remark. She blew gently on her tea before gingerly taking a sip. "But you do understand what I mean. If your father were here, he could put things so much better than I can."

"You w-want me to marry an heiress." His voice was growing louder. Mary could surely hear them arguing. But trying to hide anything from his sister was pointless. They'd known intuitively of each other's sufferings and triumphs since childhood. Even if she didn't hear their conversation, Mary probably already knew how he felt.

"Shush. Your servant might hear." Mother carefully settled her teacup back in the saucer and turned her bright blue eyes on him, facing him squarely. "You've known for some time what I expect of you. Why do you act so defensively now? Your duty is to the family, and that means marrying someone who can restore our lost fortunes. Someone who, in exchange, would appreciate the value of our family name." She dabbed at her mouth with her starched handkerchief. "Goodness, I detest having to put the facts so baldly, but since you insist on a confrontation..."

"Enough." He turned away from the mantelpiece, his hands clenched. "Lucy is a sight too good for this family if you ask me. She's intelligent, witty and kind and has made her own way in this world. She helped me when I was at my lowest ebb. And I must mention the obvious—she's a beautiful woman." He paced the floor, the boards squeaking in protest. "Speak ill of her, and you might as well insult me."

Mother's mouth dropped open. "Where is your stammer? Do you lose it when you grow agitated?"

"S-sometimes. Yes." As if that mattered at this particular moment.

"Well then, I say it's too bad you don't get furious all the time. Our family fortunes might improve." Mother gave a sharp little laugh. "Now, then, I don't doubt that Miss Williams is all the things you say she is. But that doesn't change the simple fact that she doesn't have money or a family name. We must have one or both, James. Surely as a practical man, you see the wisdom of this."

A white-hot shaft of anger pierced through James, painful in its intensity. Talking and arguing with Mother would get him nowhere. She was as determined in her way as he was in his. This was futile. He must convince Lucy to marry him with or without his mother's approval. In time, his mother might soften when she saw what a lovely person Lucy really was. But until then—

"I am determined, Mother. We shall never speak of this again."

"Your mind is set, then?" Mother folded her hands in her lap with the same calm deliberation that a man might use when choosing his dueling pistols.

He nodded. She might as well know the truth. He'd never budge.

"Well, then. There's nothing for this poor old woman to do but slink off to bed." She rose and planted a kiss on his cheek and stalked out of the room. But something in the tilt of her head—the stiff carriage of her back—told him that the battle had just begun.

Mother would have been an excellent soldier. Even Wellington himself would find her formidable.

'Twas going to be a long fortnight.

Chapter Eighteen

Thank the good Lord, a man could still attend his veterans' group meetings without Mother or Mary by his side. James mounted the stone steps of the chapel two at a time, a spring almost in his step. He might even whistle. An hour or two away from Mother's agitated company was like a furlough. Macready had been dancing attendance on Mary since the disastrous dinner party a week ago, and Mother was frothing at the mouth that Mary hadn't attracted a more lucrative prospective husband. Getting away from her frustration was a tremendous relief.

And there was the chance to see Lucy today. He hadn't seen her since she left with Macready after dinner that night. An urge to apologize, to soothe and to bolster her flagging confidence fought for primacy in his being. She must know what she meant to him, no matter how Mother behaved.

The door of the chapel banged open, and Lieutenant Cantrill stormed out, his face as dark as a thundercloud.

"What ho, L-Lieutenant?" James called. Perhaps something was amiss, and he could help.

"Rowland," Cantrill acknowledged with a brief nod. Cantrill reached out and caught the lieutenant's good arm.

"M-may I b-be of assistance?" By Jove, Cantrill looked ready for a fight. Even his arm was tensed as though he were prepared to strike a blow.

Cantrill hesitated a moment, as though weighing his words. "That cur Bradbury made an improper offer to my Sophie. And now she has fled. She's gone home to Tansley." He spat the words out as though they choked him. "When I lay hands on that…that deceitful wretch I will thrash him within an inch of his life."

Well, that would be disastrous. Lord Bradbury was one of the wealthiest men in Bath—if not in all of England. His power was far-reaching, his influence extensive. Cantrill should confront him for his improper actions, of course, but in a less belligerent frame of mind. He must stall his friend until his temper was a little less…combative. "How d-did you find out? Are you certain it's the t-truth?"

"Of course it's true. Lucy Williams just told me everything." Cantrill withdrew a leather pouch from his coat pocket, giving it a shake so it jingled. "She gave me this, too. Money. My dearest Sophie sold the bracelet that blackguard gave her to help fund a ministry for the women here in the veterans' group." He gave a long, shuddering sigh. "What a fool I am. I should never have listened to my brother. My family—they poisoned my mind against her."

He could well relate to that. A wrench of pain seized his gut. If meddling mamas had their way, there would be no happy marriages in all of England. He nodded, looking Cantrill squarely in the eye. "If Lucy says it's so, then you c-can be assured it's the truth, no m-matter how sordid the circumstances sound. But you must g-gain some c-control over yourself. You c-can't thrash a man like B-Bradbury. Have some sense."

"I must be allowed to do something," Cantrill muttered, his mouth twisted into a grimace. "It's not right for him to get away with that."

"C-confront him, certainly," James agreed. "But leave physical violence out of the matter unless you want to end up in gaol. I work for the m-man. His influence in this city is p-profound." If all else failed, he could interfere on his friend's behalf, but he hoped it would not come to that.

Cantrill gave a long, shuddering sigh. "I will go and brazen this out now."

"You must p-promise me not t-to use violence to settle the matter." James laid a restraining hand on Cantrill's arm. 'Twas odd to be holding back a superior officer; in the army, he would never have attempted to do so. But now, in civilian life, he gained an authority that the uniform never leant him.

"I give my word." Cantrill clenched his jaw as though wishing he could bite the words back. He flung off James's hold and tore down the rest of the steps, fury evident in every line of his body.

James turned and continued his progress up the steps. He must find Lucy. She was, in all likelihood, quite shaken from her encounter with Cantrill.

The church was abuzz with activity. Men stood shoulder to shoulder and hailed James in hearty voices as he entered the narthex. "If ye're looking for Miss

Williams, she's in the back with the young'uns," a grizzled veteran said, jerking his thumb over one shoulder. "She's right patient with them, despite their high spirits."

The corner of James's mouth quirked. Everyone knew that he and Lucy spent far too much time together. He'd have to marry her. If not, he had a sneaking suspicion that the veterans' group would have his hide for leading her a pretty dance.

And there she was. She sat on the stone floor—two children nestled in her lap and a group of half a dozen urchins kneeling on the floor in a half circle around her. She was bestowing upon them her loveliest smile, a smile that lit her eyes with an amber glow. He caught his breath, watching her as she told the children a story, her lilting voice carrying over the din from the men gathered at the front of the church.

As he drew near, she looked up and caught his gaze. A pretty pink flush stole over her cheeks and she finished her tale rather abruptly as he came to stand beside her. He took her hand, and as the children tumbled from her lap, he helped her to rise. Her hand, so small within his, was cold. He chafed the top of her hand with his thumb.

"I just saw C-Cantrill," he murmured into her ear as he drew her to her feet. "That was a brave thing you d-did. Most women would have merely sent round a note or some such."

"I thought the direct approach was best." She withdrew her hand from his, keeping her eyes cast down. "I did it rather more quickly than Sophie wanted, but I wanted the lieutenant to know as soon as possible."

"I've missed you," he whispered. If only he could

recapture her hands again, just for a moment. He'd been deprived of her for only a week, but it felt like an eternity.

"Hush." She took a step backward, the rosiness in her cheeks deepening. "You shouldn't speak so."

"We're engaged," he responded, closing the distance between them with a single step. "If I weren't t-to speak t-to you in this fashion, something would b-be sorely amiss."

"We're not engaged—not formally," she admitted, and placed her hands on his chest in a warning gesture. "And we are in church. I would ask you to remember where you are and what you are about."

"When may we b-be formally engaged?" His voice held an urgent note. "You've m-m-met my family. When m-may we announce it?"

"Your mother sent around a note to invite me to tea tomorrow." She removed her hands from his person and folded them across her chest. "I don't feel it's right to say anything until after I've met with her."

"Very well." He looked at her from under his brows. "You are very stubborn, Miss Williams. Has anyone ever t-told you that?"

She shrugged, the ghost of a smile crossing her pretty lips. "I'm not being stubborn. Merely wise and prudent." She leaned over, looking past him, and nodded. "Macready? How are you this morning?"

Oh, blast. He'd only had Lucy to himself for a few moments. Why couldn't Macready make himself scarce? He turned to face his brother in arms, warning writ plain on his face. "Macready."

"Miss Williams, Rowland." Macready nodded to

each in turn. "I hate to interrupt, but—could I speak to you in private, Rowland?"

Lucy gathered her books into her leather satchel and scooped it into her arms. "Of course, Lieutenant. I was just leaving." She curtsied and brushed past them, and as she passed, he touched her silken sleeve.

"T-tomorrow," he murmured.

She kept her head bent down but nodded—the gesture so slight that if he'd blinked, he would have missed it.

After she was out of earshot, Macready turned to James. "Are you going to marry her?"

"If she'll have me." Whether or not his mother liked her was no longer an impediment. Mother asked her to tea, didn't she? So that boded well.

"Good. I'm glad to hear it." Macready pulled him over to the side of the pew, glancing back over his shoulder. "Sit, won't you?"

"What's this all about?" 'Twas thoroughly annoying to have Macready interrupt his few precious moments with Lucy and then this nonsense about looking over his shoulder and making sure no one overhead—he was behaving like an inept robber in a farce. But Macready looked so serious that worry started to gnaw. What could this be about? Was his friend ill, or in some sort of trouble?

Macready leaned up against the wall, staring down at James with an inscrutable expression on his face. "I love your sister. And I am asking your permission to seek her hand in marriage."

The coiled tension within James broke. He laughed—the first time he'd really laughed in a fortnight. "You l-love M-Mary?"

Macready's face grew pale, and his eyes darkened. "It's not funny. Cease with your laughter."

"No, no." James shook his head. He'd seen the glow in Mary's eyes at dinner that night. She, no doubt, returned Macready's feelings tenfold. "I'm just so relieved. Mary is a g-good girl and will make you a fine wife. I should love to call you b-brother-in-law."

Macready's shoulders, which had risen defensively, settled back into position. "Thank the good Lord above. I thought for a moment you found the idea too ridiculous to even entertain. I am, after all, penniless and wounded. Hardly much of a man."

"W-well, I know you. You're a g-g-good fellow. I know you'll p-p-provide for M-Mary." He hesitated briefly. 'Twas odd to be asking these questions of Macready but so tradition dictated. He'd nearly died that night at Waterloo. So his character was, in some ways, quite apparent to James. No further character references would be necessary. On the other hand, one's sister had to have food and clothing and shelter—the necessities. "I s-s-suppose I should ask h-how."

"My father wants me to return to Essex and help manage the estate. My elder brother, Samuel, will take over, but I can help manage the tenants. We'd have our own little home and a small living. It's not much, but it would be enough." Macready looked down at the floor, as though fascinated by its surface. "I was planning on leaving Bath soon anyway. My wounds have healed enough that I can begin working again. And seeing your progress with Felton, I was inspired to work. Then, when Mary came, I knew the necessity of it."

James nodded and rose, extending his hand. "Well

then, my good fellow, I look forward to calling you 'brother' soon."

Macready clasped his hand warmly. "There's just one thing," he added. "Your mother. I am sure she will object to me, as penniless as I am."

"I won't d-deny that Mother has some rather high-flown plans for Mary, but my sister has no d-dowry and few connections. Our name is respectable but not illustrious. The likelihood of her finding a spectacular match is highly unlikely." James shrugged. "B-besides, I'd rather she m-m-marry for love. She d-deserves happiness."

"I shall spend the rest of my life trying to make her happy," Macready said gallantly. "And what of you? When will you marry your love? Sooner rather than later, I hope."

"The s-s-sooner the b-better. If I have m-my way, Lucy and I will share in each other's h-happiness b-b-before long," he admitted.

"Good. I was afraid that your mother would interfere there, as well. She didn't seem very enamored of Lucy at dinner the other evening."

"My mother thinks she is a lot more influential than she is," James replied with an uneasy laugh. Macready's conversation was not adding to his feelings of certainty. He'd put a stop to it now. "I'll marry Lucy. Even if we have to elope to Gretna Green."

Lucy smoothed her lavender skirts with a nervous gesture. This gown, like the buttercup-yellow one she'd worn to dinner, had been part of Sophie's wardrobe, left behind when she fled Bath. The rest of the gowns were in the satchel she'd brought with her. Perhaps if she arrived with a peace offering of several pretty gowns for Mary, Charlotte Rowland would look more kindly on her.

She let herself in the gate and permitted herself a moment's luxury of looking at James's home one more time. How peaceful it was and how lovely. Not imposing like Lord Bradbury's residence but snug and comfortable as a home should be. This was a home meant for a family. A home that asked only to be lived in. The kind of home that she'd dreamed about in the orphanage. Just a place of her own—to be with people she loved.

She knocked on the door, and Mrs. Peyton answered. "Oh, bless you. What on earth have you got there?" She took the satchel from Lucy's shoulder and beckoned her in. "Come in, come in. Mrs. Rowland is waiting for you in the parlor." The housekeeper smiled kindly. "I made cinnamon scones, my specialty. I hope you like them."

Lucy nodded, her heart warming to Mrs. Peyton. What a good find she was. James was certainly lucky to have her.

Mrs. Peyton led the way to the parlor and opened the door with a flourish. Charlotte Rowland sat near the empty hearth, a small table laid before her. Lucy's nose wrinkled appreciatively at the scent of those scones. Goodness, she was hungry. She had been so nervous she hadn't been able to eat all day. But now that she was actually going through with the meeting, and now that she could smell those delicious scones, her head swirled. She sought a chair near the table before her knees gave out.

Charlotte waited to speak until Mrs. Peyton had retreated, closing the door behind her with a gentle click. "How good of you to spend some time with me, Miss Williams." Her voice was so quiet, so well bred. Why, just from her tone, you could tell that she came from a cultured, cosseted background. "Here, have some tea. You look rather peaked."

"Thank you." Lucy accepted the steaming teacup gratefully. "It smells wonderful. But please, call me Lucy. I feel like I know you so well already. Your son has always spoken so highly of you." It was a little white lie, but still—one had an obligation to be socially polite.

There was a brief knock at the door, and Mrs. Peyton bustled back in. "I forgot to leave your satchel, Miss Williams. Here you go." She laid the leather bag on a nearby settee and bowed back out of the room.

"What did you bring?" Charlotte arched an elegant eyebrow in surprise.

"A friend of mine is a modiste here in Bath, and she left me several gowns when she moved away," Lucy explained. "But as a governess, I have very few occasions to wear pretty clothes and bright colors. I thought Mary might like them."

The frozen polite look on Charlotte's features thawed ever so slightly. "That's very kind of you."

"Not at all," Lucy replied, smiling warmly. "I am glad they will go to good use. Mary has such fair coloring with that golden hair and those lovely eyes—these gowns will suit her beautifully. They might well have been made just for her."

"You seem rather fond of Mary." Charlotte passed the plate of scones. "You have struck up a friendship quickly, haven't you?"

Was that a thread of suspicion running through Charlotte's tone? Lucy hastened to cover any damage she'd done. "Well, growing up as I did, I warm to people rather quickly. It may seem odd to others, I am sure."

"Growing up as you did? How did you grow up?" Her tone remained polite, but her large eyes bored into Lucy over the rim of her teacup.

There was nothing to do but tell the truth. The cinnamon scone, so tender and flaky just moments before, crumbled into ashes in her mouth. She swallowed, choking down the lump of pastry with difficulty. "In an orphanage," she mumbled.

"Gracious." Charlotte set her teacup aside. "That must have been difficult."

"Good things came from it, and I am quite grateful for the experience. It made me value what I've earned," Lucy continued.

Charlotte nodded. "I understand. My family lost everything, so I have come to value not only what we no longer have but what we were able to salvage."

"Yes, I understand what you mean." It was nice to have common ground. Charlotte Rowland no longer seemed formidable. She was now very much like Lucy, trying to eke out an existence and making the best out of difficult circumstances.

Charlotte sighed deeply. "This is rather a thorny issue to broach, Miss Lucy, but I feel I must forge ahead. I asked you here today with an ulterior motive. You see, it has come to my attention that my son is quite enamored of you."

A strange buzzing sounded in Lucy's ears, and the

tips of her fingers went numb. "Yes." 'Twas all she could manage.

"Has he proposed to you?" Charlotte's voice was so quiet she could hardly hear over the buzzing in her ears.

"Yes."

"And what did you say?"

Lucy could not meet Charlotte's gaze, but it burned her skin like a candle flame. "I told him I would not say yes unless I met with your approval."

Charlotte's chair creaked as she sat back. "Thank you for that. I appreciate your caution."

Lucy's lips trembled so badly she couldn't form any words. She pressed them together to still them, and blurted out her desperate question—the question that would decide her fate. "And have I your approval?"

Chapter Nineteen

Lucy attempted to swallow as she scanned Charlotte Rowland's patrician features for any sign that she was considering a positive reply. But her throat was suddenly dry. She picked up her teacup with trembling hands. Charlotte's face belied no change of expression. Lucy took a single burning mouthful of tea and waited. After an eternity, Charlotte spoke.

"My son is determined to have you for his wife," she began. "He told me as much the night of our dinner party. While he respects me, he loves you more. So, in his mind, what I feel about the matter makes not one whit of difference."

"But it does matter to me," Lucy whispered. She set her teacup aside and clasped her hands together to still them. She wanted Charlotte Rowland's approval more than anything. "Having lost my own dear parents, I know the sadness of no longer having family in my life. I would not wish that for your son. I won't marry him if you do not consent."

"It's not that I don't like you, my dear Lucy. You seem a bright girl and a generous one. I am rather fond of you, even though we've only met recently. But our family is quite destitute. I have every reason to suspect that Lieutenant Macready will make an offer for Mary. I can hardly say no—for Mary has no chance on the marriage mart. Her stammer and her lack of dowry preclude any spectacular matches. But I had planned on James to restore our fortunes."

"Why is it dependent on James?" Lucy licked her lips nervously. Surely Mary had as much responsibility to the family as her brother. Why should she be allowed to marry for love if James couldn't?

"The flaws that are insurmountable in a woman can be excused in a man." Charlotte ticked off the reasons on her fingertips. "Stammer...lack of dowry... But a woman might marry James for his title, even though it's impoverished. Some heiresses are like that. They want the cachet of a title in exchange for money. And James is handsome, though I say so myself. His military record speaks well of him. A woman might be willing to overlook his flaws because he has so many good things in his favor."

Lucy shuddered a little inside. What Charlotte said was true. But on the other hand, it was so cold. So impersonal. And it reduced love and marriage to a mere contract. But perhaps it was not truly that emotionless. Many women likely found James attractive. She'd been dreaming of his dark green eyes, his angular face and his unruly sandy hair since their first meeting. Another woman would come along who would love him and care for him. There were probably girls standing in line to take her place. Girls who could offer him love in addition to wealth or position.

"James has a good job with Felton," she argued hesitantly. "He's trying to earn the money to make you and Mary more comfortable. He's been able to afford this house on the strength of his work for Lord Bradbury, and he has already secured more commissions. Perhaps he doesn't need to marry money."

"Ah yes, his work with a carpenter." Charlotte waved her hands with a dismissive gesture. "A gentleman does not work with his hands. He manages his estate, he collects from tenants. As soon as James marries well, he will stop working in the shop. And the money he makes is nothing compared to what an heiress can bring him."

"You sound as though you already have someone in mind." Lucy's stomach churned violently.

"There are a few girls in Essex who would fit the bill quite nicely." Charlotte folded her hands in her lap. "Daughters of merchants, farmers, you know—money but no title."

Lucy nodded slowly. She'd known this moment would come, but it was still a slap in the face. "Then I do not have your approval."

"I would never withhold my approval. As I said, you seem like a sweet girl, and I know James is besotted with you. But I am asking you as his mother to let him go. Let him move on to great things. By relinquishing your hold on him, our family may gain comfort and peace at last." The expression in Charlotte's eyes changed from haughty to pleading in a matter of seconds. "You have all the power in the world at this moment. Use it well."

Lucy stood, her knees wobbling so badly she grasped her chair for support. "I would never do anything to hold James back. From the first moment I saw him, I wanted only good to befall him. You have my word, Mrs. Rowland. I will not accept his proposal."

"Thank you." Charlotte sank against the back of her chair as though winded from a long hike. "Do not tell him I asked this of you. He might not understand."

Her eyes clouded with tears, obscuring her vision through a thick, watery haze. "I'll keep quiet. Excuse me. I must go." She couldn't burst into tears in front of James's mother. She must hold herself together until she reached the sanctuary of her room. She fled from the room and out the front door, running through the streets of Bath as though a highwayman chased her heels. She bumped into passersby, and her bonnet was knocked off her head by the force of their collision, but it did not matter. The bonnet dangled on its strings, hitting her shoulders with every step she took. Her hair tore loose from its pins and tumbled about her shoulders.

She reached the Crescent and let herself in the back door of his lordship's home, uttering little broken cries that sounded foreign to her own ears. She raced up the stairs and threw open the door of her room, the hot tears she had suppressed finally pouring down her cheeks.

"Lucy? Whatever is the matter with you?" Louisa rose from the settee and threw her arms about Lucy. "Are you ill?"

Lucy's body was numb. Funny, she couldn't even feel Louisa's embrace. She stood as still as a statue and allowed her tears to spill over her eyelids, wetting the Aubusson rug beneath her feet.

"I've never seen you like this. I'm calling the doctor." Louisa turned to go, but Lucy caught her arm.

"I'm...not ill." She untied her bonnet and cast it onto her vanity table. Then she sank onto the settee, her teeth chattering loudly.

"Tell me what happened." Louisa began removing the few remaining pins from her hair, combing through the dark waves with her fingers.

She had to tell someone. She could never tell James the truth of what happened. She had promised she would not. And Sophie was gone. She had no one to confide in but her charge. 'Twas improper to do so, but the ache in her heart demanded a release. Haltingly, she murmured her conversation with Mrs. Rowland to Louisa. When she finished her tale, Louisa sat back and regarded her, her wide brown eyes filled with tears.

"And so you're going to refuse him? Oh, Lucy. Don't do it. Papa will get more commissions for the ensign, just you wait and see. He'll be the most famous cabinetmaker in all of Bath. He doesn't need to marry some old farmer's daughter for money." Louisa shuddered.

"What she says is true, though." Lucy took a long, deep breath to calm her nerves. "If I were an heiress, this wouldn't even be a question. But I am penniless, too. I knew all along this would be the case—that's why I refused to accept him the first time he asked."

"I'll give you my money," Louisa avowed stoutly. "You can have half of my dowry. I'll make Papa sign it over to you as a wedding gift."

Despite her heartache, Lucy couldn't suppress a chuckle. "Louisa, you are a dear. But I could never, ever accept your money." She sniffed and blew her nose in her sodden handkerchief. "I love James and so I must let him go. I don't have such a bad life. Better than most, I admit. It's just that I was silly enough to believe in something that can never, ever happen."

"When do you see the ensign again?" Louisa asked. "Is he expecting an answer from you?"

"I suppose he is coming to show his lordship the library tomorrow," Lucy answered. "I think he wanted us to meet today, but I can't. I need a little time to compose myself so I don't break down completely." She sought a dry spot on her handkerchief and wiped her eyes. They burned as though she had rinsed them in salt water. And she was tired. So very, very tired. A weariness that invaded her bones.

"Lucy, why don't you rest." Louisa grasped her hand and tugged, pulling them both to their feet. "I'll go study my French while you nap." Lucy began to protest, but Louisa shook her head firmly. "No, I won't hear of it. You've had a terrible shock, and you need to sleep."

Sleep would be nice—just an hour or so to forget. Her nerves were so tightly wound of late. It would be good to stop thinking of James and Mary and Charlotte—of his lovely home. Of the look on his face when he whispered, "Tomorrow." Of the thought of a merchant's daughter wearing his ring.

She removed her lavender gown. She would never wear it again. She would send it 'round to Mary with a note on the morrow. She pulled a soft cotton night rail over her head and settled deep under her coverlet. 'Twas odd to be sleeping in the middle of the day with the sunlight pouring in through the windows. It was like being sick abed. Which, in a sense, she was. Sick at heart.

James whistled merrily at his work. He had but one table leg to finish and his lordship's library would be complete. Tomorrow he would meet with Lord Bradbury and get his final approval for the room. After that, he would begin working on the library and ballroom of the Earl of Cavendish's home in Bath. 'Twas twice the work of Lord Bradbury's library, and the Earl was paying accordingly. There was a certain emerald and diamond ring that winked alluringly to him from a shop window that morning—a ring that was just suited for Lucy's slender fingers. Thanks to his commissions, he could go purchase the ring in the morning on his way to his lordship's home.

The door to his workroom opened, and Felton stuck his head inside. "A visitor for you."

James rose, a smile hovering on his lips. Perhaps it was Lucy, there to give him the answer he sought. His grin faded as the door opened wider, admitting Miss Louisa Bradbury.

"M-Miss Louisa? Is everything all right? D-d-does his lordship have a m-message for me?" How very odd. Louisa shouldn't be here all by herself.

Louisa turned and looked at Felton, who obliged her by backing out and closing the door behind him. "Lucy came home this afternoon after having tea with your mother in an absolute state." She spoke so rapidly that he had trouble discerning what she was saying. "She agreed not to marry you."

He set the table leg down on the workbench. Her words were like a blow to his midsection. "D-d-did she say why?"

"Only that your mother was going to try to find an heiress for you. I tried reasoning with Lucy. I even tried to give her my money." She shrugged her shoulder helplessly. "I wanted you to know so that you can plan. Lucy is going to refuse you tomorrow unless you can find a way to convince her otherwise."

James looked at Miss Louisa, a dawning respect for her growing within him. "You m-must love Lucy very m-much to be willing to lose her to m-m-marriage."

"I want her to be happy," she said simply. "She's a wonderful teacher. Far too good for Amelia and myself. But she will never be as happy teaching as she could be with you." She came forward and propped her elbows on the workbench. "What are you going to do?"

"I d-don't know." Talking to Louisa was as refreshing as talking to Mary, back when they were children. He'd always been able to talk to his sister about things easily, despite her stammer. Louisa had that same frankness, that same easiness of manner that Mary had. Despite the fact that her father could buy and sell all of Bath.

"Well, in novels the hero and the heroine always elope to Gretna Green," she said, her voice rising with excitement. "What about that? Couldn't you two just elope? I could have one of Papa's carriages ready and waiting. I can pack Lucy's trunk while she is sleeping this afternoon—"

He shook his head and laughed. He might have joked about Gretna Green but to actually plan for it? Beyond ridiculous. Not to mention, Lucy would never agree. No, he'd have to think of some other way to convince her. "I d-doubt that would work. You know Lucy. Her word is as g-good as g-gold."

"She promised your mother she would never tell you the truth of why she's refusing you," Louisa added. "But she didn't make me promise not to tell. So that's why I came here. Are you going to tell your mother you know of her interference?"

His hand tightened on the workbench. He shook his head. No, he'd brazen it out. He'd work as late as he possibly could, and then he would go home, eat dinner in his room and go to bed. The less time he spent in Mother's company, the better. Otherwise, he might say things he'd regret later.

"Thank you for c-coming to warn m-me." He walked around the workbench and bowed briefly to her. "Shall I escort you h-h-home? Surely you d-didn't walk all this way b-b-by yourself."

"No indeed," she replied with a laugh. "Lucy would faint if I ever did that. I have one of Papa's carriages waiting for me." She curtsied. "Whatever you decide to do, please know that Lucy is incomparable. She's an extraordinary governess. She's pretty, she's kind-hearted and she's smart. And if you won't marry her, then I shall have no choice but to find a husband for her myself." She raised her chin defiantly. "I'd rather Lucy go with you for it's all so romantic. But I won't have her languishing away as a governess, hiding herself from the world."

"Agreed." He shook her hand solemnly. "I understand that in you, I have b-both a formidable ally as w-w-well as a formidable foe."

Louisa laughed, showing her dimples, and took her leave. The door closed gently behind her. Despite his jesting, James was sick to his stomach. Coldly sick, as he was very close to losing the only thing that mattered in this world.

Of course, Lucy would never go back on her word to his mother. And therein lay the problem. If Lucy were less of a woman, they could both defy his mother and never give her displeasure with the match another thought. But Lucy was so good. She would never defy anyone, even if it meant breaking her own heart in the process.

But what if he refused to marry anyone but her? Hope began to dawn within him. Lucy had said she would not marry him, and all he'd done was let her have the last word in the matter. If he told her that his mother's plans were for naught, that he had eyes for no one but her, then she'd have to listen to reason. For it didn't matter whom his mother had picked out for him. He'd marry no one but Lucy Williams. If she continued to refuse him, then he'd live a life of solitary bachelorhood.

He picked up the table leg, scraping some of the sawdust off with his thumbnail. Gretna Green was out of the question. Wasn't it? At least it held the allure of certain marriage. For propriety's sake. Lucy couldn't refuse to marry him if they were traveling for days on end. The corner of his mouth turned down in a rueful grin. It was all right to laugh about silly novels, but the heroes always managed to get what they wanted in the end. No one would stop them. What if life imitated literature, just this once?

That emerald and diamond ring in the jeweler's window. He'd go there this afternoon and buy it. He'd rent a carriage—not just any carriage but a traveling carriage. He'd go to his lordship's tomorrow and find a way to speak to Lucy alone. And when they were finally together, he'd tell her the truth. He'd have no one but her. If his words alone didn't convince her, then the ring or the traveling coach might.

He began to whistle as he finished the table leg, but 'twas a false show of bravado. His problem lay in Lucy's formidable character. A lesser woman might be swayed by jewels and carriages. His beloved, on the other hand, would not.

No, he would bring these things along. But it would be his words alone that would convince her. And for a fellow with a poor command of words, this was a seemingly insurmountable task.

He ceased his whistling and bowed his head, a prayer for strength flowing through him. He'd never make it through without some help from above. If only he could be certain his words would be enough to convince Lucy.

Chapter Twenty

Nancy, the cheeky downstairs parlor maid, poked her head around Lucy's door frame after a brief knock. "His lordship wishes to see you. The man is here about the library." Her black eyes twinkled as she closed the door. She, like everyone else in the house today, must sense that something was afoot.

Lucy was a coward. She'd sat in her room all day long, avoiding the kitchens, the schoolroom and any place she might encounter the servants—particularly the library. The whole house was abuzz with news that the new library was finally ready. But today was much more than the celebration of a completed project for her. Today was the day that she and James must part ways forever.

She cast a glance in the mirror as she rose from the window seat. Her dress, a funeral black, suited her mood perfectly. Her face was drawn and pale, the freckles across the bridge of her nose standing out as though drawn on with a pencil. Her hair was twisted into a severe knot at the back of her neck. Her days of being pretty, or even being thought of as passably attractive, were now over. It was just as well. She was, after all, merely the governess.

How strange—nothing felt or sounded right as she quit her room and descended the staircase to the main corridors of the house. Her senses were muffled. The usual morning hubbub of his lordship's home was muted, and the brilliant scarlet of the scattered rugs was, to her eyes, faded to pink. Her breath came in painful, rapid hitches. She must brazen this out as best as she could. Then, once it was over, she could regain the solitude of her room.

She opened the door latch to the library and strode in. Practicality and calm settled over her like a well-worn cloak. Lord Bradbury and James, who had been in conversation, glanced over at her and nodded as she came in. James stared at her, his emerald green gaze searing her skin, but she could not meet his eyes.

"Well, Miss Williams, I must say this is a splendid success." His lordship waved his hand about the room, indicating the golden oak bookcases and the sky-blue silk curtains. "It's the very opposite of how the room looked before, and so I shall be able to spend more time here in the future."

"Thank you, sir," she murmured. "But your praise belongs to Louisa and Ensign Rowland. I merely supervised some of the planning. Louisa and the Ensign chose the materials."

"M-Miss Williams is too m-modest," James interrupted. "She c-came up with the c-colors and selected the wood so the room would b-become b-brighter. She has g-good t-taste and excellent style."

"Indeed." His lordship nodded coolly, his hands clasped behind his back. "I would never have guessed it, but you have a lady's touch. Encouraged, perhaps, by my own Louisa." His lordship turned to Rowland. "I am very pleased with the room. Very pleased. I shall make sure that you are kept quite busy from now on. I've told all of my friends about your work."

Of course, his lordship meant the "lady's touch" as a compliment, but Lucy burned with shame and indignation at his surprise over her good taste. It was rather tiring to have people continue to harp on your lack of family or connections. After all, she'd never hidden her background from anyone. Had never struggled or schemed to rise above her station. And all his lordship did was widen the gulf between James and herself.

The door to the library banged open, and Louisa peeked around the corner. "Papa," she cried, "I want to show you something in the parlor."

"Can't it wait, my dear? I was just looking over your handiwork." Lord Bradbury raised one eyebrow as he surveyed his daughter.

"No. You must come now." Louisa captured her father's hands and pulled him toward the door.

"Ensign—just send the bill…" his lordship called as he followed Louisa. As Louisa turned to close the door behind her, she winked—actually winked—at James. Embarrassment welled in Lucy's chest. Louisa was ever determined to remain the matchmaker, even when the circumstances were highly unfavorable to love.

James crossed the distance between them with one stride. "Lucy," he murmured, "do you have an answer for me? Are we going to be wed?"

"I'm sorry, James, but I must say no." The answer, long-practiced, fell from her lips like a stone. She kept her eyes down, tracing the pattern of the Aubusson rug to stay calm.

"I w-w-was afraid you'd s-s-say that." He placed his hands on her shoulders and drew her closer. His touch, warm and gentle, brought tears to her eyes. "I s-s-suppose this is d-due to some s-silly notion that m-my family d-d-doesn't approve of you."

What could she say? If she admitted the truth, she would be breaking her vow to his mother. So she fell silent, biting her lip. If only he would release her, she could stay strong. But his touch lulled her into a sense of protection, and she stayed put.

"You might as well know how I feel in the matter. I've asked you and begged you and put off announcing our marriage for weeks because you wanted my mother's approval. But no one asked me what I want." He kissed the top of her hairline. "And here it is: I want to marry you, Lucy Williams. In fact, I will marry none but you."

Lucy gave a little sob at this admission—'twas a dear thing to hear. Something she'd remember forever. But they both had a duty to move beyond themselves. "A marriage built on selfishness would be no kind of union at all," she whispered. "You owe your mother and sister a living. I owe my charges the best of my devoted care. Would you have us throw our obligations over to satisfy ourselves?"

"Yes." His hold tightened on her shoulders. "Lucy—I love you. Do you love me?"

"That's not the point," she interjected. If she began confessing her love for him, all would be lost. "What we must decide is if we can hurt those who depend upon us out of the selfish desire to stay together."

"My mother's gotten to you," he muttered, pulling her closer. "Tell me what she said at tea."

"Nothing I didn't already understand and feel for myself," she replied defensively. She placed her hands on his chest and pushed away a bit, her breath coming more quickly. "James, I can't marry you. I just can't."

"If you are refusing because my mother has some other woman picked out for me, then it won't matter." His voice was a low growl now, causing her heart to flutter wildly in her chest. "I'm not marrying anyone but you. No matter what any of my family says." He fidgeted in his coat pocket and withdrew a ring. It sparkled in the light streaming in from the windows—prisms of rainbows scattered about the room, refracted from the emeralds and diamonds in the setting. "This is for you and no one else."

"I can't accept it." She choked out the words. Pain seared through her as though a knife had been thrust into her midsection. She must go, or else she would break down entirely. She rushed past him toward the library door, but he grasped her arm, halting her progress.

"So you would condemn us both to a life without love merely to satisfy a few obligations?" His voice shook with anger, and her heart pounded at the sound. James's temper was not something to trifle with, and he was growing more hurt and angry by the second.

"Please understand, James." She pitched her voice so that it was low and pleading, trying desperately to placate him. "It's not that I don't love you. But if you married me as I am, with no family connections, no money—it could lead to bitterness and strife later on. Years later, you might regret marrying me, and then what could we do? 'Tis better to leave things as they are. Surely you know that what I am saying is true."

"I know nothing of the sort." His hand still about her wrist, he pulled her close enough to murmur in her ear, "I've a carriage outside. We can go anywhere we wish to go. Even," he hesitated, his eyelashes tickling her cheek, "even Gretna Green."

That was her breaking point. How easy it could be to just flee to the border with James and follow only her selfish desires. But she would hate herself for it for the rest of her life. His family would be miserable. His mother would likely take every opportunity to point out the disparity in their situations. James couldn't see it now, but in time he would come to understand and even respect her decision. She wrenched free of his grasp and ran to the door.

"You're not marrying me because I stammer," he called after her. "I embarrass you."

She stopped and turned around, willing herself to look him in the eye, but his expression—sick and broken—made her turn away. "That's not true. I could never be embarrassed of you. Never." She tugged open the door and fled down the hallway, up the stairs and to her room. She locked herself in and huddled on the bed, her knees drawn to her chest.

Hot tears trickled down her cheek, wetting her pillow.

Love was horrid.

Novels and poems lied about it.

She'd never, ever allow herself to fall in love with a man again.

After Lucy left the room, there was nothing to do but go as well. So James flung himself out of Lord

Bradbury's house and into the street, ignoring the carriage that waited so patiently on the curb. He needed to walk. He needed purpose, even if it was just putting one foot in front of the other. Otherwise, he would go mad.

He directed his steps toward Felton's shop. He could not go home. If he did, he might wring his mother's neck. He was not a violent man, but so help him—she was responsible for his misery. And for Lucy's, too. Her expression, as she turned to face him that last time, would be burned into his mind for all eternity. How pale she was, her enormous eyes ringed with dark smudges. His beloved Lucy, sick and wounded. And no matter what he'd said, no matter what arrows he flung her way, she'd dodged them expertly, determined not to let him talk her into a marriage she believed he would someday regret. She valued his future peace of mind more than her own happiness. What could he do with a woman like that?

He jostled past street vendors, servants, lords and ladies alike who thronged the sidewalk in the morning. He had to get to his workshop. There, he knew what he was doing. There, he reigned supreme. At home and elsewhere, he had no idea what he was doing with his life.

When he, at length, reached Felton's shop, he let himself in through the back door. That meant passing the Assembly Rooms. It meant a quick glance up at the window he'd spied Lucy sitting in, so many nights before. He crushed the grief that welled within him and opened the back door. He could avoid the workmen this way. Anyone who saw him at this moment would know, just by looking at him, that something was amiss.

In his workroom, he took out a large length of oak and several pegs. Then, methodically, he began smashing each peg into the solid wood beam. The sound of each blow of the hammer ricocheted off the walls of the room with a satisfying crash. He pounded and pounded until blisters formed on his palms. Then he cast the hammer aside and buried his face in his hands, too exhausted to do anything but close his eyes.

A knock sounded on the door, and Felton let himself in. "I take it your meeting with Lord Bradbury did not go very well? What more did the man want? You did a splendid job."

"It w-w-wasn't his l-lordship," James mumbled, scrubbing his face with his sweaty palms.

"Well, there must be something amiss. Did one of the workmen do a poor job?" Felton pulled a stepstool over to the workbench and sat down.

"N-no. They all d-d-did quite w-well." He breathed deeply. In and out. In and out. "N-nothing with the job w-went wrong."

"Then, by Jove man, why did you come here in such a state? I thought at first a madman had come in and started shooting up the place, your hammer blows were so loud." Felton rested his arms on the table, his grizzled visage open and expectant.

He hated to talk about the matter. It was a private thing between him and Lucy, no matter how angry and frustrated he became. So he merely shook his head, and with trembling fingers, swept the splinters of oak off the bench.

"I imagine it had something to do with the Honorable Miss Louisa Bradbury's visit the other day." Felton steepled his hands beneath his chin. "She seemed to have a great deal weighing on her mind."

James's head snapped up. "You're w-worse than a g-gossiping old b-biddy," he snarled. Felton would simply not drop the matter and leave him in peace.

"That was a mighty fine piece of oak you destroyed," Felton responded coolly. "Worth about twenty pounds. Now, you can tell me why you ruined it, or I shall wheedle the truth out of you. Either way. Admit the truth or let me pester you." His voice softened. "You're like a son to me, Rowland. I hate to see you like this."

James stilled, grasping the workbench. He didn't remember his father. It had always been Mother directing and dictating his life. What if he talked to a man about this matter? A man who was old enough to be his father? It could relieve some of the anxiety and the pressure. At worst, he would reveal himself as a coward and a blackguard to Felton. At best, Felton's sympathy could help restore his spirit. He closed his eyes and took a deep breath.

"I'm in l-love with Lucy W-W-Williams, the g-governess to Lord B-B-Bradbury's daughters," he began, and spilled the whole sordid tale. Felton sat back, his expression unchanging, until James finally reached the end of his story and fell silent.

"So the lady will not change her mind until your mother changes hers," he surmised, his arms crossed over his chest. "Thus, it remains your duty to change the minds of both women."

"I d-don't care about M-Mother," James spat. "I would have m-married Lucy t-t-today, despite M-Mother's objections. It's Lucy's mind I must change. But she is so d-d-determined—how c-c-can I?"

Felton shrugged. "You've made tremendous strides since you first came to me. Do you remember what you were? You shrank within yourself. You stammered. No—it wasn't merely a stammer. You could hardly speak two words together. Do you remember?"

James nodded, his mouth twisting ruefully at the memory. "I l-lived with M-Macready, and I had no p-purpose in life. That all changed b-b-because of L-Lucy. Without her, I would not be the m-man I am today. She is the one who t-t-transformed me. Without her, I am n-nothing."

Felton nodded. "And so it usually is. With a good woman behind you—a woman like the 'virtuous wife' described in Proverbs, 31—you can do anything. My own wife, Anna, was like that. She passed away six years ago." His eyes misted over, and he rubbed at them with a fierce gesture. "She encouraged me to do my utmost. I did, and this shop is a testament not just to her faith but her faith in me." He glanced at James, his gaze piercing in its intensity. "If you feel this way about her, you cannot let her slip away."

"I—I—I know that," James agreed. "B-b-but how c-c-can I convince her to d-d-defy my m-mother?"

Felton's expression softened, as though he were admitting defeat. "I don't know. Maybe you can't. You cannot blame her for being too good to go against your mother, no matter how much she loves you. So it's up to you to convince your mother that you will have no one but Lucy."

"You might as well t-t-tell me to move a m-mountain." James pounded on the workbench with his clenched fists. "Mother is unyielding. She clings to the p-p-past the way a burr c-clings to your clothing."

"Well, my boy, I have no advice to offer you, save to tell you it's worth the fight," Felton said, rising. "After all, you can always pluck a burr from your trousers. It may prick your finger, but you can get rid of it."

James nodded. The task before him was overwhelming. Charging into battle again would be more welcome than convincing his mother she was wrong. After all, he knew what to expect in battle now. He wouldn't be a coward any longer.

Felton turned toward the door, his hand resting on the latch. "And mind you, don't destroy any more of those oak beams. If you need to relieve your temper, there are plenty of knotty pine logs in the back of the shop." With a sympathetic grin, he departed, leaving James alone once more.

James rubbed his thumb along the rough surface of the workbench. This was a formidable task indeed. Was he equal to it? He was never much of a praying man, but the need to ask for help overwhelmed him. He said a silent prayer, begging for wisdom and strength. He would need it in the weeks to come.

Chapter Twenty-One

Lucy sat in the dusky twilight of her room, her forehead pressed against the window glass. She was dizzy and, truth be told, a little light-headed. She'd taken nothing to eat or drink all day. And she'd cried until her eyes felt gritty, as though sand were abrading them. The mere fact that no one had come to knock on her door spoke volumes. Everyone must know her business. Should she be embarrassed by that fact? No, she was too tired to care. Tomorrow she would be back to her usual practical self. Today she could wallow in her own misery.

A knock sounded on the door. "Yes?" she called. The door was locked. No one could bound in without her permission.

"It's me, Lucy." Louisa answered, her voice slightly muffled by the closed door. "I have a tray for you. I thought you might be hungry."

Lucy smiled faintly and rose. Louisa was a good girl—it spoke well of her maturity that she was thinking of others instead of just herself. She crossed the room and turned the key in the lock, allowing the door to swing open. Louisa came in, bearing a heavy white tray from which issued an array of tantalizing scents.

"I wanted to bring this to you myself, and not entrust it to that horrid Nancy," she panted, relieving herself of her burden by placing it on a nearby table. "She gossips entirely too much." Louisa lifted the covers, sniffing at each dish in turn. "I brought a roast chicken breast, some rice, a few *haricots verts* and a chocolate bombe," she pronounced. "My favorite things—but then, I thought you might like them, too. They're most comforting."

"Thank you, dear," Lucy murmured, pulling a chair before the table. "Have you eaten? Would you like to share?"

"I ate already," Louisa admitted. "Although I would take a bite of the chocolate if you don't mind sharing."

"Take it all," Lucy urged. She handed the dish and a spoon to Louisa, who settled on the settee. "I'm afraid I can't eat chocolate right now. My stomach's too upset."

They ate in silence. The food smelled wonderful but tasted like ashes in her mouth. Still, she dined anyway. It would do no good to get sick and faint. She still had a duty to take care of her charges, and it would do her no favors to appear weak-willed and sickly to Lord Bradbury.

Louisa finished the bombe and licked the spoon. Then, setting the dish aside, she surveyed Lucy frankly. "I suppose you told the ensign no."

Lucy sighed, closing her eyes for a moment. Of course, she had assumed that Louisa would guess the truth, but still—oh bother, she'd have to talk about it. "Yes. After all, I gave my word to his mother."

"Oh, Lucy." Louisa bit her lip, her large brown eyes

widening. "I hoped you would say yes. I hoped you would elope to Gretna Green."

"Gretna Green." Lucy stared at her charge, her mind working rapidly. "How did you know he'd try to tempt me to Gretna Green?"

"Well—" Louisa's cheeks turned a mottled shade of red. "I spoke to the ensign a little while ago. After you got home from tea with his mother."

Lucy's heart sank. Had her charge actually tried to play matchmaker? How humiliating. "What did you tell him?" she asked, her suspicions rising.

"The truth." Louisa looked at Lucy with a frank expression on her face. "And I told him not to take no for an answer. I suggested he spirit you away to Gretna Green if necessary." She tilted her chin and gazed at Lucy. "Did he say anything about eloping?"

Lucy sat back in her chair, defeated. She was so tired. So very, very tired. "Yes. But I still turned him away." She clasped her hands and looked back at Louisa, returning her gaze for gaze. "You see, as an honorable person, I had to adhere to what I promised his mother," she explained. "And my feelings shouldn't enter the matter at all. If we wed without his mother's blessing, our marriage would be rocky from the very beginning. It could spell trouble for us all our lives. So, in telling him no, I was actually sparing us all from a great deal of unhappiness."

"Oh, Lucy. What are you going to do now?" Louisa's eyes welled with tears. She sniffled and rubbed her nose on her sleeve.

"Well, first I am going to retrieve a handkerchief for you." She rustled about in her workbasket until she found a clean, folded square of linen. "Here, don't cry."

She handed the handkerchief to Louisa. "I've cried all day, and I can't bear any more. If you start, then I won't be able to stop again."

"You seem so resigned to your decision, Lucy." Louisa blew her nose. "How can you be so cool and practical about it?"

"You must understand that I grew up with very low expectations. The fact that I get to love and nurture you and Amelia is beyond anything I could have expected growing up. I never dreamed of a home and family. At most, I dreamed of having my own school, when I could save up the money to start. Already I have surpassed what most women in my station can hope to get out of life." She stopped, biting her lip. She could not say it to her charge, but just knowing that once she had the love of a man like James Rowland would give her sustenance for the rest of her life. When she was old and lonely, she would sit in a corner and recall the look on his face as he bared his soul to her. It was something she could remember and treasure forever.

"I just want you to be happy, Lucy." Louisa sniffled. "You've been like a mother to me. The best comfort I could hope for after Mama passed away. What would make you happy?"

As Lucy looked at her charge, a warm glow kindled in her heart. The girls needed her now. Other children would need her once Amelia and Louisa had grown. While she did not have the kind of romantic love that made for exciting novels, what she had was quite enough for a penniless orphan. Wasn't it? "I want to help nurture you girls onto the right path. And when you have made your debut and no longer need me, I will move on to another house with other little girls who need a governess." She smiled faintly at Louisa. "And, in the meantime, I shall work with the children of the veterans' group, educating them so that they can go out and take their places in the world."

Louisa nodded. "Very well, Lucy. But it isn't a bit like anything in one of my novels."

"You read too many novels," Lucy admonished, a thread of reproof running through her tone. "And I want you to make a promise to me. Don't go to see the ensign any longer. Don't try to interfere. I know you meant well, and I love you for it. But he is very hurt and angry. We must give him time to heal. After a while, he will know that I was right." For his mother was right, too. He could do so much better than her. Any woman would be happy to marry James. His handsome, angular face—the stubborn cowlick of sandy hair—his dark green eyes that could change from mischievous to tender in a matter of moments—and, of course, his temper and his endearing stammer and his large hands that could transform a block of wood into a work of art. He was an attractive man, whether he had a title or not, and in time, some pretty merchant's daughter would make him a fine wife.

Louisa promised she would no longer interfere, and in a show of complete helpfulness and usefulness, she took her tray back down to the kitchens. What a fine young lady she was becoming—far removed from the self-absorbed little miss Lucy had met just a few years ago. Lucy changed into her sturdy cotton night rail and bathed her face and hands with rose-scented soap, using the basin and pitcher. Then she plaited her long curls and donned a nightcap. Already she was as set in her ways as an old maid. In no time, she would be sporting a pince-nez.

If she'd said yes to James, she might at this moment be speeding toward Gretna Green, breathless with laughter and excitement. But it would be a selfish pleasure all the same. There was something to be said for self-sacrifice. Even if it was the sacrifice of your own joy.

She blew out the candle and sank into an exhausted slumber.

It was well past dark when James finally came home. He'd worked in the shop all afternoon and well into the evening. When he could delay the inevitable no longer, he walked back to his home—the home that was meant for Lucy, himself and their children. Mother would be there—and Mary. And he didn't want to face either of them.

Candles burned low in the parlor, giving off a guttering light as he let himself in the front door. Someone was still awake.

"James," Mother called.

He groaned quietly. There was no chance at even sneaking upstairs and falling into bed. Mother had waited up for him.

He crossed the hallway and entered the parlor. "Yes?"

"You're very late," she said crossly. "Come in and sit with me for a moment. I've waited for you."

He glowered at her from under his brows and sank into a chair near the hearth. "What is it?"

"Well, I shall come straight to the point. Macready and your sister are to be wed." She heaved a gusty sigh. "He came here today in such a state—practically swept Mary off her feet. And when I objected, he insisted that you had given your blessing and that as head of our family, he was beholden to no one but you. Is that true?"

"Macready spoke t-to me about the matter recently," he admitted, crossing his arms over his chest. "Mary seems to adore him. And he's a g-g-good fellow. So I t-told him that he c-c-could p-pursue her."

"Well, I don't suppose we could have done better for Mary, with her stammer and all, and no dowry." Mother sighed. "Still, I had hoped—"

"Mary's happy. Macready's ecstatic. Who are we t-to stand in the w-way?" He cleared his throat. "Macready will make a g-good husband, and they will live c-comfortably on his father's estate. I d-don't see why you are so upset."

"Well, I had rather hoped to restore the Rowland fortune," Mother admitted, a hopeful smile flitting across her face. "However, I may still depend upon you to do that, my dear son."

He stood abruptly, sending his chair scraping across the floor. "We will talk no more about marriage tonight," he snapped roughly. "Good night."

He took the stairs two at a time, ignoring his mother's protests as he quit the room. He was in no humor to talk about the Rowland fortune or marriage. He was barely able to contain his rage. He needed to bathe his blistered fingers in cool water and to rest his weary head on his pillow. He could deal with Mother's hopes of restoring faded glory tomorrow when he had more strength.

Mary popped her head out of her bedroom door as

he came up the stairs. "James." Her eyes shone with a gentle light. "Come and sit with me for a moment."

He gave Mary a brief hug and followed her into her room. "I hear c-congratulations are in order."

She nodded, a shy smile lighting her pretty face. "And I have you t-to thank for it. Thank you for g-giving your b-blessing."

The last thing he wanted to do was talk about weddings, but Mary looked so happy and so hopeful that he squashed his personal turmoil. "When's the d-date?"

"Six months from now. In February. M-M-Mother wanted us t-to b-be engaged for at least a year, and Macready wanted only three months. So we c-c-compromised."

James chuckled. "S-s-sounds like a fine c-compromise."

"I even have my t-trousseau already." Mary waved her hand at half a dozen brightly colored gowns scattered across her bed. "Lucy Williams gave them t-to me. They were g-given her by a friend, but she says she has no use for them. Aren't they lovely?"

"They are." He choked down the bile rising in his throat. "'Twas a thoughtful g-gift."

"She seems like such a lovely g-girl. I like her very much. D-do you think she would b-be willing to stand up with me at my wedding? I have so few friends and all of them married. I'd like Lucy to be there. She's a part of B-Bath, and a part of my c-courtship with Macready."

He winced but pasted a grin on his face anyway. "I'm sure she'd be d-delighted." He couldn't even imagine what that meeting would be like, but then—'twas six months away. By then he'd have his Lucy by his side. He knew not how but it would happen.

"Oh, g-g-good." Mary smiled at him and fell silent. They'd always been comfortable in silence together since childhood, and it was a welcome respite from making polite chatter.

At length, Mary spoke again. "Are you c-coming home to Essex, James? We m-miss you s-s-so."

"No," he replied. "My home is here n-now. I have more work c-c-coming in than I know how t-to handle. And I took p-possession of this home..." He trailed off. How much did Mary know of his romance with Lucy? She knew him well and had a strong sense of intuition; it was quite likely she had guessed at the truth from the first few moments of meeting Lucy. Yet, he had no strength to speak the words aloud to tell her what had occurred. He'd spent all day mastering his temper, and now he could not afford to let one spark of his anger flare anew.

She studied his face, her eyes growing softer as he spoke. "Of course, I t-t-told Mother as much," she murmured. "After all, this is the home you hope t-to share with Lucy Williams. Am I right?"

"Yes." 'Twas folly to try to keep the truth from Mary. She'd always been able to read him, just like she would read any book in Papa's library.

"It would be very nice to c-call her my sister." Mary clasped her hands in her lap. "Have you p-proposed yet?"

How much of Mother's meddling should he keep from Mary? Did she know that Mother would have prevented a match between Macready and herself if she could? Did she know that Mother prevented Lucy from saying yes? He looked into her guileless eyes, her mouth upturned into a hopeful smile. She had a great deal of intuition, but he also longed to protect her from anything unpleasant. He ran his hands through his hair, defeated. He had no idea what to say.

Mary sat back in her chair. "I t-take it from your silence that something is amiss. Don't worry, James. I won't p-pry it from you. Just t-take heart and know that everything will work out well in the end. It d-did for me, and it will for you t-too."

Sweet Mary and her innocent faith in the good in all things. He could not bear to taint her view of the world. He would take his bitterness and go—and leave her with her happiness and with the bloom still on her roses. She deserved happiness. He would not ruin it by telling her the truth. He managed a tight smile and rose.

"Again, my b-best wishes to you and to Macready. He'll make a fine husband for you." He kissed the top of her head. "G-good night."

"G-good night, James. Oh! I forgot t-to t-tell you. Mother s-says we shall j-journey back to Essex earlier than we p-planned t-to begin the wedding p-preparations. I expect we will l-leave in the next d-d-day or so." Mary's eyes sparkled with excitement.

That was the best news he'd heard all day. He nodded and quit the room. He could keep up the pretense of good cheer no longer. Another moment and he'd lose his temper altogether. Or break down crying like a fool.

Alone in his chamber at last, he bathed his sore hands and grimy face in the basin of water next to his bed. He was so weary that even the thought of making a quick supper seemed like too much work. He'd just go on to sleep and eat a hearty breakfast in the morning.

As he climbed into bed, his head swirled with thoughts and words and images from the day. Mary's shy smile. Lucy's wan expression, the hurt in her dark eyes.

He'd find a way to win Lucy back and to get her acceptance whether Mother approved of it or not. He was making his own way in the world, supplementing the paltry income left from Father's estate, paying his mother's bills and providing a roof over her head. He had a right to his own happiness and so did Lucy. He must find a way to break through her resistance and win her hand just as he'd won her heart.

He was a coward no longer.

He ground his teeth in the darkness.

Finally he'd found a cause for which he was willing to fight with his whole heart. And fight he would.

Chapter Twenty-Two

Summer faded as autumn's chill nipped the air. Amelia's grand debut drew to a close, and already Lord Bradbury was besieged by offers for her hand. Amelia herself had grown dreamy and silent, blushing furiously whenever a certain Lord Spencer was mentioned teasingly by Louisa. Lucy immersed herself in her charges' affairs, living through them, vicariously enjoying their thrills and pleasures. She'd stopped attending the veterans' group meetings, for the possibility of seeing James outstripped, for now, any chance to educate the young children of the widows and veterans. One day, perhaps, she could run the risk of seeing him, when emotions no longer ran high. But it had only been a matter of a few weeks, and the ache in the pit of her heart had not yet abated.

His lordship entered the schoolroom after a brief knock. "I hope I am not intruding."

"Not at all, sir." Lucy swept her notebook and pen aside. "I was merely making lesson plans for the week. How may I be of assistance?"

His lordship sat rather heavily onto a spare wooden

chair. "I am sure you've heard of some of the rumors circulating about Amelia. The *on dit* is that young Spencer is quite enamored of her." He ran his hand distractedly through his graying hair. "If her mother were here, I could confer with her. But as it is, I must prevail upon you."

"Of course, your lordship. I shall do whatever is needed to help." She gave him a comforting smile. He'd always been a good father, despite his dalliances with young blond things. Despite his great wealth, he seemed to care about his daughters and their welfare.

"I must know if you feel that Amelia is too young to be wed," Lord Bradbury blurted. "You've seen her every day for several years. Is she ready to become a wife? To leave her father's home?"

Lucy fell silent, considering the matter. Amelia was, of the two daughters, the more mature and worldly. Although Louisa was always her favorite, Lucy had to admit that Amelia had come into her own quite gracefully over time and was every day becoming more of a woman while Louisa was still in many ways a little girl. "I think that Amelia is a great deal more grown up than she was even just before her debut," she began slowly. "On the other hand, she's only sixteen. And she hasn't had a London season yet, just her season in Bath. She's hardly begun to experience what the world can offer."

"True." Lord Bradbury sighed. "But she is very taken with Spencer and he with her. The lad's only two years older than she but has already come into his inheritance. He's as solid and steady as they come, not like those London bucks who gamble and drink away their livings."

"Have you spoken to Amelia at all about this matter?"

"No," he admitted. "I find myself unable to broach the subject. Spencer came around to ask my permission just yesterday. I told him I would consider the matter." He chuckled dryly. "It came as rather a shock to hear a young man asking for my Amelia. I suppose I still thought of her as being in leading-strings."

Lucy laughed, tears springing to her eyes. "Come to think of it, so did I." Here she'd been planning their lessons for the following week as though both her charges were still mere girls. No, one of them at least was already a woman. A pang of regret and nervousness tore through her.

"Ah, I knew it. You love them as I do. I see the tears in your eyes." He laughed again, more softly this time. "What shall I do? Shall I give him permission to ask her?"

"As you said, Spencer is a good lad and a steady one. He has money of his own and cares for Amelia a great deal." She sighed. "Her youth and inexperience make me want to hold her back. There's nothing wrong with either of them. I just want them to be sure."

"A long engagement, perhaps? I could stipulate that they wait a year."

She shook her head. No, that would not work. Amelia would want to wed right away—she'd never been good at waiting for what she wanted. She glanced at his lordship with his bowed head and the wrinkles radiating from the corners of his eyes. He was growing older, and he wanted what was best for his daughter.

Parents always wanted the best for their children. If her own father and mother had been alive just a few short weeks ago, when James asked her—what would they have said? She had no doubt they would want her to be happy. Charlotte Rowland wanted what she thought was best for James, but would it make him happy?

"I don't think parents should interfere in a match," she blurted. "After all, it's between the two of them. If you have no objections, then you should let matters unfold as they will. Great harm can come from parents who meddle too much in affairs of the heart."

"So I should tell them yes. Or no?" His lordship scrubbed at his face with a weary hand. "I have no idea how to proceed. If this were a business negotiation or a political race then I would know exactly what to do. But when it comes to my little girl…tell me what to do, Miss Williams."

"My advice is to sit with Amelia and talk to her about the matter. Tell her that Spencer has offered for her hand. Explain our reservations. And then tell her that you will back her decision no matter what." If only Charlotte Rowland had done just that—aired her reservations and then left them to decide the best course for themselves. But then she made Lucy promise—and Lucy couldn't go back on her word. As unhappy as the situation made her, she had the sense that somehow the universe would be made right again if Amelia got what she wanted. It would, in a way, right the wrong.

"I wish I'd had sons sometimes," his lordship admitted wearily. "I can see now that having two attractive daughters will make me old and gray before my time." He rose, smiling down at Lucy. "Thank you for having this conversation with me. Time and again we ask you to perform outside your duties. But know that we would not lean so heavily upon you if we did not care for your opinion."

"Thank you, sir." A brief spark lit within Lucy. What a kind thing for his lordship to say. And he was not one given to flattery. If he said the family valued her, then it was true.

His lordship turned to go, and then he swung back with a snap of his fingers. "Speaking of wedding madness, I had a letter from Charles Cantrill. Did you know that he and Sophie Handley are to be wed next month?"

"Yes, I had a letter from Sophie this week." How very odd that Cantrill would write to his lordship. After all, he'd threatened to thrash the man for his improper advances to Sophie.

"We've been invited to the wedding—you, me and the girls," Lord Bradbury added. "So, we shall plan to journey to Tansley in the next few weeks. I've a residence in the country out there. I'll send word for them to start making it ready in anticipation of our visit."

She couldn't help it. Her mouth dropped open. How very cosmopolitan of his lordship to attend the wedding of the woman he'd asked to be his mistress. Just when she was coming to see his lordship as nothing more than an aging, doting father, he changed direction. She would never understand the gentry. Never.

His lordship smirked at her expression, his face growing a trifle red. "I know what you must be thinking, Miss Williams, but Cantrill and I had a bet. And I promised I would dance at his wedding if he carried through. It will all be perfectly friendly and respectable. Louisa and Amelia will be delighted to see Sophie again, and I am sure you will enjoy the trip too."

"Of course, your lordship." She bobbed a curtsy.

After all, it wasn't her place to condemn or criticize his actions. And besides, it sounded like this wedding invitation were an olive branch of sorts—a way for his lordship to make peace with Sophie and Cantrill.

Lord Bradbury nodded and quit the schoolroom, his shoulders slightly more stooped than when he came in. He did look older and a trifle more defeated. Funny how one simple matter was enough to age him so quickly, taking him from a carefree *bon vivant* to a tired, nervous father.

She gathered her things and prepared to close the schoolroom for the day. 'Twould be lovely to see Sophie again and to get out of Bath. In Tansley, she wouldn't have to worry about running into the ensign. She could relax and enjoy the countryside, allowing her raw emotions to heal. And perhaps, by the time they returned, she would be helping Amelia prepare for her wedding. Yes, his lordship had the right of it. Wedding madness, indeed. She suppressed the twinge of jealousy that gnawed within her. She would not have a wedding, herself. But she could always enjoy the weddings of others.

"His Grace is very pleased with the way the ballroom is progressing." The Earl of Cavendish's man of business looked over the ledger before him. "The work is coming along quite well—you are on schedule and staying within your means. As a consequence of your good work, his grace would like to offer a bonus to you. He is gifting you the sum of two thousand pounds and asks if you will consider working on his country home, as well."

James sat back in his chair, unsure he'd heard the

man aright. The gentry, particularly well placed and wealthy gentry like the Earl, were not known for paying their bills in a timely manner. In fact, it was quite fashionable for the duns to seek them out. How very odd to get extra money—and in advance, too. "I'm not sure I understand," he admitted. "More money? In advance?"

The man's mouth quirked a little. "His grace is not like the gentry you've heard about. He's very generous with his wealth when he feels it has been earned. Your worksmanship has made him quite happy. He's prepared to give you enough work to keep you busy for a long time to come." He pushed a leather pouch across the desk. "This is no advance on payment owed but a gift to show his intentions to keep you well occupied for the future. Two thousand pounds, with his grace's gratitude."

James's head was still spinning wildly when he stepped out into the street. He'd earned the money Mother needed to restore the family's fortunes, and he'd done so without marrying an heiress. No, indeed. He'd done it by his own hand. He would purchase a home for Mother in Essex, better than the cottage she had now, and he could give Mary a bit of a dowry. He was, in truth, the head of the family now.

He was ready to burst with the news, but there was no one to tell. Macready had gone home to his family estate, vacating his flat in Bath forever. Cantrill was in Tansley, making preparations to marry Sophie Handley in just a month or so. Felton had gone home to stay with his daughter and her family in Derbyshire. If only he could tell Lucy. He was only a few steps away from the Crescent. She'd be so proud of him, her large velvety eyes lighting up, and her generous mouth quirking in a welcome smile. But he'd avoided her these past few weeks. He was ashamed of the way they'd parted. How could he ever make it right? How could he convince her to be his?

Without knowing he'd done so, the Earl of Cavendish had given Ensign James Rowland the keys to his prison cell. With this money, he could convince his mother to change her mind. And then he could ask Lucy to be his once more.

He continued his progress, walking down into the heart of York Street. A sign caught his eye: Jennings and Crowley. Ah yes. Estate agents. Now was the time to take over and assert himself as head of the Rowland family.

"Can I help you, sir?" the clerk asked as James entered, the bell on the door tinkling merrily.

"Yes, I need to p-purchase t-two homes. One for m-m-myself and one for my m-mother. C-can you assist me with finding s-s-something small b-b-but nice in the Essex area?"

"I daresay we can, sir." The clerk rose. "Just let me ask one of the gentlemen to come out and assist you. Did you want the two residences to be in Essex?"

"No." James couldn't suppress a chuckle. The clerk probably thought he was mad, but there it was. He would purchase his home here in Bath, and he and Lucy would make it theirs forever. And Mother would have her place in Essex. And if she were nice, she could come visit on occasion. On rare occasions.

"Very good, sir." The clerk looked at him quizzically over the rim of his glasses but said nothing more.

When James stepped back out of the office a scant

forty five minutes later, he was a landed man. He now owned his own cottage and had purchased what the agent described as a very pretty property for Mother not very far away from her current residence.

For the first time since Waterloo, he was himself again. Only better. More sure in his purpose. He'd go home now—to his home, the home he would share with Lucy for the rest of their lives—and write to Mother at once. And he'd send a letter to Mary, too, promising her a small dowry.

Mrs. Peyton greeted him as he opened the door. "The post just came," she said. "There was a big fat letter from Tansley Village, so I put it on the top of the stack."

"Thank you." He went into his study and retrieved the missive from the silver tray on his desk. Yes, it was from Tansley. From Cantrill, actually. He broke the seal and poured over the contents.

> As you know, Sophie and I are to be wed in November. We are asking all of our friends from the veterans' group to join with us to share in our joy. Lord Bradbury has graciously offered to provide transportation to Tansley for any veteran or widow who cannot afford the journey on their own. We should love for you to be there, Rowland, not just as our friend but as a powerful reminder of what the veterans' group means to all of us.
>
> Of all of the men I have worked with, you have come the furthest. Your progress over the past few months is nothing short of astonishing. I know I sound like a schoolmaster or elder

brother, but there it is. I am proud of you, and Felton is, too. He's said as much to me, though he is old-fashioned and won't praise you so highly to your face. I am sure he thinks it could inflate your vanity grotesquely or cause you to defect and start your own shop. But you can take it from me, as your fellow brother in arms—you have come far.

Sophie reminds me that while you are to be highly commended, your progress would not have been as swift or as complete without the help of her friend Lucy Williams. She claims nothing more than that but only wishes to add that Lucy will also be at the ceremony, since she will be there to chaperone Louisa and Amelia Bradbury.

And there it was. James threw the letter down, exultation pouring through his being. He had a month to settle matters. A month to help his mother move, and to assert himself as head of the family. When he came to the wedding in November, he would be able to offer for Lucy's hand freely, unencumbered by the dictates of his mother or anyone else.

He turned and, in doing so, knocked a stack of books from his desk with his elbow. The top volume was his favorite book of poetry, and it fell open to the very page Lucy Williams had playfully selected during one of their first meetings. He picked the fragile book up, rubbing his hand gently over its smooth pages. This book was symbolic of how far he'd come, but it was also the bond between them. When he offered for her again, he would do so differently. Not proudly. Not arrogantly. He wouldn't push or shove, he wouldn't flash an emerald before her eyes or hire a coach for Gretna Green.

He would come to her as she'd come to him—pure of heart, radiant in love, full of hope. He'd show her all he'd become because of her.

Sophie Handley was right. He could take all the credit in the world for his transformation, but it was a hollow victory indeed. He had Lucy Williams to thank for making him the man he was. And whether his family appreciated that fact or not, it did not matter. He was now head of the Rowland family, and he would make his own decisions from now on.

He closed the book and placed it back on his desk. Then, he withdrew several sheets of foolscap from his letter box, and drew up the ink in his favorite pen.

He had much to say after all.

Chapter Twenty-Three

"This house is very nice, I suppose," Mother admitted, sinking back into her chair before the fire. "Though I did not appreciate being jostled about, moving out of the cottage on my own. You should have been here to help me, James. I was quite distressed."

"As I mentioned in my letter, work p-precluded me from arriving until this week." James arched one eyebrow as he surveyed his mother's aristocratic features. "But the workmen d-did all of the heavy lifting and p-packing for you. Macready even came t-to supervise. You were hardly left on your own."

Mother sniffed. "It matters not a whit. The thing is done now. At the very least, I am in a home befitting our station." She waved her hand languidly around the room. "Four bedrooms, two parlors, a dining room, and a study. It's at least twice as big as our old cottage, and the gardens are far prettier."

"I'm g-glad you like it, Mother. We were lucky to find it on such short notice."

"So I take it your work with the Earl of Cavendish and Lord Bradbury has not gone unrewarded," Mother added, looking at him squarely. "Perhaps now that you have a bit of money, you can cease with this ridiculous nonsense. Working with your hands? You are a Rowland, after all. Now's the time to begin seeking a mate so you can take your place as a gentleman."

He straightened in his seat. Well, Mother had certainly come straight to the point—and to the heart of his purpose for visiting her in her new home. Of course, she had raised two arguments just then—arguments he never, after today, wanted to discuss again.

Mother smiled at him and picked up her teacup, stirring it with a tiny silver spoon. "There's a young lady in the village, her name is Elizabeth Warren. She's the daughter of George Warren, a merchant. She's a pretty thing, rather buxom for my tastes, but one can't have everything. She has a sizable dowry, and rumor has it that she is hunting for a title." Mother set her spoon aside and took a careful sip of her tea. "I've invited her to dine with us this evening."

In years past, such a pronouncement would have hurled James into a mad, impotent rage—but no more. Whether Mother admitted to it or not, he was the head of the Rowland family, and he would have no woman but Lucy Williams. Now was the time to make that clear.

"That sounds lovely," he replied in an easy tone, "but I am afraid I w-won't be able to stay. I shall be dining at the inn t-tonight."

Mother drew her eyebrows together crossly. "Really, James—"

"Enough, Mother." He rose and crossed over to the hearth, placing one booted foot upon it. "For years you have c-clung to the absurd notion that the Rowlands are still of the gentry and that a successful marriage on my p-part—to a woman chosen by you, of course—will restore our lost fortunes." He cleared his throat. "I've c-come from Bath to disabuse you of this notion."

Mother set her teacup aside with a defiant clink. "You are being disrespectful, James."

"I mean no disrespect, Mother. But you must understand that, henceforth, I am the leader of this family." He kept his tone cool and even, his expression open and frank. As always, when his emotions ran high, his stammer vanished. "I will not cease in my work for Felton. Besides putting a roof over your head and a dowry in Mary's pocket, my work provides me great personal satisfaction. When I do marry, I will continue to be a cabinet and furniture maker."

Mother tsked, her mouth turned downward, and she shook her head. "If your father were here—"

"If Father were still alive, I'd like to think he would applaud my decision. I intend to stand on my own feet and face the world on my own terms. I will be a coward no longer. I've made a rather good career for myself with Felton, and I refuse to cast it aside for any tarnished dreams you hold for our family."

Mother's china-blue eyes widened. "I did not say you were a coward, my son."

James sighed, clasping his hands behind his back. "No, you did not. But, Mother, you must know the truth. Until very recently, I lived my life afraid of everything. It all began at Waterloo, when I feigned death to keep from being killed. After that, everything I did was in reaction to that one act. I could find no purpose in my life because I was afraid to act. One person helped me to overcome that cowardice. She is the reason that I stand before you as I am today. Lucy Williams. Lucy is the reason I can look myself in the eye." Now was the time to tell the truth. It was easier than he'd worried it would be, after all these years. "Mother, I intend to marry Lucy. She is my intended and no one else."

"Oh, James." Mother dropped her head in her hands. "I had intended you to marry so well."

"If you mean that you wanted me to marry a woman who loves me, who makes me a better person, who nurtures me as a helpmeet—then you have no better choice than Lucy." This was it. He was putting his foot down. There was no turning back. "But I refuse to marry a woman for her money, which is—I'm afraid—your definition of marrying well."

"I don't deny that Lucy is a sweet girl." Mother sniffled, her eyes growing misty. "I grew quite fond of her despite myself." She heaved a gusty sigh. "It's just…if you could but remember how wealthy our family used to be—the carriages and the homes, the food and the gowns—you would know how very badly I wanted it all back. Not just for me, but for you and Mary, to have everything that should have been your birthright. And Lucy, despite her goodness, was keeping me from attaining those things once more."

"Look around you, Mother." He indicated the cozy parlor with a sweep of his hand. "C-could you ask for better than this? A nice home and two happily married children? Mary and Macready are as happy as I will be with Lucy. We w-want nothing more than what we have. How many of the gentry c-could say the same?" She was softening. He could feel it. And with the conviction that he would get his Lucy, he relaxed. And of course, his stammer returned. It would always return.

Mother laughed and sobbed at the same time, a strange noise issuing from her throat. "I see your mind is made up, then."

"It is." Never had he been so firm in his conviction before. "You might as well know that I already tried to p-persuade Lucy to marry me despite your wishes, and she refused. She would not c-consent to wed me until she received your approval. Mother, I ask that you g-give your approval to Lucy. She is a virtuous woman, just like the B-Book of P-Proverbs describes. In her, I will have no lack of g-gain."

"Well, at least you are asking for something instead of just telling me what you intend to do." Mother withdrew a handkerchief from her sleeve and blew her nose. "You are determined, so what more can I say? If I say no, I run the risk of losing you. You may not convince her to marry you without my consent, but I could see you drifting away from my life altogether." She sighed. "I cannot lose you. It was difficult enough to see you off to war. If you are set on staying a furniture maker for life, then I cannot deny you your Lucy."

"Thank you, Mother." He swooped down from his spot on the hearth and kissed his mother's finely wrinkled cheek. "I shall b-b-be happy the rest of my life." His heart pounded in exultation. 'Twas just a matter of a fortnight before Cantrill's wedding—and he would see Lucy there—

Mother gave him a sad smile. "I want you to be happy. That's why I wanted you to marry an heiress. I wanted our family to be well provided for. But since you're resolute about making your own way in the world, what am I to do? Stand in the way of true love?"

James grasped her cold hand. "Mother, I know this is hard for you to accept, but I wouldn't change things. Not for all the t-t-tea in China. I'm attending Lieutenant Cantrill's wedding in T-Tansley in just a matter of weeks. I w-w-want you to write a l-letter t-t-to Lucy, removing your objections t-t-to the match. She'll never b-believe me if I t-t-tell her you have c-consented. It m-must come d-d-directly from you."

"Lucy will be in Tansley, then?"

"Yes, Sophie Handley—Lieutenant C-C-Cantrill's bride—is a d-dear friend of Lucy's. So I am certain she will b-be in attendance as w-w-well." In fact, Sophie was making sure that the two of them would meet. She must know that something was afoot. And for once, he was grateful of another woman meddling in his wedding plans. At least Sophie had chosen the right woman to match him with.

"Very well." Mother sighed. "I shall post a letter this afternoon. Shall I send it in care of Sophie? That way, it will be ready and waiting for her when she arrives in Tansley."

"Yes, M-M-Mother. That would b-be a wonderful idea." He rose. He had a few more matters of business to attend to before he could strike out for Tansley Village. And now that he was certain that Mother would give Lucy her blessing, he could finish making his preparations. "If you are s-s-still having d-d-dinner with Miss Warren, then I shall t-t-take my m-m-meal at the inn."

"What would be the point?" Mother pouted. "I shall

cancel our dinner engagement and feign illness. As it is, I feel rather peaked at the moment."

"P-p-poor Mother." He pecked her cheek once more. "I have work to attend to out in the stable. I'll be b-back to wash up before d-dinner."

Mother made a little sound indicating acceptance and shrugged her shoulders. Well, she'd likely sulk for a few days. After all, her entire world had changed in the space of a fortnight.

He walked out of the house and toward the stable. The brisk October breeze ruffled his hair. The clouds gathered in a silver mass over the horizon, and the leaves on the trees were a kaleidoscope of reds, yellows and browns. If he were uncertain of his future, this autumn weather might add to his depression. But now, it served merely to remind him that November was on the way, and with it, his chance to make Lucy Williams his once more.

He creaked open the door to the stable and stepped inside, allowing his eyes to adjust to the dim, filtered light. His saddlebag rested on a bench nearby. Reaching inside, he withdrew a length of a willow branch. The wood was smooth and had dried rather well. It would be perfect for his purposes.

He set about to work, whittling the wood down to a manageable size. Good thing he'd brought a few tools along from Felton's shop. This was, perhaps, the most delicate thing he'd made so far and it was certainly the most important. He had to get it right. Fortunately, he had about a week to work on it for his beloved.

His lordship's carriage rounded through the gates of Brookes Park. What a pretty part of the country this was. Lucy pressed her face against the window, straining for a better look. And 'twas nice of his lordship to allow her to use one of his carriages, for riding all this way on horseback would have been quite tiring. As it was, she'd covered the distance between Windmere, the Bath country seat, and Brookes Park in a mere quarter of an hour.

Louisa and Amelia had begged to come along, but Sophie had insisted that Lucy come for tea alone. The girls would have to wait until the wedding, which was but two days away, before visiting with their former modiste and friend again. Lucy was sorry to leave the girls behind but also excited at the prospect of having a real visit with Sophie. It had been far too long since they'd had a conversation.

The carriage drew to a halt before Brookes Park's dignified façade. But as Lucy stepped down, the front doors were flung open by none other than Sophie, her blond curls bobbing merrily.

"Lucy!" She fairly flew down the steps, smothering Lucy in an embrace redolent of violets. "I cannot believe you are here! It has been too long."

"Too long, indeed," Lucy agreed, returning the embrace warmly. "I am so happy for you, my dear."

"Thank you." Sophie drew back, her wide blue eyes sparkling. "Come inside. This weather is wet and chill, even for a November. I've a fire burning in the parlor, and Rose promised to bring in some of her biscuits and scones. We'll sit and have a proper chin-wag, as Aunt Katherine says. And Hattie gave her word that she won't pop her head in until after we've had a jolly good chat."

They mounted the wide stone steps and went inside. Brookes Park was a stately home, rather grand in its way but not smug or self-important like most country homes.

The two friends sat in the parlor, which was as warm and cozy and friendly as Sophie had described. It was good to be with a friend again. Lucy realized with a pang that she'd retreated into solitude these past few weeks, just as she had in the orphanage. In the warmth of the parlor, and aided by Sophie's sunny smile, her very soul began to defrost.

"Oh, goodness. I am so glad you are finally here. I've been on the edge of my seat with excitement, and now I can finally know the truth." Rifling under a pillow, Sophie withdrew an envelope and held it out to Lucy. "It's from Charlotte Rowland, for you. I'm dying to know what it says. Read it right away."

Lucy's heart pounded in her chest with a force that was painful. Her fingers trembled as she grasped the envelope and broke the seal. It would be bad news. It had to be. Perhaps she had arranged a marriage between James and another girl—a wealthy girl. She closed her eyes and held the letter still in her lap.

"Oh, botheration. I'll read it." Sophie snatched it from her grasp. Lucy opened her eyes, watching her friend's face as she scanned the sheet of foolscap. If it were something truly awful, she would be able to tell from Sophie's expression.

"How marvelous!" Sophie dropped the letter and clapped her hands. "She's withdrawn her objection to your courtship with James. She says you can marry him, and she will be happy to call you daughter."

"No," Lucy gasped. "I don't believe it." She dropped her face into her hands, breathing deeply.

"It's true! She says right here, 'James has made it clear to me that the only woman who can make him happy is you. I want my son to be happy, and so I withdraw my objection to your marriage.'" Sophie handed her the letter. "Read it for yourself."

Lucy grasped the foolscap, willing her hands to stop trembling so she could read the words. *Dearest Lucy,* it said, *I shall be happy to call you daughter someday...* The lines blurred together as her eyes filled with tears.

"Now, we must plan for the wedding—and decide what you shall wear," Sophie pronounced as she grabbed a plate from the tea tray, filling it with chocolate biscuits. "With your coloring, I rather think something in a yellow or perhaps in gold would look very well. Do you still have all my gowns from Bath?"

"No," Lucy choked on a sob. Her head was whirling. There was no longer any impediment to marrying James Rowland. Why, it was all over. If he but asked her again she could say yes. Freely and happily—yes. And they would be together. And she would never be alone again.

"Gracious, what happened to them? Never mind. I have a gold gown here that will do quite nicely. We may have to make some adjustments, for I made it for Hattie, and she is taller than you. But she's increasing, and it will no longer fit her. I think we shall do very well with the gold and perhaps a few ribbons woven into your hair?"

Whatever was Sophie talking about? "Of what importance is my appearance at your wedding? What does it matter what I wear? All eyes will be on you." She took a deep, steadying breath.

"Because Ensign Rowland will be there, silly."

Lucy raised her eyes to her friend's face, unsure she had heard aright.

Sophie chuckled at Lucy's expression. "Yes, it's true. All the veterans have been invited. Charlie wrote to James quite a while back, insisting that he come to the wedding, as well. So, you see? 'Tis of utmost importance that you look your best." Sophie passed the plate of biscuits to Lucy. "First, you must eat something. I vow you've grown thinner since I left Bath, and you've gotten all wobbly since reading Mrs. Rowland's letter. Eat all these biscuits, and then we will go upstairs and try on gowns."

Lucy bit into one of the biscuits, like a well-behaved child obeying her mother. They were delicious. Of course, his lordship always employed good cooks, but the cook here at Brookes Park must be quite extraordinary. The biscuits were so light that they melted in one's mouth.

"Rose will be pleased to see you eating so hearty." Sophie smiled, filling her plate. "We'll fatten you up before the wedding for sure."

"But it's only two days away," Lucy protested. "Surely there's no time—"

Sophie rolled her eyes merrily. "Not my wedding, you goose. Your wedding. Come, bring the biscuits with you, and I shall bring mine along, too. I am in a fever to get to those dresses. We shall make you an incomparable, for certain."

Chapter Twenty-Four

St. Mary's was in Crich, just a few miles away from Tansley Village, and the wedding ceremony filled the little country church to overflowing. James recognized many of his fellow men from the veterans' group as he approached the chapel. He nodded and smiled in passing but did not stop for conversation. He was a man on a mission. He had eyes for only one person—and thus far, she seemed not to have arrived.

He ducked inside the chapel, but Lucy's dark curls and wide, laughing brown eyes did not materialize within the crowd. There was nothing to do but wait. He'd promised himself that he would be patient and not press his suit as he had before but blast it all. He'd waited an eternity for this day, and it was finally here.

"Excuse me, Ensign," a familiar voice piped up behind him. He whirled around to see Louisa Bradbury standing there, a knowing grin pasted on her young face.

"How d-do you d-d-do, Miss Louisa." He bowed.

She bobbed a quick curtsy and leaned forward. "Lucy just finished helping Sophie dress. There's a little side room over there," she whispered urgently, flailing her hand over toward the side of the church. "She's there now."

He nodded, giving her a conspiratorial grin. "Thank you," he murmured. Then he strode off in the direction she'd indicated. Stepping just inside the back of the church, he caught a glimpse of Lucy. In the dim light of the hallway, she shimmered in a captivating gold dress, her abundant chestnut locks swept up and bound with ribbons. The sight of her took his breath away, and he could only gasp. "L-Lucy."

She turned, regarding him, her almond-shaped eyes growing wider. "James."

"I need t-to t-t-talk with you." Again, the urgency. He had to calm himself—to approach her as he would a skittish colt. He'd behaved so badly before. This time, he must do everything right. "When and where c-can we m-meet?"

Behind Lucy, a door opened and Sophie stuck her head 'round the door frame, wreathed in a bridal veil. "She can speak with you now," she replied merrily. "There's a little room on the other side that the reverend uses as an office. I believe it's open."

Lucy whirled around to look at Sophie. "We might miss the ceremony. I don't want to ruin it."

"Go on." Sophie waved her gloved hand. Then she ducked back into the dressing room and shut the door firmly.

James took a deep breath. Calm and steady. *Show her how far you've come.* He offered her his arm. "Shall we?"

She took his elbow and a jolt of warmth ran up his arm at her touch. How he'd missed her. He couldn't make a hash of things now, not when he was so close. He led her through the back hallway to another room, which must be the office. Just like Sophie had indicated, it was open and deserted. Almost as if it had been left for the two of them. He led Lucy inside. "Do you mind if I c-close the d-door? I wish to speak to you p-privately."

"No, not at all." If it weren't for her white face and troubled eyes, her bright, false tone could have been a cheery response to some mundane question. No—Lucy knew what was coming. And somehow, that made it all the more difficult for him to form the right words.

"Lucy…." He paused and closed the door. "I d-don't suppose you received a letter from my mother."

She swallowed, then ran her tongue nervously over her lips. "I did."

"G-good." He took a deep, shuddering breath. "I have to t-t-tell you something. You've m-m-made me the m-man I am. I'll never forget the d-d-day that we met, and I walked you back to the C-Crescent. You s-s-see, up until that d-day, I had been wrapped in c-cotton wool. Everything was d-d-dull and g-g-gray. Even sounds, ordinary s-sounds, were m-muffled. I lived in fear and c-c-cowardice after W-Waterloo."

She nodded slowly, her dark eyes sparkling with unshed tears.

"But you c-cared enough about me to ask if I wanted to be healed. And then you w-worked with me and encouraged m-me, even when I acted like an idiot. B-Because of you, the c-c-cotton wool fell away. I began to earn a l-living with my own hands. I took my p-place as head of my family. You d-did this, Lucy. Without you, I would still be the m-man I was—and I shudder to recall those d-days."

He rifled in his pocket, withdrawing a small wooden box. Conviction, strong as a river, flowed through his being as he held the box in his hand. "I finally had the c-c-courage to s-s-speak up to my m-mother, and to tell her the t-truth of what you've d-d-done for me. And she's withdrawn her objections. And now I m-m-must ask you—will you b-b-be my wife?" He opened the box.

Lucy gasped, and took a step forward to peer inside. "James—it's lovely."

He withdrew the wooden band that he had whittled. "I m-m-made this ring from the b-branch of the willow t-t-tree at Saint Swithin's. I never p-pass that t-t-tree without thinking of you and r-remembering how you helped me t-t-to become a better man." He smiled, taking her little cold hand in his. "It s-s-seemed m-more fitting than emeralds and d-d-diamonds—but I s-s-still have those, t-t-too," he hastened to add. Perhaps she would be offended by his simple offering after the dazzling jewels he'd offered before.

"It's perfect," she whispered, her eyes cast down.

He pulled her close, not in the same possessive manner he had before but tenderly. "Lucy, you m-m-must know something. My s-s-stammer may never g-g-go away. It disappears in some m-m-moments, but I fear it's as m-m-much a part of me as a s-s-scar that will never c-c-completely heal."

"I've never minded your stammer," she protested, leaning against him. Her slender frame was light as a feather. "Never. It has never bothered me as much as it has bothered you."

"S-s-so, as imperfect as I am, will you c-consent to be my w-wife?" He closed his eyes, willing his heart to keep its same steady rhythm. She was standing so close that she would be sure to feel its pounding.

"I am flawed, too," she whispered. "And there is no one I would rather live imperfectly with than you."

James released his tightly held breath and slipped the wooden band onto Lucy's ring finger. Then he tilted her chin up, kissing her tentatively at first. As Lucy softened against him, he deepened the embrace until she broke away breathlessly.

"Gracious," she murmured. He chuckled softly, pressing kisses onto her hairline.

"I hope you l-l-like the h-house," he murmured. "I p-purchased it outright just a few w-weeks ago. It's ours n-now, Lucy. Our h-home."

"Our home," she repeated. "Oh, James, I love it. I love you. You have no idea how happy you've made me. Everything was so dreadful and lonely—I felt like I had lost half of myself."

"So d-did I." He held her tightly and they stood together, wrapped in each others' embrace, until the notes of the wedding processional echoed through the little church.

"Sophie's wedding! We must go." Lucy broke away from his hold.

He took her arm and led her into the church, settling beside the Bradbury family in a back pew. Miss Louisa looked over at them, a broad grin lighting her face. He returned the grin and winked at her. Life was complete—his cup ran over. In just a few short months, he and Lucy would be having a wedding of their own. He said a silent prayer of thanks.

With Lucy by his side, he could do no wrong.

* * *

Sophie's wedding breakfast was a jolly affair, made jollier by the appearance of all the veterans, who took turns telling jokes and singing songs. Lucy couldn't stop smiling. She simply couldn't. Life was too sweet now. She glanced over at her handsome fiancé as he stood talking to Lieutenant Cantrill. What a good man he was. She touched her wooden ring. This was exactly what she'd always wanted but had never dared to hope for for herself.

Sophie passed by on her sister's arm. The bride had been so busy that Lucy hadn't had a moment to share her news. But Sophie grasped Lucy's left hand as she drew close and smiled merrily. "I see I shall be dancing at your wedding in a few months' time!" she cried as she disappeared up the stairs with her sister, who was rather obviously with child. Lucy watched them depart with a glow warming her heart. It was good to see the two of them together—rather like watching Amelia and Louisa in the old days.

"Miss Williams." Lord Bradbury came up to her, with Louisa hanging on his elbow. "My daughter has brought it to my attention that you are engaged to be married."

Oh, dear. His lordship was very particular about his female employees remaining unmarried. She should have said something—but it all had just taken place. "Forgive me, your lordship…I should have told you first…."

He nodded slowly, his graying temples flashing in the candlelight. "We shall be sorry to lose you, Miss Williams. You've been an outstanding governess. Almost like a mother to my girls. But Amelia has told me that she wishes to marry young Spencer, and that means Louisa will make her debut soon after." He pulled his youngest daughter close. "I'm sorry to be losing both of my daughters, but that is the way of the world."

"Of course." She smiled at Louisa—little Louisa who would need a governess no longer. Overnight she had grown into a lady.

"Tell her about the gift, Papa," Louisa whispered urgently in his lordship's ear.

"Oh, yes. Louisa says you have a sort of pet project—something about starting a school for the children of the veterans' group. I like that organization. They are doing good work for men and women who sorely need it." His lordship pursed his lips for a moment and then continued. "I was thinking that—in light of the fact that you essentially raised my daughters for the past several years—I owe you more than just a trifling wedding present. Rather ridiculous to give someone of your standing in our family a set of dishes or some old lace. No, indeed. I'd like to gift you the money to start your school."

Lucy wasn't sure she'd heard correctly. Long inured to expecting nothing out of life, she had never expected such a generous gift from his lordship. She looked from father to daughter in turn, trying to comprehend all she'd heard. "Money for the school?"

"Yes, for all those children who need you, Lucy," Louisa added. "We were lucky to have you all those years, and now you can share your gift for teaching with children who couldn't afford an education."

"Would five thousand pounds be sufficient?" his lordship queried. "I don't wish to stint you, but I have no idea what the costs would be."

Lucy gasped. "Oh, no, it's too kind," she whispered, shaking her head. "I couldn't accept it."

"It's not for you, not exactly." Louisa smiled cheekily. "It's for those children. And I should consider it repayment in kind if you drill all of them on their Latin declensions, just as you used to torture me with them."

"It's settled then." His lordship clapped his hands. "I'll gather the money for you when we return home. And of course, you may stay with us until your marriage. I'll bend the rules this once. Now, where can I find some port?" He drifted away, leaving Louisa behind.

"Oh, Lucy." Louisa embraced Lucy so hard that the breath was knocked out of her. "I shall miss you dreadfully, but I shall come to visit and perhaps help at your school. Would that be all right?"

"Of course it will. I should love to have you," Lucy responded warmly. "With Amelia leaving, will you be lonely?"

"No," Louisa said decisively. "Now we have weddings to plan—yours and Amelia's. And I shall help with the school. And then, of course, I have my own debut to plan. This next year is going to be quite the social whirl. I cannot wait." She smiled, but tears crowded her eyes. "And I shall have a brilliant debut, and find my prince—for I want to live happily ever after, too."

"Of course, you will." Lucy hugged her tightly, smoothing her hair. She wished nothing but happiness for Louisa.

A general hubbub broke out amongst the crowd, and Lucy spied Sophie and the lieutenant gathering their things. "It must be time for the bride and groom to depart," she told Louisa. "Come, let us see them off in style."

The chilly, wet November day dampened no spirits as the guests streamed out of the manse and onto the lawn. They lined up on either side of the pathway and showered the couple with rice as they ran, panting and laughing, toward the carriage waiting nearby.

After seeing Sophie and the lieutenant off, the assembled throng of guests began to drift away. James came to her side. "Shall we t-t-take a walk together? I c-can t-take you home if his lordship wishes t-to leave early."

"Of course. Just let me get my wrap." She'd neglected to grab her shawl before coming out to see Sophie off, and now she was shivering. When she returned, her heavy cloak swirling about her ankles, James was waiting there for her. For her alone. She touched the ring under her glove. It was a novel feeling, knowing that he was there and would be there for her the rest of their lives.

They walked along the scrubby hills, the frost covered moor grass crunching beneath their feet. "I just wanted to have a moment with you before we parted once more," he explained, his breath showing on the air. "I m-must apologize that it's so awfully c-c-cold out here."

"Don't apologize." She was warmed from within, a glowing fire that made the weather seem positively balmy. "I am happy simply to be here with you."

"I s-suppose you will have to t-tell his lordship about us," he muttered. "D-do you think he will m-m-make you leave his home? If s-s-so, we c-can wed immediately."

She laughed. "Gretna Green?" She shot a sidelong glance at him and was rewarded by the blush that crept over his angular cheeks. "No, do not worry. His lordship has already spoken to me, and he will not make me leave. Not until we are wed. Louisa Bradbury is rather poor at keeping secrets, so he knew by the time the ceremony had ended."

"G-good, I am g-glad to hear that." He still looked rather embarrassed, though, and was studying the moor grass as if it were the most fascinating thing in the world. "I'm sorry I b-behaved so b-badly when I b-begged you to marry me last time, Lucy. I was scared—scared to d-death, actually—that I w-would lose you. I c-couldn't bear it. And so I l-lashed out."

"Think no more of it." This must be a happy occasion. She wanted to think no more about that day—or the weeks that followed it, gray and bland and unending. "His lordship has even given us a rather sizable wedding gift. Enough money to start the school I wanted for the veterans' group."

James's face lit up with a grin, and he picked her up off her feet, whirling her around. "Lucy, that is phenomenal. You are such an excellent t-tutor. I know you will do those children a p-power of g-good."

She laughed breathlessly, her head spinning at the sight of the clouds and trees spiraling around them. "What do you know of my teaching skills?"

"I know this." He set her back on her feet, holding her close as she dizzily tripped over his boots. "You t-taught me how to become the man I am. With infinite patience, you helped remove the c-cotton wool from my eyes." He bent forward and captured her lips, increasing her dizziness until he pulled away. "If you can help a p-poor scrap of a human being like me, I cannot imagine what more you c-can d-do for others. I love you."

"I love you, too." She rested her head against his chest, savoring the feel of him—strong and solid—under her cheek. She stayed so as the world stopped spinning and her sense of balance was restored. "When shall we be married?"

"My sister is marrying Macready in February. She's already asked if you would stand up at her wedding." He chuckled softly, rubbing his chin on the top of her head. "My sister is rather intuitive. I wonder if she had this in mind?"

"A double wedding?" Lucy smiled. There was no better way to start her life as part of James's family than sharing a wedding day with his sister. "Do you think she would like that?"

"I think she w-w-would be ecstatic. She adores you already. And it will help t-t-take some of the nervousness away for M-Macready and I if we c-can stand at the altar looking like l-lovestruck fools together. What d-do you think? W-would that m-make you happy?"

"It's wonderful." She sighed, a deep sense of peace washing over her. She was the luckiest woman in the world. How could a penniless governess receive so much from life?

"What of your r-r-ring? Would you l-like to have your emeralds and d-d-diamonds as well? I've k-kept them all this t-t-time just for you."

"No, indeed. What you've given me is worth far more than emeralds or diamonds." She held him tightly and gazed out over the moors, at the clouds gathering over the steeple of St. Mary's, at the people who streamed out of the church, so far away they were mere blurs of color. James's heart beat steadily against her back; his breath was warm on her ear.

She could ask no more from life than this.

Epilogue

Saint Swithin's Church of England
February 1819

"Oh, Lucy, I am s-s-so nervous," Mary murmured, brushing out her white satin skirts. "I j-just know I will s-s-stammer like a fool when I am up there. Thank g-g-goodness you're with me. I wouldn't b-b-be able to g-g-go through this alone."

"There's no need to worry." Lucy tucked a rosebud back into place in Mary's coiffure and stood back, admiring her handiwork. "All that matters is one thing only. Today is the day you marry Macready. He's the love of your life. What does it matter if you stammer?"

"It's just s-s-so inelegant. I wish I were as c-c-confident as you." Mary grasped her wedding bouquet from the bench nearby. "D-d-do I look all right?"

"Pretty as a picture," Lucy pronounced. "How about me? Do I look presentable?"

"Oh, Lucy, you look lovely. J-James will not b-b-be able to k-keep his eyes from you."

Lucy surveyed her reflection in the looking glass.

Sophie's skills with a needle were unparalleled. Her wedding gown was a triumph. Ecru silk trimmed in lace and a little jacket to match. She took up her bouquet of roses—pale pink, just blushing with color. Courtesy of his lordship's hothouse. Every detail, every little thing a bride's heart could ask for, had been given her by those she loved today.

Charlotte Rowland entered the little dressing room, gorgeously arrayed in dark blue velvet. "They're ready to begin. Oh, my darling girls," she sighed, pulling them close. "You both are the sweetest brides a mother could hope for. I wish nothing but happiness for you both."

Lucy blinked. She was still trying to adjust to Charlotte Rowland's kindness. 'Twas a new thing to her. And yet, the warm, caring look in her future mother-in-law's blue eyes was genuine. Despite her earlier objections, Charlotte really had overcome her objections to Lucy. Someday, it wouldn't be as hard to fathom. Charlotte beckoned them out of the dressing room and to the back of the church. The glorious notes from the organ swirled around her, bathing her in the beauty of Bach. Snow swirled against the windowpanes, blanketing the view of Bath in white. She smiled and linked arms with Mary, now soon to be her sister in both name and nature.

Was she worthy of all of this? She started down the aisle with Mary by her side. The last time she had spent any length of time in this chapel, she was teaching the urchins of the veterans' group to read and to write. And she was certain, back then, that she would never marry. That James would never be hers. That her school would limp along without much success.

How much had changed in the space of a few months.

As they marched up the aisle, she caught glimpses of friendly and much-loved faces. The children she taught. Lord Bradbury. Amelia and Louisa. Sophie and Lieutenant Cantrill. Henry Felton. Reverend Stephens. And there, waiting for her at the altar, her own Ensign James Rowland. The sandy cowlick of hair stood up on the crown of his head, and this time, she did not resist the urge. She patted it into place with her gloved hand. He captured her hand and tucked her close beside him.

She smiled. If only Mother and Father could have lived to see this. How sweet it would be to have them here on this day. And yet, she was no longer alone. These dear people, gathered together in the familiar chapel, had become as much of a family to her as her own flesh and blood.

She repeated her wedding vows, smiling into James's emerald eyes. She would never be alone again. James talked a great deal about how she had transformed him, but in truth, he had transformed her, as well. He taught her to ask more of life. He tore away the curtain she left between herself and the world. And because of him, she would never be lonely again. He'd made her a family member—not just of his family, but of the greater community of people who surrounded them and who loved her as much as she loved them.

* * * * *

Dear Reader,

This is the third—and last—book in the Brides of Waterloo trilogy. It makes me rather sad to bid these characters farewell. They have become like family to me over these past two years. It all started with an idea—"What if there were two poverty-stricken sisters?" and grew from there. Although I love to read about lords and ladies—that is, after all, what's so fun about the Regency era—I wanted to write about the "little" people who would have been living and working, loving and growing, during that same era. And so writing about the Handleys and their dear friend Lucy has been a real labor of love—and a real eye opener about what life was like for regular people back then.

I am working on a new series now, but I would always like to hear from you. Do you want to hear more stories about people like the Handleys, or are you ready to hear about more lords and ladies? Drop me a line at lily@lilygeorge.com. I would love to hear your thoughts.

Blessings,

Lily George

Questions for Discussion

1. Lucy Williams feels that, because she is an orphan and has to work for a living, she has no time for love. Is that a common feeling nowadays? Do you agree with the limits she places upon herself?

2. Ensign James Rowland is immediately attracted to Lucy but feels he must overcome his cowardice and his stammer before he can court any woman. Is he being too hard on himself? Or should he work on himself before seeking love?

3. James seeks a position with a cabinet maker, even though he is worried he cannot prove himself in his new position. Have you ever been overwhelmed by a new job or career change? How did you deal with it?

4. Lucy and James grow closer by working on the library. They become friends first, and then fall in love. Is it better for a couple to be friends before they cherish romantic feelings for each other?

5. Lucy decides to start a school for the children who attend the veterans' group meetings. What kind of charitable endeavor would you start if you could?

6. James Rowland prefers to make his own way in the world rather than marry a woman for money. Was this the right choice?

7. Lucy loves Louisa and Amelia Bradbury like her own sisters. Have you ever been close enough to a friend that it was like you were related by blood?

8. Lucy chooses not to accept James's suit because his mother persuades her not to. Was this the right thing to do? What would you have done?

9. Lucy resigns herself to a life without love once she refuses James. Was this the right choice? How would you have handled James's proposal?

10. James is determined to make his own way in the world, even though his mother is originally against his choice of lifestyle. Have you ever gone against someone's expectations of you, even though you knew it would be difficult to do so?

11. Louisa meddles in Lucy's affairs constantly, though she means the best for her governess. Have you ever had someone try to change your life for the better? If so, did things work out all right in the end?

12. Have you ever met anyone like Charlotte Rowland, James's mother, who is so devoted to her family name? How do you feel about family background and wealth?

13. James gives Lucy two rings: one made of emeralds and diamonds and one made of the wood from the willow tree in the churchyard. Which would you prefer if given the choice?

14. Lord Bradbury gives Lucy the money to start her school in Bath. Have you ever been the recipient of a large gift? If so, how did it change your life?

15. Lucy and James have a double wedding with Macready and Mary. Do you like the idea of a double wedding, or should the bride have the day (and all the attention) for herself?

COMING NEXT MONTH
from Love Inspired® Historical
AVAILABLE SEPTEMBER 3, 2013

FALLING FOR THE TEACHER
Pinewood Weddings
Dorothy Clark

Cole Aylward may be helping Sadie Spencer's grandfather, but he's the last man Sadie wants to see when she comes home. He *must* have an ulterior motive. Can Cole convince her that his intentions—and feelings—are genuine?

KEEPING FAITH
Hannah Alexander

After her husband's death, Dr. Victoria Fenway is determined to find his murderer. But could her quest for revenge ruin her second chance at love with wagon-train captain Joseph Rickard?

THE DUTIFUL DAUGHTER
Sanctuary Bay
Jo Ann Brown

Sophia Meriweather knows she's expected to marry her late father's new heir. But when widower Charles Winthrop, Lord Northbridge, and his two young children arrive, Sophie must choose between duty to her family or to her heart.

A PLACE OF REFUGE
Boardinghouse Betrothals
Janet Lee Barton

Kathleen O'Bryan was searching for a safe refuge, and Heaton House boardinghouse gave her the shelter she needed—and reunited her with the man who had rescued her in the past. Can Luke Patterson offer her a safe haven where she can risk opening her heart once more?

Look for these and other Love Inspired books wherever books are sold, including most bookstores, supermarkets, discount stores and drugstores.

LIHCNM0813

SPECIAL EXCERPT FROM

Love Inspired

Gracie Wilson is about to become the most famous runaway bride in Bygones, Kansas. Can she find true happiness? Read on for a preview of THE BOSS'S BRIDE by Brenda Minton. Available September 2013.

Gracie Wilson stood in the center of a Sunday school classroom at the Bygones Community Church. Her friend Janie Lawson adjusted Gracie's veil and again wiped at tears.

"You look beautiful."

"Do I?" Gracie glanced in the full-length mirror that hung on the door of the supply cabinet and suppressed a shudder. The dress was hideous and she hadn't picked it.

"You look beautiful. And you look miserable. It's your wedding day—you should be smiling."

Gracie smiled but she knew it was a poor attempt at best.

"Gracie, what's wrong?"

"Nothing. I'm good." She leaned her cheek against Janie's hand on her shoulder. "Other than the fact that you've moved one hundred miles away and I never get to see you."

What else could she say? Everyone in Bygones, Kansas, thought she'd landed the catch of the century. Trent Morgan was handsome, charming and came from money. She should be thrilled to be marrying him. Six months ago she had been thrilled. But then she'd started to notice little signs. She should have put the wedding on hold the moment she noticed those signs. And when she knew for certain, she should have put a stop to the entire thing. But she hadn't.

"Do you care if I have a few minutes alone?"

"Of course not." Janie gave her another hug. "But not to long. Your dad is outside and when I came in to check o you the seats were filling up out there."

"I just need a minute to catch my breath."

Janie smiled back at her and then the door to th classroom closed. And for the first time in days, Gracie wa alone. She looked around the room with the bright yello walls and posters from Sunday school curriculum. Sh stopped at the poster of David and Goliath. Her favorite She'd love to have that kind of faith, the kind that knocke down giants.

"You almost ready, Gracie?" her dad called throug the door.

"Almost."

She opened the window, just to let in fresh air. She leane out, breathing the hint of autumn, enjoying the breeze o her face. She looked across the grassy lawn and saw…

FREEDOM.

To see if Gracie finds her happily-ever-after, pick up
THE BOSS'S BRIDE
wherever Love Inspired books are sold.

LIEXP0813